W9-BXX-542

another day

also by david levithan

Boy Meets Boy

The Realm of Possibility

Are We There Yet?

The Full Spectrum (edited with Billy Merrell)

Marly's Ghost (illustrated by Brian Selznick)

Nick & Norah's Infinite Playlist (written with Rachel Cohn)

Wide Awake

Naomi and Ely's No Kiss List (written with Rachel Cohn)

How They Met, and Other Stories

The Likely Story series (written as David Van Etten,
with David Ozanich and Chris Van Etten)

Love Is the Higher Law

Will Grayson, Will Grayson (written with John Green)

Dash & Lily's Book of Dares (written with Rachel Cohn)

The Lover's Dictionary

Every You, Every Me (with photographs by Jonathan Farmer)

Every Day

Two Boys Kissing

Hold Me Closer: The Tiny Cooper Story

another day

david levithan

alfred a. knopf
new york

536960

THIS IS A BORZOI BOOK PUBLISHED BY ALFRED A. KNOPF

This is a work of fiction. Names, characters, places, and incidents either are the product of the author's imagination or are used fictitiously. Any resemblance to actual persons, living or dead, events, or locales is entirely coincidental.

Text copyright © 2015 by David Levithan
Jacket art copyright © 2015 by Adam Abernethy

All rights reserved. Published in the United States by Alfred A. Knopf, an imprint of Random House Children's Books, a division of Penguin Random House LLC, New York.

Knopf, Borzoi Books, and the colophon are registered trademarks of Penguin Random House LLC.

Visit us on the Web! randomhouseteens.com

Educators and librarians, for a variety of teaching tools, visit us at
RHTeachersLibrarians.com

Library of Congress Cataloging-in-Publication Data
Levithan, David.
Another day / David Levithan. — First edition.
pages cm.
Companion book to: Every day.
Summary: "Rhiannon is disappointed that her neglectful boyfriend Justin doesn't remember the one perfect day they shared, until a stranger tells her that the Justin she spent the day with, the one who made her feel like a real person . . . wasn't Justin at all." —Provided by publisher
ISBN 978-0-385-75620-4 (trade) — ISBN 978-0-385-75621-1 (lib. bdg.) —
ISBN 978-0-385-75622-8 (ebook)
[1. Love—Fiction. 2. High schools—Fiction. 3. Schools—Fiction. 4. Identity—Fiction.]
I. Title.
PZ7.L5798Ano 2015
[Fic]—dc23
2015005798

ISBN 978-1-101-93136-3 (intl. tr. pbk.)

The text of this book is set in 11.5-point Goudy.

Printed in the United States of America
August 2015
10 9 8 7 6 5 4 3 2 1

First Edition

Random House Children's Books supports the First Amendment
and celebrates the right to read.

For my nephew, Matthew
(May you find happiness every day)

Chapter One

I watch his car as it pulls into the parking lot. I watch him get out of it. I am in the corner of his eye, moving toward its center—but he isn't looking for me. He's heading into school without noticing I'm right here. I could call out for him, but he doesn't like that. He says it's something needy girls do, always calling out to their boyfriends.

It hurts that I can be so full of him while he's so empty of me.

I wonder if last night is the reason he isn't looking for me. I wonder if our fight is still happening. Like most of our fights, it's about something stupid, with other non-stupid things right underneath. All I did was ask him if he wanted to go to Steve's party on Saturday. That was it. And he asked me why, on Sunday night, I was already asking him about Saturday. He said I'm always doing this, trying to pin him down, as if he won't want to be with me if I don't ask him about it months ahead of time. I told him it wasn't my fault he's always afraid of plans, afraid of figuring out what's next.

Mistake. Calling him afraid was a big mistake. That's probably the only word he heard.

"You have no idea what you're talking about," he said.

"I was talking about a party at Steve's house on Saturday," I told him, my voice way too upset for either of us. "That's all."

But that's not all. Justin loves me and hates me as much as I love him and hate him. I know that. We each have our triggers, and we should never reach in to pull them. But sometimes we can't help ourselves. We know each other too well, but never well enough.

I am in love with someone who's afraid of the future. And, like a fool, I keep bringing it up.

I follow him. Of course I do. Only a needy girl would be mad at her boyfriend because he didn't notice her in a parking lot.

As I'm walking to his locker, I wonder which Justin I'll find there. It probably won't be Sweet Justin, because it's rare for Sweet Justin to show up at school. And hopefully it won't be Angry Justin, because I haven't done anything *that* wrong, I don't think. I'm hoping for Chill Justin, because I like Chill Justin. When he's around, we can all calm down.

I stand there as he takes his books out of his locker. I look at the back of his neck because I am in love with the back of his neck. There is something so physical about it, something that makes me want to lean over and kiss it.

Finally, he looks at me. I can't read his expression, not right away. It's like he's trying to figure me out at the same time I'm trying to figure him out. I think maybe this is a good sign, because maybe it means he's worried about me. Or it's a bad sign, because he doesn't understand why I'm here.

"Hey," he says.

"Hey," I say back.

There's something really intense about the way he's looking at me. I'm sure he's finding something wrong. There's always something wrong for him to find.

But he doesn't say anything. Which is weird. Then, even weirder, he asks me, "Are you okay?"

I must look really pathetic if he's asking me that.

"Sure," I tell him. Because I don't know what the answer is supposed to be. *I am not okay*—that's actually the answer. But it's not the right answer to say to him. I know that much.

If this is some kind of trap, I don't appreciate it. If this is payback for what I said last night, I want it over with.

"Are you mad at me?" I ask, not sure I want to know the answer.

And he goes, "No. I'm not mad at you at all."

Liar.

When we have problems, I'm usually the one who sees them. I do the worrying for both of us. I just can't tell him about it too often, because then it's almost like I'm bragging that I understand what's going on while he doesn't.

Uncertainty. Do I ask about last night? Or do I pretend it never happened—that it never happens?

"Do you still want to get lunch today?" I ask. It's only after I ask that I realize I'm trying to make plans again.

Maybe I am a needy girl, after all.

"Absolutely," Justin says. "Lunch would be great."

Bullshit. He's playing with me. He has to be.

"No big deal," he adds.

I look at him, and it seems genuine. Maybe I'm wrong to assume the worst. And maybe I've managed to make him feel stupid by being so surprised.

I take his hand and hold it. If he's willing to step back from last night, I am, too. This is what we do. When the stupid fights are over, we're good.

"I'm glad you're not mad at me," I tell him. "I just want everything to be okay."

He knows I love him. I know he loves me. That is never the question. The question is always how we'll deal with it.

Time. The bell rings. I have to remind myself that school is not a thing that exists solely to give us a place to be together.

"I'll see you later," he says.

I hold on to that. It's the only thing that will get me through the empty space that follows.

I was watching one of my shows, and one of the housewives was like, "He's a fuckup, but he's *my* fuckup," and I thought, *Oh, shit, I really shouldn't be relating to this, but I am, and so what?* That has to be what love is—seeing what a mess he is and loving him anyway, because you know you're a mess, too, maybe even worse.

We weren't an hour into our first date before Justin was setting off the alarms.

"I'm warning you—I'm trouble," he said over dinner at TGI Fridays. "Total trouble."

"And do you warn all the other girls?" I replied, flirting.

But what I got back wasn't flirtation. It was real.

"No," he said. "I don't."

This was his way of letting me know that I was someone he cared about. Even at the very beginning.

He hadn't meant to tell me. But there it was.

And even though he's forgotten a lot of other details about that first date, he's never forgotten what he said.

I warned you! he'll yell at me on nights when it's really bad, really hard. *You can't say I didn't warn you!*

Sometimes this only makes me hold him tighter.

Sometimes I've already let go, feeling awful that there's nothing I can do.

The only time our paths intersect in the morning is between first and second periods, so I look for him then. We only have a minute to share, sometimes less, but I'm always thankful. It's like I'm taking attendance. *Love? Here!* Even if we're tired (which is pretty much always) and even if we don't have much to say, I know he won't just pass me by.

Today I smile, because, all things considered, the morning went pretty well. And he smiles back at me.

Good signs. I am always looking for good signs.

I head to Justin's class as soon as fourth period is over, but he hasn't waited for me. So I go to the cafeteria, to where we usually sit. He's not there, either. I ask Rebecca if she's seen him. She says she hasn't, and doesn't seem too surprised that I'm looking. I decide to ignore that. I check my locker and he's not there. I'm starting to think he's forgotten, or was playing with me all along. I decide to check his locker, even though it's about as far from the cafeteria as you can get. He never stops there before lunch. But I guess today he has, because there he is.

I'm happy to see him, but also exhausted. It's just so much work. He looks worse than I feel, staring into his locker like there's a window in there. In some people, this would mean daydreams. But Justin doesn't daydream. When he's gone, he's really gone.

Now he's back. Right when I get to him.

"Hey," he says.

"Hey," I say back.

I'm hungry, but not that hungry. The most important thing is for us to be in the same place. I can do that anywhere.

He's putting all of his books in his locker now, as if he's done with the day. I hope nothing's wrong. I hope he's not giving up. If I'm going to be stuck here, I want him stuck here, too.

He stands up and puts his hand on my arm. Gentle. Way too gentle. It's something I'd do to him, not something he'd do to me. I like it, but I also don't like it.

"Let's go somewhere," he says. "Where do you want to go?"

Again, I think there has to be a right answer to this question, and that if I get it wrong, I will ruin everything. He wants something from me, but I'm not sure what.

"I don't know," I tell him.

He takes his hand off my arm and I think, okay, wrong answer. But then he takes my hand.

"Come on," he says.

There's an electricity in his eyes. Power. Light.

He closes the locker and pulls me forward. I don't understand. We're walking hand in hand through the almost-empty halls. We never do this. He gets this grin on his face and we go faster. It's like we're little kids at recess. Running, actually running down the halls. People look at us like we're insane. It's so ridiculous. He swings us by my locker and tells me to leave my books here, too. I don't understand, but I go along with it—he's in a great mood, and I don't want to do anything that will break it.

Once my locker's closed, we keep going. Right out the door. Simple as that. Escape. We're always talking about how we want to leave, and this time we're doing it. I figure he'll take me out for pizza or something. Maybe be late to fifth period. We get to his car and I don't even want to ask him what we're doing. I just want to let him do it.

He turns and asks, "Where do you want to go? Tell me, truly, where you'd love to go."

Strange. He's asking me as if I'm the one who knows the right answer.

I really hope this isn't a trick. I really hope I won't regret this.

I say the first thing that comes to my mind.

"I want to go to the ocean. I want you to take me to the ocean."

I figure he'll laugh and say what he really meant was that we should go to his house while his parents are gone and spend the afternoon having sex and watching TV. Or that he's trying to prove a point about not making plans, to prove that I like being spontaneous better. Or he'll tell me to go have fun at the ocean while he gets lunch. All of these are possibilities, and they all play at the same time in my head.

The only thing I'm not expecting is for him to think it's a good idea.

"Okay," he says, pulling out of the parking lot. I still assume he's joking, but then he's asking me the best way to get there. I tell him which highways we should take—there's a beach my family used to go to a lot in the summer, and if we're going to the ocean, we might as well go there.

As he steers, I can tell he's enjoying himself. It should put me at ease, but it's making me nervous. It would be just like Justin to take me somewhere really special in order to dump me. Make a big production of it. Maybe leave me stranded there. I don't actually think this is going to happen—but it's possible. As a way of proving to me that he's able to make plans. As a way of showing he's not as afraid of the future as I said he was.

You're being crazy, Rhiannon, I tell myself. It's something he says to me all the time. A lot of the time, he's right.

Just enjoy it, I think. Because we're not in school. We're together.

He turns on the radio and tells me to take over. What? *My car, my radio*—how many times have I heard him say that? But it seems like his offer is real, so I slip from station to station, trying to find something he'll be into. When I pause too long on a song I like, he says, "Why not that one?" And I'm thinking, *Because you hate it.* But I don't say that out loud. I let the song play. I wait for him to make a joke about it, say the singer sounds like she's having her period.

Instead, he starts to sing along.

Disbelief. Justin *never* sings along. He will yell at the radio. He will talk back to whatever the talk radio people are saying. Every now and then he might beat along on his steering wheel. But he does *not* sing.

I wonder if he's on drugs. But I've seen him on drugs before, and it's never been like this.

"What's gotten into you?" I ask.

"Music," he says.

"Ha."

"No, really."

He's not joking. He's not laughing at me somewhere inside. I am looking at him and I can see that. I don't know what's going on, but it's not that.

I decide to see how far I can push it. Because that's what a needy girl does.

"In that case . . . ," I say. I flip stations until I find the least-Justin song possible.

And there it is. Kelly Clarkson. Singing how what doesn't kill you makes you stronger.

I turn it up. In my head, I dare him to sing along.

Surprise.

We are belting it out. I have no idea how he knows the words. But I don't question it. I am singing with everything I've got, never knowing I could love this song as much as I do right now, because it is making everything okay—it is making *us* okay. I refuse to think about anything other than that. I want us to stay inside the song. Because this is something we've never done before and it feels great.

When it's done, I roll down my window—I want to feel

the wind in my hair. Without a word, Justin rolls down all the other windows, and it's like we're in a wind tunnel, like this is a ride in an amusement park, when really it's just a car driving down the highway. He looks so happy. It makes me realize how rare it is for me to see him happy, the kind of happy where there isn't anything else on his mind besides the happiness. He's usually so afraid to show it, as if it might be stolen away at any moment.

He takes my hand and starts to ask me questions. Personal questions.

He starts with, "How are your parents doing?"

"Um . . . I don't know," I say. He's never really cared about my parents before. I know he wants them to like him, but because he's not sure they will, he pretends it doesn't matter. "I mean, you know. Mom is trying to hold it all together without actually doing anything. My dad has his moments, but he's not exactly the most fun person to be around. The older he gets, the less he seems to give a damn about anything."

"And what's it like with Liza at college?"

When he asks this question, it's as if he's proud that he's remembered my sister's name. That sounds more like Justin.

"I don't know," I tell him. "You know we were more like sisters living under a truce than best friends. I don't know if I miss her that much, although it was easier having her around, because then there were two of us, you know? She never calls home. Even when my mom calls her, she doesn't call back. I don't blame her for that—I'm sure she has better things to do. And really, I always knew that once she left, she'd be gone. So I'm not shocked or anything."

I realize as I'm talking that I'm getting close to the nerve, talking about what happens when high school is over. But Justin doesn't seem to be taking it personally. Instead, he asks me if I think school is much different this year than last year. Which is a weird question. Something my grandmother would ask. Not my boyfriend.

I tread carefully.

"I don't know. School sucks. That's not different. But, you know—while I really want it to be over, I'm also worried about everything that's going to come after. Not that I have it planned out. I don't. I know you think that I have all of these plans—but if you actually look at the things I've done to prepare myself for life after high school, all you'll see is a huge blank. I'm just as unprepared as anyone else."

Shut up, shut up, shut up, I'm telling myself. *Why are you bringing this up?*

But maybe I have a reason. Maybe I'm bringing it up to see what he'll do. He tests me all the time, but I'm not exactly innocent in that department, either.

"What do you think?" I ask him.

And he says, "Honestly, I'm just trying to live day to day."

I know. But I appreciate it more when it's said like this, in a voice that acknowledges we're on the same side. I wait for him to say more, to edge back into last night's fight. But he lets it go. I am grateful.

It's been over a year, and there've been at least a hundred times when I've told myself that this was it—this was the new start. Sometimes I was right. But not as much as I wanted to be.

I will not let myself think that things are suddenly better.

I will not let myself think that we've somehow escaped the us we always end up being. But at the same time, I will not deny what's happening. I will not deny this happiness. Because if happiness feels real, it almost doesn't matter if it's real or not.

Instead of plugging the destination into his phone, he's asking me to keep giving him directions. I screw up and tell him to get off the highway one exit too soon, but when I realize this, he doesn't freak out at all—he just gets back on the highway and goes one more exit. Now I'm no longer wondering if he's on drugs—I'm wondering if he's on *medication*. If so, it's kicking in pretty quickly.

I do not say a word. I don't want to jinx it.

"I should be in English class," I say as we make the last turn before the beach.

"I should be in bio," Justin says back.

But this is more important. I can make up my homework, but I can't make up my life.

"Let's just enjoy ourselves," he says.

"Okay," I tell him. "I like that. I spend so much time thinking about running away—it's nice to actually do it. For a day. It's good to be on the other side of the window. I don't do this enough."

Maybe this is what we've needed all along. Distance from everything else, and closeness to each other.

Something is working here—I can feel it working.

Memory. This is the beach my family would come to, on days when the house was too hot or my parents were sick of staying in the same place. When we came here, we'd be surrounded by other families. I liked to imagine that each of our blankets was a house, and that a certain number of blankets made a town. I'm sure there were a few kids I saw all the time, whose parents took them here, too, but I can't remember any of them now. I can only remember my own family—my mother always under an umbrella, either not wanting to burn or not wanting to be seen; my sister taking out a book and staying inside it the whole time; my father talking to the other fathers about sports or stocks. When it got too hot, he would race me down into the water and ask me what kind of fish I wanted to be. I knew that the right answer was *flying fish*, because if I told him that, he would gather me in his arms and throw me into the air.

I don't know why I've never brought Justin here before. Last summer we stayed indoors, waiting for his parents to leave for work so we could have sex in every room of the house, including some of the closets. Then, when it was done, we'd watch TV or play video games. Sometimes we'd call around to see what everyone else was doing, and by the time his parents came home, we'd be off at someone's house, drinking or watching TV or playing video games or some mix of the three. It was great, because it wasn't school, and we were with each other. But it didn't really get us anywhere.

I leave my shoes in the car, just like I did when I was a kid. There are the first awkward steps when I'm still in the parking lot and the pavement hurts, but then there's the sand and everything's fine. The beach is completely empty today, and even though I didn't expect there to be a lot of people here, it's still surprising, like we've caught the beach napping.

I can't help myself. I run right down into it, spin around. *Mine*, I think. The beach is mine. The time is mine. Justin is mine. Nobody—nothing—is going to interfere with that. I call out his name, and it's like I'm still singing along to a song.

He looks at me for a moment, and I think, *Oh no, this is the part where he tells me I look like an idiot.* But then he's running down to me, grabbing hold of me, swinging me around. He's heard the song, and now we're dancing. We're laughing and racing each other to the water. When we get there, we splash-war, feeling the tide against our legs. I reach down for some shells, and Justin joins me, looking for colors that won't be the same when they're dry, looking for sea glass and spirals. The water feels so good, and standing still feels so good, because there's a whole ocean pulling at me and I have the strength to stay where I am.

Justin's face is completely unguarded. His body is entirely relaxed. I never see him like this. We are playing, but it's not the kind of playing that boyfriends and girlfriends do, where there's strategy and scorekeeping and secret moves. No, we have scissored ourselves away from all that.

I ask him to build a sand castle with me. I tell him how Liza always had to have her own, next to mine. She would build a huge mountain with a deep moat around it, while I would make a small, detailed house with a front door and a garage. Basically, I was building the dollhouse I was never able to have, while Liza was creating the fortress she felt she needed. She would never touch my castle—she wasn't the kind of older sister who needed to destroy the competition. But she wouldn't let me touch hers, either. We'd leave them when we were done, for the tide to take away. Sometimes our parents would come over. To me, they'd say, *How pretty!* To Liza, it would be, *How tall!*

I want Justin to work on a sand castle with me. I want us to experience what it's like to build something together. We don't have any shovels or buckets. Everything has to be done with our hands. He takes the phrase *sand castle* literally—starting with the square foundation, creating a drawbridge with his finger. I work on the turrets and the towers—balconies are precarious, but spires are possible. At random moments, he compliments me—little words like *nice* and *neat* and *sweet*—and I feel like the beach is somehow unlocking this vocabulary from the dungeon where he's kept it all these months. I always felt—maybe hoped—that the words were in there somewhere. And now I know they are.

It isn't very warm out, but I can feel the sun on my cheeks and my neck. We could gather more shells and begin to decorate, but I am starting to tire of the building, and putting our focus there. When the last tower is complete, I suggest we wander for a little while.

"Are you pleased with our creation?" he asks.

And I say, "Very."

We head to the water to wash off our hands. Justin stares back at the beach, back at our castle, and seems lost for a moment. Lost, but in a good place.

"What is it?" I ask.

He looks at me, eyes so kind, and says, "Thank you."

I am sure he has said these two words to me before, but never like this, never in a way that would make me want to remember them.

"For what?" I ask. What I mean is: *Why now? Why finally?*

"For this," he says. "For all of it."

I want so much to trust it. I want so much to think we've finally shifted to the place I always thought we could get to. But it's too simple. It feels too simple.

"It's okay," he tells me. "It's okay to be happy."

I have wanted this for so long. This is not how I pictured it, but nothing ever is. I am overwhelmed by how much I love him. I don't hate him at all. There's not a single part of me that hates him. There is only love. And it isn't terrifying. It is the opposite of terrifying.

I am crying because I'm happy and I'm crying because I don't think I ever realized how much I was expecting to be unhappy. I am crying because, for the first time in a long time, life makes sense.

He sees me crying and doesn't make fun of it. He doesn't get defensive, asking what he did this time. He doesn't tell me he warned me. He doesn't tell me to stop. No, he wraps his arms around me and holds me and takes these things that are only words and makes them into something more than words. Comfort. He gives me something I can actually feel—his presence, his hold.

"I'm happy," I say, afraid he thinks I'm crying for a reason besides that. "Really, I am."

The wind, the beach, the sun—everything else wraps around us, but our embrace is the one that matters. I am holding on to him now as much as he is holding on to me. We have reached that perfect balance, where each of us is strong and each of us is weak, each taking, each giving.

"What's happening?" I ask.

"Shhh," he says. "Don't question it."

I don't feel any questions—only answers. No fear, only fullness. I kiss him and continue our perfect balance there, let our separate breaths become one breath. I close my eyes and feel the familiar press of his lips, the familiar taste of his mouth. But something is different now. We are not just kissing with our whole bodies, but with something that is bigger than our bodies, that is who we are and who we will be. We are kissing from a deeper part of our selves, and we are finding a deeper part of each other. It feels like electricity hitting water, fire reaching paper, the brightest light finding our eyes. I run my hands down his back, down his front, as if I need to know that he's really here, that this is really happening. I linger on the back of his neck. He lingers on the side of my hip. I slip below his belt, but he leads me back up, kissing my neck. I kiss beneath his ear. I kiss his smile. He traces my laugh.

Enjoying this. We are enjoying this.

I have no idea what time it is, what day it is. I have nothing but now. Nothing but here. And it is more than enough.

Eventually my hand slides down his arm and holds his hand. We stand there for a few seconds, or maybe a few minutes, hand in hand, forehead on forehead, lips gently on lips, drained entirely of longing, because everything's been found.

Then we pull away, keeping our hands together. We begin to walk down the beach, like couples do. Time comes back, but not in a scary way.

"This is amazing," I say. And then I cringe despite myself, because this is what Justin would usually call *an obvious statement*. But of course, on this day, in this place, all he does is nod in agreement. He looks at the sun, which is coming closer to the horizon. I think I can see a boat offshore, but it could just be driftwood, or a mirage.

I want every day to be like this. I don't understand why it can't be.

"We should do this every Monday," I say. "And Tuesday. And Wednesday. And Thursday. And Friday."

I'm joking. But not really.

"We'd only get tired of it," Justin says. "It's best to have it just once."

Once? I don't know what he means. I don't know how he could say that.

"Never again?" I ask. I don't want to be wrong here. I really don't want to be wrong.

He smiles. "Well, never say never."

"I'd never say never," I promise him.

Company. There are other couples on the beach now. Only a few, all of them older than us. Nobody asks us why we aren't in school. Nobody asks us what we're doing here. Instead, they seem happy to see us. It makes me feel like we belong here, that we are right to be doing what we're doing.

This is how it's going to be, I tell myself. And then I look at Justin and think, *Tell me this is how it's going to be.*

I don't want to ask him. I don't want to have to ask. Too often, it's my questions that push things off course.

I don't want this to be fragile, but I still treat it like it is.

I'm starting to get a little cold. I have to remind myself that it isn't summer. When I shiver, Justin puts his arm around me. I suggest we go back to the car and get the make-out blanket he keeps in his trunk. So we turn around, head back to where we started. Our castle is still there, still standing, even as the ocean comes closer.

Once we have the blanket, we bring it back to the beach. Instead of wrapping it around our shoulders, we put it on the sand and press ourselves beside each other. We are lying down, staring up at the sky. Clouds push by us. Every now and then a bird appears.

"This has to be one of the best days ever," I say.

Without turning his head, he puts his hand in mine.

"Tell me about some of the other days like this," he asks.

"I don't know . . . ," I say. I can't imagine another day like this.

"Just one. The first one that comes to mind."

I think about times when I was happy. Really happy. Balloon-floating happy. And the strangest memory comes into my mind. I have no idea why. I know I need to give him an answer, but I tell him it's stupid. He insists I share it anyway.

I turn to him and he moves my hand to his chest, making circles there.

He is here. This is safe.

I tell him, "For some reason, the first thing that comes to mind is this mother-daughter fashion show."

I make him promise not to laugh. He promises. And I believe him.

"It was in fourth grade or something," I say. "Renwick's was doing a fund-raiser for hurricane victims, and they asked for volunteers from our class. I didn't ask my mother or anything—I just signed up. And when I brought the information home—well, you know how my mom is. She was terrified. It's enough to get her out to the supermarket. But a fashion show? In front of strangers? I might as well have asked her to pose for *Playboy*. God, now there's a scary thought."

Some girls have moms who partied all the time when they were young, who laughed and giggled and flirted and dressed in super tight clothes. I don't have a mom like that. My mom was, I think, always the same as she is now. Except maybe this one time.

I tell Justin, "But here's the thing: she didn't say no. I guess it's only now that I realize what I put her through. She didn't make me go to the teacher and take it back. No, when the day came, we drove over to Renwick's and went where they told us to go. I had thought they would put us in matching outfits, but it wasn't like that. Instead, they basically told us we could wear whatever we wanted from the store. So there we were, trying all these things on. I went for the gowns, of course—I was so much more of a girl then. I ended up with this light blue dress—ruffles all over the place. I thought it was so sophisticated."

"I'm sure it was classy," Justin says.

I hit him playfully. "Shut up. Let me tell my story."

He holds my hand on his chest. Before I can go on, he kisses me. I think the story might end there, but he pulls back and says, "Go ahead."

I forget for a second where I was, because for a moment I fall out of the story and back into now. Then I remember: My mom. The fashion show.

"So I had my wannabe prom dress," I say. "And then it was

Mom's turn. She surprised me, because she went for the dresses, too. I'd never really seen her all dressed up before. And I think that was the most amazing thing to me: It wasn't me who was Cinderella. It was her.

"After we picked out our clothes, they put makeup on us and everything. I thought Mom was going to flip, but she was actually enjoying it. They didn't really do much with her—just a little more color. And that was all it took. She was pretty. I know it's hard to believe, knowing her now. But that day, she was like a movie star. All the other moms were complimenting her. And when it was time for the actual show, we paraded out there and people applauded. Mom and I were both smiling, and it was real, you know?"

Real like this is real—Justin listening next to me, the sky above, the sand underneath. It is real in such an intense way that it feels unreal, too. Like I had no idea it was possible to feel so much at once, and have it all be true.

"We didn't get to keep the dresses or anything," I go on. "But I remember on the ride home, Mom kept saying how great I was. When we got back to our house, Dad looked at us like we were aliens, but the cool thing is, he decided to play along. Instead of getting all weird, he kept calling us his supermodels, and asked us to do the show for him in our living room, which we did. We were laughing so much. And that was it. The day ended. I'm not sure Mom's worn makeup since. And it's not like I turned out to be a supermodel. But that day reminds me of this one. Because it was a break from everything, wasn't it?"

"It sounds like it," Justin says. And the way he looks at me—it's like he's finally realized how real I am, how *here* I am.

What I've just said isn't worth that. Which means I must be worth that.

"I can't believe I just told you that," I say. It's like I'm giving him a chance to change his mind.

"Why?"

"Because. I don't know. It just sounds so silly."

"No," he says, "it sounds like a good day."

"How about you?" I ask. I know I'm pushing it. It's one thing for him to listen. It's another to have him actually tell me something.

"I was never in a mother-daughter fashion show," he says.

Ha ha. So maybe he isn't taking this seriously after all. I hit him on the shoulder and say, "No. Tell me about another day like this one."

I can see him thinking about it. At first, I think he's debating whether or not to tell me anything. But then I realize that, no, he's just trying to come up with a good answer.

"There was this one day when I was eleven," he starts. He's not staring out to the ocean or looking anywhere else, distracted. He's looking right into my eyes, his way of saying this story is for me. "I was playing hide-and-seek with my friends. I mean, the brutal tackle kind of hide-and-seek. We were in the woods, and for some reason I decided that what I had to do was climb a tree. I don't think I'd ever climbed a tree before. But I found one with some low branches and just started moving. Up and up. It was as natural as walking. In my memory, that tree was hundreds of feet tall. Thousands. At some point, I crossed the tree line. I was still climbing, but there weren't any other trees around. I was all by myself, clinging to the trunk of this tree, a long way from the ground.

22

"It was magical. There's no other word to describe it. I could hear my friends yelling as they were caught, as the game played out. But I was in a completely different place. I was seeing the world from above, which is an extraordinary thing when it happens for the first time. I'd never flown in a plane. I'm not even sure I'd been in a tall building. So there I was, hovering above everything I knew. I had made it somewhere special, and I'd gotten there all on my own. Nobody had given it to me. Nobody had told me to do it. I'd climbed and climbed and climbed, and this was my reward. To watch over the world, and to be alone with myself. That, I found, was what I needed."

I'm almost crying, imagining him there. Every now and then he'll tell me something about when he was little, but not like this. Usually he only tells me the bad things. The hard things. Mostly as an excuse.

I lean into him. "That's amazing."

"Yeah, it was."

"And it was in Minnesota?"

I want to show him I remember what he tells me—his family's moves, how cold it was there—so he'll feel he can tell me more.

I want to tell him more, too. I always want to tell him more, but now that I know he's listening—really listening—it means something different.

"You want to know another day like this one?" I ask, moving even closer, like I'm building a nest of our bodies in order to catch all the memories.

He pulls me in, settles the nest. "Sure."

"Our second date," I tell him.

"Really?" He seems surprised.

"Remember?"

He doesn't. Which is fair, because it's not like we labeled everything as a date. I mean, there were plenty of times before our first date where we were in the same place with other people, flirting. I'm talking about the second time we arrived together and left together and spent most of the time together.

"Dack's party?" I say.

"Yeah. . . ."

Still unclear. "I don't know," I say. "Maybe it doesn't count as a date. But it was the second time we hooked up. And, I don't know, you were just so . . . sweet about it. Don't get mad, alright?"

I don't want to ruin it. I am afraid I'm ruining it. Why don't I just stop when things are good?

But then he says, "I promise, nothing could make me mad right now." And he crosses his heart. Something I've never, ever seen him do before.

Smile. I'm not ruining it. I'm really not. "Okay," I say. "Well, lately—it's like you're always in a rush. Like, we have sex but we're not really . . . intimate. And I don't mind. I mean, it's fun. But every now and then, it's good to have it be like this. And at Dack's party—it was like this. Like you had all the time in the world, and you wanted us to have it together. I loved that. It was back when you were really looking at me. It was like—well, it was like you'd climbed up that tree and found me there at the top. And we had that together. Even though we were in someone's backyard. At one point—do you remember?—you made me move over a little so I'd be in the moonlight. 'It makes your skin glow,' you said. And I felt like that. Glowing. Because you were watching me, along with the moon."

I have never said this much to him. In all the time we've been together, I'm not sure I've ever let the words come out like this, without inspecting them first. I thought I knew what we were, and that was good enough for me.

What is this? I think. Because now he's leaning over and kissing me, and it's making everything romantic. Justin has been able to do romantic things before, sure. But he's never made everything seem romantic before. The universe, at this moment, is romantic. And I want it. I want it so badly. I want the touch of his lips on mine. I want the way my heart is pounding. I want this nest, my body and his body. I want it because it's that unreal kind of real.

There are so many other things we could say, but I don't want to say any of them. Not because I'm afraid of ruining it. But because right now I have everything. I don't need anything more.

We close our eyes. We rest in each other's arms.

We've somehow made it to the better place you always want to be.

I don't even realize I'm falling asleep. We're just so comfortable that I guess we go there.

Then my phone is ringing, the ringtone so much shriller than the ocean. I know who it is, and even though I want to ignore it, I can't. I open my eyes, shift away from Justin, and pick up the phone.

"Where are you?" Mom asks.

I check out the time. School's been over for a while now.

"I just went somewhere with Justin," I tell her.

"Well, your father's coming home tonight, so I want us to all have dinner."

"That's fine. I'll be home before that. In an hour or so."

As soon as those words leave my mouth, the clock that had stopped begins to tick again. I hate my mother for causing this to happen, and I hate myself for letting it.

Justin's sitting up now, looking at me like he knows what I've done.

"It's getting late," he says. He picks up the blanket and shakes it out. Then we fold it together, drawing nearer and farther and back nearer again, until the blanket is a square. Usually we just roll it up and throw it back in the trunk.

It feels different, driving home. It's no longer an adventure; it's just driving home. I find myself telling him all the things he never wants to hear about—other people's relationship drama, the way Rebecca's really trying hard to get into a good school and leave the rest of us behind (which I fully believe she should do), the pressure I feel to do well, too, or at least good enough.

After a while, the sun has set and the headlights are on and the songs we're choosing are quiet ones. I lean on his shoulder and close my eyes, falling asleep again. I don't mean to do it, but I'm just so comfortable. Usually I'm leaning into him to prove something, to claim something. But now—it's just to have him there. To rebuild that nest.

When I wake up, I see we're getting close to my house. I wish we weren't.

The only way for me to avoid being depressed is to create a bridge between now and the next time we'll be like this. I don't need to plan exactly when we'll get there. I just need to know it's there for us to get to.

"How many days do you think we could skip school before we'd get in trouble?" I ask. "I mean, if we're there in the morning, do you think they'd really notice if we're gone in the afternoon?"

"I think they'd catch us," he says.

"Maybe once a week? Once a month? Starting tomorrow?"

I figure he'll laugh at that, but instead he looks bothered. Not by me, but by the fact that he can't say yes. A lot of the time I take his sadness in a bad way. Now I almost take it in a good way, a sign that the day has meant as much to him as it has for me.

"Even if we can't do this, I'll see you at lunch?" I ask.

He nods.

"And maybe we can do something after school?"

"I think so," he says. "I mean, I'm not sure what else is going on. My mind isn't really there right now."

Plans. Maybe he's right—maybe I always try to tie him up instead of letting things happen. "Fair enough," I say. "Tomorrow is tomorrow. Let's end today on a nice note."

One last song. One last turn. One last street. No matter how hard you try to keep hold of a day, it's going to leave you.

"Here we are," I say when we get to my house.

Let's make it always like this, I want to say to him.

He pulls the car over. He unlocks the doors.

End it on a nice note, I think, as much to myself as to him.

27

It's so natural to drag a good thing down. It takes a lot of control to let it be what it is.

I kiss him goodbye. I kiss him with everything, and he responds with everything. The day surrounds us. It passes through us, between us.

"That's the nice note," I tell him when it's through. And before we can say anything else, I leave.

Later that night, right before sleep, he calls me. I never get calls from him—he always texts. If he wants to let me know something, he lets me know, but he rarely wants to talk about it.

"Hey!" I answer, a little sleepy but mostly happy.

"Hey," he says.

"Thank you again for today," I tell him immediately.

"Yeah," he says. Something's a little bit off in his voice. Something has slipped. "But about today?"

Now I'm not happy or sleepy. I'm wide awake. I decide to make a joke.

I say, "Are you going to tell me that we can't cut class every day? That's not like you."

"Yeah," he replies, "but, you know, I don't want you to think every day is going to be like today. Because they're not going to be, alright? They can't be."

It's almost like he's talking to himself.

"I know that," I tell him. "But maybe things can still be better. I know they can be."

"I don't know. That's all I wanted to say. I don't know. Today was something, but it's not, like, everything."

"I know that."

"Okay."

"Okay."

He sighs. Again, I have to tell myself this sadness is not something directed at me. It has to be directed at the fact that he can't be with me.

"That's all," he says.

I don't know what I'm supposed to say. If he's worried that I'm really going to expect this from him every day—he can't think that, can he? I decide to leave it alone. I say, "Well, I'll see you tomorrow."

"Yeah, you will."

"Thanks again for today. No matter what trouble we get into tomorrow for it, it was worth it."

"Yeah."

"I love you," I say.

It's not like Justin to say *I love you* back. Most of the time, he resents it when I say it, accuses me of saying it just to see if he'll say it next.

Sometimes he's right. But that's not why I'm saying it tonight. And when he responds by saying "Sleep well," that's more than enough for me.

I don't know what's going to happen tomorrow, but for once I'm really looking forward to it.

Chapter Two

Mom is up before me, as usual, in the same place at the kitchen table. It's like she thinks Dad or I will steal her seat if she doesn't beat us to it—and if she loses the seat, where will she spend the rest of the day?

"You look nice," she tells me. Which would be a compliment, if she didn't sound suspicious.

I don't tell her that I made sure to look nice because it's the one-day anniversary of everything getting better. She'd shoot that down real quick.

"I have to give a report," I tell her. "In class."

I know she's not going to ask me what report, or what class.

Eager. I want to get to school as soon as possible, to see him. I hope he's feeling the same way over at his house. I could text him and ask, but if things are going to change, then I can change, too. I don't need to know everything all the time.

Mom and I say more to each other, but neither of us is really listening. I want to go, and she wants to stay. It's the story of our lives.

• • •

I have to take the bus because my car is still at school. I could ask Rebecca or someone else to drive me, but then I would have to spend the whole ride talking about things instead of thinking about them.

His car isn't there when my bus gets in. In fact, he doesn't show up until almost everyone else has pulled in.

But this time he notices me waiting. Walks over. Says good morning.

I am trying hard not to barrage him with happiness. It's still early in the morning. He's barely awake.

"Sure you don't want to run away?" I ask. Just to pull a little bit of yesterday into today.

He looks confused. "Are you serious?"

"No," I tell him. "But a girl can dream, right?"

"Whatever." He starts walking, assuming I'll fall in step right beside him. Which I do.

I get it. Kind of. Since it's not like we're going to do it again today, it's probably best not to think of it as an option. Otherwise, whatever we do today will feel pathetic in comparison.

I reach for his hand.

He doesn't take it.

"What's gotten into you?" he asks.

Yesterday, I want to tell him. But from the way he looks straight ahead, I figure now's not the right time.

He doesn't even wait to hear my answer to his question.

He just keeps moving.

I tell myself it's not Angry Justin. It's Lost Justin. It has to be.

When you picture someone lost, it's usually in someplace like the woods. But with Justin, I imagine a classroom. It's not that he has a learning disability or anything. That would be a good reason. But no. He's just bored. So he doesn't keep up with what's going on. And it only gets worse, and he only gets more lost, which only makes him hate it more.

I am trying to stay on the beach. As the teachers talk and as Justin and I barely say hello between first and second period, I am reminding myself what it was like. I am turning my mind into a time machine, because I need to.

I know Rebecca's going to pin me down third period, when we're sitting next to each other in art. And that's exactly what she does.

"Where were you?" she whispers. "What happened?"

Art is one of the only classes we have together, because my school likes to keep the smart kids away from the not-smart kids, as if being in class with me might hurt Rebecca's test scores. In art, some of the not-smart kids get their revenge. I like that it gives me and Rebecca a chance to be together.

Mr. K has put a car engine at the front of the room, and has asked us to draw it in charcoal. He always says we're not supposed to talk while we're working, but as long as we're not too loud and we're getting our work done, he doesn't really mind.

Rebecca's engine is turning out worse than mine, and I feel bad that this makes me feel better.

I tell her that Justin and I escaped to the beach. I tell her it was an in-the-moment thing, and that it was wonderful.

"You should have asked me and Ben to come along," she says.

Ben is her boyfriend. He's smart, too. Justin doesn't like him at all.

"Next time," I tell her. We both know it'll never happen, but we're okay with that. Our friendship doesn't need her to skip school, and it doesn't need Ben and Justin to get along. She and I have enough history that we don't need to make a whole lot happen in the present to be close.

"Wasn't it cold?" she asks.

"Too cold to swim," I say. "But warm enough to be there."

She nods. Whatever I say to her usually makes sense.

I'm just leaving out some of the details.

I wonder if I'm supposed to meet him at his locker like yesterday. But lunchtime habit takes me to the cafeteria first, and there he is, at our usual spot.

"Hey," I say.

He nods. I sit down.

"Has anyone said anything to you about yesterday?" I ask. "I mean, you haven't gotten into any trouble, have you?"

He dips a French fry into some ketchup. That's all he's having for lunch.

"It's all good, I think," he says. "You?"

"Rebecca was curious. But that's it so far."

"Rebecca? Curious? Now there's a shocker."

"She said next time she and Ben want to go driving with us."

"I'm not sure Ben would let us inside his Mercedes. We'd have to take our shoes off first."

This one time, we went over to Ben's house and he asked all of us to take off our shoes before we came inside. Justin and I found that hysterical. "Doesn't he know that our socks are much nastier than our shoes?" Justin asked. It became one of our jokes.

"Don't say anything to Rebecca," I make Justin promise. He pretends to be zipping his lips. I relax.

I go and get my lunch, and when I come back, Rebecca and some other friends are at the table, so Justin and I are part of the big conversation instead of having our own. When the bell rings, I ask him if he can do something after school, and he says no, he has to work. He says it like I should have his work schedule memorized. But Target sends the email to him, not me.

I do not point this out. Instead, I remind myself that I am lucky I don't have to work yet. I remind myself that Justin hates his job. I remind myself that yesterday was all about a choice, but not every day allows us to make our own choices.

The important thing is that when he had a chance, he chose me. And I have to hope that next time, he'll choose me again.

He texts me when he gets home from work. Two words.
Long day.
I text him back one word.
Yeah.

• • •

Patterns. The next day, I think about patterns. Or, really, I think about ups and downs. I am used to ups and downs. Monday, when we were at the beach, was an up. I can see that.

But now—it's neither an up nor a down. It's like we've disappeared from the chart.

He's not mad at me. I can feel that. But his love has gone passive.

I don't understand. And there's no one to talk to about it. Not Justin. Every time I mention the beach, it's like it never happened. Not Rebecca. If I told her more, it might sound crazier than it really is. Not my mom. She and I don't talk about ups or downs, as a way of not having them.

I know what he and I had on Monday is worth fighting for. But I have no one to fight, so I turn on myself instead.

I know I wasn't imagining things.

But I seem to have been sent back to my imagination now.

Chapter Three

Thursday I get to school first and wait for him. I don't think that much about it. It's just what I do.

"Jesus, Rhiannon," he says when he gets out of the car. I step aside as he pulls out his bag and slams the door.

"What?" I ask.

"*'What?'*" he mimics in a high, girly voice. It's a voice his bad moods like to use.

"Crappy morning?"

He shakes his head. "Look. Rhiannon. Just let me have two minutes, okay? All I ask is for two minutes each day where nobody wants anything from me. Including you. That's all."

"I don't want anything from you," I protest.

He looks at me, tired, and says, "Of course you do."

He's right, I know. He's right, and that hurts a little.

Space. I want a boyfriend and he wants space.

Since I have plenty of space—empty space—I guess it's hard for me to understand.

"I'm sorry," I say.

"It's alright. It's just—you should see how you look there.

Nobody else is just standing in the parking lot. I'm fine with seeing you. But when you stand like that, it's like you're waiting to pounce."

"I get it," I assure him. "I know."

We're at the doors now.

He sighs. "I'll see you later."

I guess I'm not going to his locker. I guess that's okay.

"Sure you don't want to run away?" I ask. I can feel the beach, the ocean, talking through me.

"You have to stop saying that," he says. "Keep giving me the idea, and one day I just might do it."

He's not asking me to come along.

I get my books out of my locker, get ready for the day. My heart isn't in it, because my heart doesn't feel like it's anywhere near me.

I hear a voice say "Hey" and don't realize at first that it's talking to me. I turn to my left and see this small Asian girl looking at me.

"Hey," I say back. I have no idea who she is.

"Don't worry—you don't know me," she says. "It's just—it's my first day here. I'm checking the school out. And I really like your skirt and your bag. So I thought, you know, I'd say hello. Because, to be honest, I am completely alone right now."

Join the club, I want to say. But the last thing this girl needs is a view of what's going through my mind. She already looks overwhelmed.

"I'm Rhiannon," I tell her, putting my books down and

shaking her hand. "Shouldn't there be someone showing you around? Like, a welcoming committee?"

I feel this is totally Tiffany Chase's job. She seems to take pride in showing people around. I've never understood her.

"I don't know," the girl says. She still hasn't told me her name.

I tell her I'll be happy to take her to the office. I think she's supposed to sign in there, anyway.

This does not go over well.

"No!" the girl says, like I've just threatened to call the police. "It's just . . . I'm not here officially. Actually, my parents don't even know I'm doing this. They just told me we're moving here, and I . . . I wanted to see it and decide whether I should be freaking out or not."

Oh, you're definitely freaking out, I think. But I don't say that, because it will only freak her out more. Instead, I say, "That makes sense. So you're cutting school in order to check school out?"

"Exactly."

"What year are you?"

"A junior."

That's funny—she seems like a freshman. But if she's a junior, I figure there's nothing wrong with her tagging along with me today. I can pretend I'm Tiffany Chase for a few hours. It'll give me something to think about besides Justin.

"So am I," I tell her. "Let's see if we can pull this off. Do you want to come around with me today?"

"I'd love that." She seems genuinely excited. It's a good reminder that sometimes it's easy to make someone happy.

Maybe it's easier with strangers. I'm not sure.

Maybe it's easier with someone who isn't asking you for something.

The girl's name is Amy, and it's almost funny how easily she fits in with my friends. I'd be awful at meeting so many new people at once. But she gets it.

Tiffany Chase sees me showing her around and looks pissed.

"What's her problem?" Amy asks.

"She usually gets first dibs on being tour guide," I say.

"I like this version better."

I know I shouldn't really take satisfaction from that, but I do. Like I'm so desperate to be good at something that I'll take whatever I can get.

I do not share this thought with Amy.

I don't see Justin at our usual time and place between first and second period, but he's there unexpectedly between second and third. I wonder if he went out of his way to make up for it. We don't have a chance to talk or anything, but at least I get to see him, and I get to see that he doesn't look too angry.

In math class, Amy starts passing me notes.

At first, I figure she just has a question. Or maybe she's telling me she's had enough and she's going to leave next period. But instead it's . . . chatty. Telling me that class here is just as boring as class back at her real school. Asking me where I got my skirt and whether there are any boys I like and if I think there are any boys she would like.

We go back and forth like this a few times. She picks up almost immediately on some of Ms. Frasier's mannerisms, and is pretty good at making fun of them. (*She talks like a nun, but instead of God, she's talking about trigonometry. I wonder what her habit looks like. A rhombus?*)

I'm having fun, but it's also making me a little sad, because it's making me realize that I haven't really made a new friend since I started dating Justin. It's like since he and I have been together, I've only seen the same people, and less of them. I need this new girl to come out of nowhere in order to have someone to pass notes with.

She comes with me to lunch—we put our stuff down at the table, and Preston goes crazy about all the buttons on her bag, asking her all these questions about Japanese comics. Amy seems flustered, and I'm hoping that Preston is showing his big gay self enough that she doesn't think he's flirting.

When Justin gets to the table, I notice he's got something on his mind. I introduce him to Amy and he gives her the Justin nod. Then he tells me he left his wallet at home. I say it's not a problem and ask him what he wants. He says French fries, but I get him a cheeseburger, too. When I hand them over, he thanks me, and I know he means it.

Even with Amy there, it feels like we're all falling into our usual lunchtime routine. Preston asks her about another comic thing, but instead of answering, she turns to me and asks me how far it takes to get to the ocean from here.

The word *ocean* makes me look at Justin, but it's like he hasn't heard, like his mind is stuck on *cheeseburger*.

"It's so funny you should say that," I tell Amy. "We were just there the other day. It took about an hour or so."

Justin is next to Amy, across from me. She turns her head and asks him, "Did you have a good time?"

He doesn't seem to have heard, so I say, "It was amazing."

"Did you drive?" she asks Justin.

This time he hears her.

"Yes, I drove," he says.

"We had such a great time," I chime in. And by saying that, I get to hold on to it a little longer. It's like Justin and I have this secret, and it's sitting there in front of everyone else, but nobody else can see it. Neither of us is going to point it out. It remains ours. Only ours.

I don't mind that.

I can tell Amy wants to ask more. I remind myself that she's not a new friend; she's just a visitor. She's only here for today.

Justin, meanwhile, has gone back to eating. He has nothing more to say about the thing that means so much to me.

Amy shadows me for the rest of the day, and keeps as quiet as a shadow. I imagine what it must be like, to look into the future and see yourself living in a new place. I've never done that. I've always been here, anchored by parents who never search out change, accompanied by all the other people who fear they'll never leave. For so many years, the idea of living somewhere else was about the same to me as the idea of living in a fairy-tale kingdom. There were places that existed as stories and places that existed as life, and I was taught to never confuse the two. It wasn't until Justin and I became a real couple and my sister left town that I started to wonder not only about what came next, but where. I don't want to picture us doing the same things in the same place ten years—or even two years—from now. But when I try to picture us anywhere else, it's hard to do. We both like to pull at the anchor, but the anchor is pretty strong.

As I do my work in English class, I imagine switching places with Amy. I don't even know where her school is, but I wonder what it would be like if I had a completely new start. Would I still remain me? Or would I become someone else? I would have to become someone else, because I can't imagine me without Justin. It hurts to think about it. I imagine myself walking those halls—and the alone I feel there is so much worse than the alone I feel here.

I remember the ocean, and know that, no matter where I go, I want him to come with me.

I feel silly, but I'm a little sad to see Amy go. As we head to the parking lot at the end of the day, I write down my email address and give it to her. While I'm doing this, Justin finds me. He seems so much better now that the day is over. And from the way he lingers, I know he wants to hang out, not just say goodbye.

"Walk me to my car?" Amy asks.

I look at Justin, wanting to make sure he'll wait.

"I'll get my car," he says.

It's a good thing he seems to be in a patient mood, because Amy has parked about as far from the school as you can get. As we walk over, I wonder what Justin is going to do now. I'm trying to figure it out when Amy breaks into my thoughts and says, "Tell me something nobody else knows about you."

"What?" I ask. It's such a slumber party question.

"It's something I always ask people—tell me something about you that nobody else knows. It doesn't have to be major. Just something."

I decide to go with whatever comes first to my mind. "Okay. When I was ten, I tried to pierce my own ear with a sewing needle. I got it halfway through, and then I passed out. Nobody was home, so nobody found me. I just woke up with this needle halfway in my ear, drops of blood all over my shirt. I pulled the needle out, cleaned up, and never tried it again. It wasn't until I was fourteen that I went to the mall with my mom and got my ears pierced for real. She had no idea. How about you?"

There's a beat as she thinks about it—which is a little off. If this is a question she always asks, doesn't she always have an answer ready? After a few seconds she says, "I stole Judy Blume's *Forever* from my sister when I was eight. I figured if it was by the author of *Superfudge,* it had to be good. Well, I soon realized why she kept it under her bed. I'm not sure I understood it all, but I thought it was unfair that the boy would name his, um, organ, and the girl wouldn't name hers. So I decided to give mine a name."

I can't help but laugh, and also can't help but ask, "What was its name?"

"*Helena*. I introduced everyone to her at dinner that night. It went over really well."

Helena. I can't figure if Justin would find this funny, too, or if he'd just find it weird.

We're at Amy's car now. "It was great to meet you," I tell her. "Hopefully, I'll see you around next year."

"Yeah," she says, "it was great to meet you, too."

She thanks me for taking her around, for introducing her to my friends, and for putting up with her questions. I tell her it wasn't any problem at all. Justin drives over and honks.

I almost tell him I want to go back to the ocean.

But instead I decide to see if I can bring the ocean here.

We go to his house like we always do, because my mom is always home at my house. We don't have a chance to talk on the way over, because I'm in my car, following his. But even when we get there, we don't say much. He asks me if I want something to drink, and I tell him water. He steals some scotch, but not that much. I never mind if he has a little. I like the taste of it on his tongue.

He sits down on the couch and turns on the TV. But I know what's going on. It's like he can't come out and say, *Let's make out.* A few times he's started kissing me the minute we've gotten in the door—but usually he has to make sure no one's home, get used to the gravity of being home before we can resist it a little.

So most of the time, it starts like this. Both of us watching the show but not really watching. Him leaning into me or me leaning into him. Putting our drinks down. A hand on a leg, an arm over a shoulder. Bodies starting to confuse. He won't say that he wants something from me. But it's there in the air. It's there and understood between us as his hands go under my shirt and my hands touch his cheek, his ear, his hair.

I return to him. He returns to me. But then it's not enough for us to balance like that. He pushes it. He's saying things, but they're not really directed at me. They're directed at what we're doing. They're part of what we're doing. The heat feels good. The touch feels good. But it doesn't feel like enough. Not for him, since he wants more, and more, and more. Not for me, because if it was enough, I wouldn't be thinking about whether or not it's enough. We aren't going all the way—not on the couch, only in the bedroom, where there's a door to close and protection to wear and blankets to pull up when it's over and we lie there, pleased. But we're still doing something—he does what he does when we're on the couch, and I do what I do when we're on the couch, and none of our clothes are totally on and none of them are totally off. He starts to murmur, starts to moan, and yes there's something he wants from me, there's something he really wants from me, and I am giving it to him and he's giving it back to me. I want him to get that peak, be-cause what I want more is the sweetness of breathing together afterward.

He groans. His back shudders under my hand. He kisses me. Once. Twice. Three times. We lie back. I find his heartbeat and lay my head there. He says more things.

The TV is still on, and what he does next is what makes me grateful, what makes me think that maybe all of this is worth it. Because instead of turning back to the TV, he turns it off. He stands up and gets me more water. He does not get himself more scotch. He comes back and returns to his place on the couch, then returns me to my place on his chest. We stay like that for a while. No longer in a rush. No longer wanting anything more than a quiet spot of nothing to share.

Chapter Four

I'm good. I wait until after school on Friday to ask about Steve's party.

"Will you just *stop?*" is his reply.

"Excuse me?" I say. "I don't think I deserve that."

He shakes his head. "Sorry."

We're at my locker. I know he has to get to work. That's why I'm trying to figure this out now.

"I'm just going to hate at least half the people there," he says. "As long as you can deal with that, we can go. If Steve and Stephanie start attacking each other, do *not* expect me to calm him down or take him outside or shield her bitchiness from his bullshit. Just let me sit in the corner and drink and watch like everyone else."

"They only fought that once!" I argue. These are our friends. Most of the time they behave. Tequila just makes them mean.

He snorts. "Jesus, Rhiannon—open your eyes."

"You can do whatever you want at the party," I say. "I'll drive. Okay?"

"I'm telling you right now, if I go there, I'm going to get wasted."

"I've been warned," I tell him. "I know I've been warned."

It's only when I'm driving over to pick him up on Saturday night that I wonder why *I* want to go to this party.

Rebecca won't be there. She and Ben have a "date night." Preston and his best friend Allie tend to avoid parties they find "obnoxious." And while I'm friends with Stephanie, I have to agree with Justin that being the party's center of attention might not bring out her best behavior.

Mostly, I guess, I feel that something new might happen if we go to the party. If we stay home, there's no chance that something new will happen.

We get pizza before heading over—apparently Justin's father told him he couldn't go out unless his room was clean, and Justin left the house anyway. When I first asked Justin what his dad was like, all he'd say was "military"—I couldn't tell whether this meant his career or his attitude or both. Now he's always saying, "Please God, don't let me turn into that man."

I think pretty much the same thing about my mom, so I guess we relate.

On our way to Steve's, I ask Justin if he knows who else is going to be there.

"Does it really matter?" he asks. "It's the same whoever's there."

I don't think he's in the mood for me to argue, so I stay quiet. A song I like comes on the radio, and I start to sing along. He shoots me a look like I'm a crazywoman and I stop.

When we get there, he goes, "You know where to find me"—meaning: wherever the alcohol is. He takes off as soon as I lock the car doors, acting like the party might run out of beer before he's made it inside. Which, considering Steve's last party, isn't totally off base.

Crowded. Already it feels like there are people everywhere. I don't recognize some of them. I see Stephanie for a brief moment—she gives me a squeal and a hug, then moves on to the next squeal and hug.

I know I should go to the kitchen, get a drink (only one), and stay by my boyfriend's side. But I find myself wandering away from it instead. Steve stumbles past me—he must've started drinking early. I say hi. He tells me to make myself at home.

It's really loud, some bitch-bashing rap competing with all the talking, making everyone louder. I head into the den and see a laptop there, hooked to the speakers. I look at the playlist and find that the song that's playing is called "My Dick's Got Rights!" The next song is called "Naked Like U Want Me." I think about turning it down. I think about putting on Adele. I don't do anything.

I look around and see Tiffany Chase talking to Demeka Miller. I walk over and say hi.

"Hi!" Tiffany shouts back over the music.

"Yeah, hi!" Demeka says.

I realize the flaw in my plan is that I don't have anything to say to either of these girls. I almost tell Tiffany that I get now why she likes to take people around the school, but I don't think that's the right party thing to say. It'll sound like I want to be her, when that's not it at all.

"I love your hair!" I tell Demeka. She recently added a red streak.

"Thanks!" Demeka says back.

Tiffany and Demeka look at each other. I've clearly interrupted their conversation. I know I should uninterrupt it.

"See you around!" I say. I drift off, but not that far. Again, I know I should head to the kitchen. But I don't.

Next to the laptop, there are CDs. Probably belonging to Steve's parents. (I have no idea where they are right now.) Adele is near the top. Having nothing better to do, I start to flip through.

There's Kelly Clarkson, which makes me think of the drive to the ocean. And there's Fun., who we also heard.

"I really like them," someone says to me, pointing to the CD. "Do you?"

I'm surprised to have been noticed. The boy talking to me looks totally out of place—he's worn a jacket and a tie to the party, like he's going straight from here to church in the morning. He looks really desperate to have someone to talk to, and at the same time, I feel this weird sense that he specifically wants to talk to me. Usually this would make my guard go up. But for some reason, I decide not to brush him off.

"Yeah," I say, holding up the CD. "I like them, too."

Quietly, he starts to sing "Carry On"—the same song Justin and I sang along to in the car. I decide to take this as a sign. Of what, I'm not sure.

"I like that one in particular," the boy says.

Strange. There is something so familiar about him. It's in his eyes, or in the way he's looking at me.

Harmless. I remind myself that talking to him is harmless.

"Do I know you?" I ask.

"I'm Nathan," he says.

I tell him I'm Rhiannon.

"That's a beautiful name," he replies. And it's not just something to say, like "I love your hair."

"Thanks," I say. "I used to hate it, but I don't so much anymore."

"Why?"

"It's just a pain to spell," I tell him. And because it's different. I don't tell him all the grief I got as a kid for it being so different, how badly I wished my parents had given me something easier.

The fact that he seems so familiar is still nagging at me. "Do you go to Octavian?" I ask.

He shakes his head. "No. I'm just here for the weekend. Visiting my cousin."

"Who's your cousin?"

"Steve."

"Oh, that explains it," I tell him. And then, just like with Tiffany and Demeka, I find I've completely run out of things to say. I mean, I could ask Nathan where he's from, how long he's here for, why he's wearing a tie. But I'd only be filling the time until I leave, and that doesn't seem fair.

I'm ready to pull the plug and let the conversation die. But then he surprises me.

"I hate my cousin," he says.

Scandal. But not really. Still, I'm curious why.

He goes on. "I hate the way he treats girls. I hate the way he

51

thinks he can buy all his friends by throwing parties like this. I hate the way that he only talks to you when he needs something. I hate the way he doesn't seem capable of love."

Wow. I can barely remember my own cousins' names. Nathan seems so *intense* about Steve.

"Then why are you here?" I ask.

"Because I want to see it fall apart. Because when this party gets busted—and if it stays this loud, it *will* get busted—I want to be a witness. From a safe distance away, of course."

The boy's on fire. It's amusing. I decide to add more fuel.

"And you're saying he's incapable of loving Stephanie?" I ask. "They've been going out for over a year."

"That doesn't mean anything, does it? I mean, being with someone for over a year can mean that you love them . . . but it can also mean you're trapped."

Trapped. How stupid, because my first thought is, *Stephanie is not nearly as trapped as I am.* Which is ridiculous. Neither of us is *trapped.*

I wonder what would make Nathan say such a thing. He talks like he knows.

"Speaking from experience?" I ask.

"There are many things that can keep you in a relationship," he says. His eyes are begging me to listen. "Fear of being alone. Fear of disrupting the arrangement of your life. A decision to settle for something that's okay, because you don't know if you can get any better. Or maybe there's the irrational belief that it will get better, even if you know he won't change."

He. I guess Nathan is on the Preston side of things.

" 'He'?" I say, to make sure.

"Yeah."

"I see." Maybe this explains why I'm finding him so harmless, why I'm feeling so open to him. Girls don't need to be threatened by boys who are after boys.

After a moment, he asks, "That cool?"

"Completely," I assure him. I wonder if Steve knows.

"How about you? Seeing anyone?"

"Yeah," I say. Then, seeing where this is going, I add, "For over a year."

"And why are you still together? Fear of being alone? A decision to settle? An irrational belief that he'll change?"

Ha. I'm not about to tell him it's much more complicated than that. So instead I say, "Yes. Yes. And yes."

"So . . ."

"But he can also be incredibly sweet," I add. "And I know that, deep down, I mean the world to him."

Those eyes don't let me out of it. "Deep down? That sounds like settling to me. You shouldn't have to venture deep down in order to get to love."

Enough. I don't know you. Stop.

It sounds like Justin talking in my head, even though it's my voice.

"Let's switch the topic, okay?" I say. "This isn't a good party topic. I liked it more when you were singing to me."

Justin pops into the doorway now, Corona in hand. He scans the room, sees me, looks a little happy, then sees that I'm talking to a guy and looks a little less happy.

"So who's this?" he asks, coming over.

"Don't worry, Justin," I say. "He's gay."

"Yeah, I can tell from the way he's dressed. What are you doing here?"

"Nathan, this is Justin, my boyfriend. Justin, this is Nathan."

"Hi," Nathan says.

Justin lets it hang for a second, then asks, "You seen Stephanie? Steve's looking for her. I think they're at it again."

There's an *I told you so* embedded in his voice. And he did tell me so.

I give him back an *I told you so what.*

"Maybe she went to the basement," I say.

"Nah. They're dancing in the basement."

Dancing. The last time the two of us danced was probably a very tipsy night at Preston's house a few months ago.

I miss it.

"Want to go down there and dance?" I ask.

"Hell no! I didn't come here to dance. I came here to *drink.*"

"Charming," I say. What was I even thinking, asking him? Then I figure I have another opportunity. "Do you mind if I go dance with Nathan?"

He takes another look at Nathan's tie, jacket. "You sure he's gay?"

"I'll sing you show tunes if you want me to prove it," Nathan volunteers.

Justin slaps him on the back. "No, dude, don't do that, okay? Go dance."

Then, with a Corona salute, he heads back to the kitchen.

"You don't have to if you don't want to," I tell Nathan. I know I wouldn't be crazy about the idea of dancing with someone I didn't know, so I can't really expect him to be into it.

But he says, "I want to. I really want to."

I don't know why this makes sense, but it does. So I lead the way to the basement. There's a different kind of noise down there—dance noise. In a total Stephanie touch, all the regular lights have been replaced with red bulbs. It feels like we're at the center of a beating heart.

It's hard to see who's here, but I spot Steve making his own pre-hangover moves in the corner.

I call out to him, "Hey, Steve! I like your cousin!"

He nods, so I guess the feelings Nathan expressed aren't entirely mutual.

"Have you seen Stephanie?" he yells.

"No!" I yell back, figuring it's probably best if they stay separate until they come to their more sober senses.

Maybe because he's gay, I think Nathan will leap into the dancing. But instead he looks vaguely terrified. I remind myself that he's surrounded by strangers. Then I also remind myself that I am one of those strangers, even if it doesn't feel that way. I pulled him down here, so it's on me to make him feel at home. I find myself thinking that dancing is just another form of singing along, and all I have to do is get him to sing along, the same way he was singing along to the song that wasn't playing upstairs.

He's swaying now, blocked in by all the people around us and the space they're taking up. I try to ignore that, and focus only on him and the music. I create a space to draw him into. And it works. I can feel it working. His eyes matching my eyes. His smile matching my smile. The song. The song is taking the lead. The song is telling us how to move. The song is guiding his hands to my back, to my waist. The song is generating the heat and giving it to our bodies. The song is pulling me closer. The song, and his eyes.

Then a new song. He starts to sing along, and that makes me happy. It's all making me happy, to be so loose in a place that's so crowded. To not feel Justin tugging me in any direction. To give up on everything.

"You're not bad!" I yell to Nathan.

"You're amazing!" he yells back.

More songs swimming through the red. Bodies coming and going. Nobody shouting my name. Nobody needing me, or asking for anything.

I lose track. Of time. Of what I'm thinking. Of where I am and who I am. I even lose track of the song. I lose track of everything but the boy in the tie across from me, who is releasing himself as well. I can tell, as one who knows.

Then it all ends. A song is cut short. I feel like a cartoon character, holding for a minute in the air, then looking down and falling to earth. The regular lights go on—they've been there all along, beside the red. I hear Stephanie's voice yelling that the party's over, that the neighbors have called the cops.

Even though it's not my fault, I want to apologize to Nathan. Because it's over. It has to be over.

"I have to find Justin," I tell him. "Are you going to be okay?"

He nods. "Look," he says. His hand is still on my wrist. "Would it be weird for me to ask you for your email?"

I wouldn't have thought it was weird, except for him asking if it was weird.

"Don't worry," he adds. "I am still one hundred percent homosexual."

"That's too bad," I say. Then, before my inner flirt can make more of a fool of herself, I give him my email address, take his pen, and write his email address down on a receipt.

The basement is nearly empty, and there's the sound of sirens in the distance. Stephanie isn't making it up—we really need to leave.

"Time to go," I say. We're both staying in the space we created, not wanting to leave it even though the lights are on.

"You're not going to let your boyfriend drive, are you?" Nathan asks.

"That's sweet," I say. "No. I control the keys."

There's chaos at the top of the stairs, and we're separated before we can say goodbye. Justin isn't in the kitchen, so I figure he's already at the car.

Sure enough, he's pacing there, waiting for me.

"Where were you?" he accuses as I unlock the door.

"The basement," I tell him when we're in the car. "You knew that."

He curses a little, but I know he's cursing at the cops, not me. I pull out, relieved that we didn't park in the driveway, where things are all backed up.

"We're going to make it," I assure him.

"You're beautiful," he slurs.

"You're drunk," I say.

"You're beautiful anyway," he tells me. Then he puts back the seat and closes his eyes.

I wait a few minutes. Then I discover a song I like on the radio and sing along.

As Justin snores, I find myself hoping Nathan made it out okay.

Chapter Five

I know Justin's not working on Sunday, so I'm hoping we'll hang out at least a little. But he doesn't wake up until one, and from what I can tell from the texts he sends, he's not in good shape. I offer to come over and make him whatever hangover cure he wants. He texts me back two hours later to say that all he can do today is sleep. He can even sleep through his parents yelling about all his sleeping.

Get shitfaced, then face the shit—I know the routine. It's not like I've never been there. I just don't go there as often as he does.

I asked him about it before. Not confrontational. Just curious.

"I drink to feel better," he told me. "And if I feel worse the next day, it's still worth it, because I still got to feel better for a little bit, which is more than I would've done sober."

There are times I can make him feel like that, too. There are times when I know he's drunk on me. Not just when we're making out—there are other times I can make him forget about everything else. Which is a power nobody else has with him. I know this.

Because my day is empty of him, it's empty. My mother asks

if I want to go to the grocery store with her, but I know if I do, I'll only want to buy things I shouldn't eat. My dad is on the computer, doing work, avoiding us to provide for us. I think of emailing Nathan from last night, but that thought passes. I doubt I'll ever see him again. Whatever we shared is gone, because it was destined to be gone from the minute it started.

Distraction. I turn on the TV. Housewives and nature shows. An episode of *Friends* I've seen a hundred times. Nothing I want to watch followed by nothing I want to watch followed by nothing I want to watch. I imagine doing this forever. An infinity of nothing I want to watch.

It's a day like that.

I call Justin. I can't help myself. I want to talk to him so bad. I know I won't convince him to stop being hungover. I won't convince him to get out of bed and do something with me—or even stay in bed and do something with me. I would be happy to lie there next to him.

"I've decided that whiskey is not my friend," he says.

"Still bad?" I ask.

"Better. But still bad. The day has completely crapped out."

"It's alright. I've been catching up on my TV watching."

"Fuck, I wish I were there with you. Being sick is so fucking *boring.*"

"I wish you were here, too. I could come over if you want."

"Nah. I just have to ride this one out. It wouldn't be fair to ask you to be around me when I'm so sick of being around me."

"I'm willing."

"I know. And I appreciate it. But it's not going to happen today."

The fact that he sounds disappointed makes my own

disappointment a little easier to live with. Even if it still leaves me alone for the rest of the day.

Alone. The only thing that prevents me from feeling completely alone is knowing that I have someone, that if I really need him, he will be there.

"I'm going to go now," he says to me. I don't point out he's not actually going to go anywhere. Neither of us is going to go anywhere.

"See you tomorrow," I say, because I know we're not going to talk again tonight.

"Yeah. See ya."

My mother comes home and I help her put away the groceries. We make dinner. We don't talk about anything. She talks, for sure. She talks and talks and talks. But we don't talk at all.

When I get back to my room, I check my email on my phone. I am surprised to find a message from Nathan.

Hi Rhiannon,

I just wanted to say that it was lovely meeting you and dancing with you last night. I'm sorry the police came and separated us. Even though you're not my type, gender-wise, you're certainly my type, person-wise. Please keep in touch.

N

I smile. It's so . . . *nice*. I wonder if he's single, even though I can't really imagine Preston going for him. Preston likes guys who are trendier. Or at least don't wear ties to parties.

I also wonder about being his type, person-wise. What does that mean, really? Where does that get us?

Shut up, I tell myself. A nice guy tries to be friendly with me and I immediately think, *Why bother?* There is something seriously wrong with me. The reason to bother is because he's a nice guy.

I hit reply, but I don't know what to write. I feel I need to make an excuse for not writing to him first; I'm sure the piece of paper with his email address on it is still in my pocket. I also want to sound like someone who gets this kind of email all the time.

It's weird, because the Rhiannon who comes out in what I write doesn't sound like I normally sound.

She sounds like she's really enjoying herself.

Nathan!

I'm so glad you emailed, because I lost the slip of paper that I wrote your email on. It was wonderful talking and dancing with you, too. How dare the police break us up! You're my type, person-wise, too. Even if you don't believe in relationships that last longer than a year. (I'm not saying you're wrong, btw. Jury's still out.)

I never thought I'd say this, but I hope Steve has another party soon. If only so you can bear witness to its evil.

Love,
Rhiannon

I don't know why I write "Love" like that. It's just what I always write. Everything else seems cold.

But now I'm worried I sound too eager. Not eager in the same way I'm eager with Justin. Just eager for . . . whatever's next.

As soon as I hit send, the emptiness returns. I'm back into the day I was having. Maybe this is what alone really is—finding out how tiny your world is, and not knowing how to get anywhere else.

I go on Facebook. I read Gawker. I watch some music on YouTube, including the Fun. song from the day with Justin, the one Nathan sang back to me. I feel stupid doing that. I know Nathan wouldn't find it stupid. Somehow I know that. And I know Justin would find it stupid. I asked him once if he thought we had a song. I mean, most couples have a song. But he said he had no idea, and that he didn't even understand why we'd want one, anyway.

I'd told myself he was right. We didn't need one. Every song could be ours.

But now I want one. It's not enough that every song can make me think of him.

I want one, just one, that will make him think of me.

Chapter Six

The hangover hangs over Monday as well.

It's like his personality has spoiled from lack of use. He's in school, but he still thinks he's in bed. I can't take it personally that he's not happy to see me, because he's not happy to see any of us. He won't say more than two words in any sentence, and after a few minutes I decide to leave him alone.

A lot of our Mondays are like this.

Our Monday at the beach seems like much longer than a week ago.

What is wrong with me?

"How was your weekend?" Rebecca asks when I get to third period.

"How *wasn't* my weekend?" I reply.

"What does that mean?"

"I don't know. I just mean that not much happened."

"How was the party?"

"It was fine. I danced with Steve's gay cousin. Justin got shitfaced. The cops came."

"Steve has a gay cousin? I didn't know that."

"I don't think they're close."

"Well, if he's still around, Ben and I were going to hang out with Steve and Stephanie during assembly period this afternoon. Just get coffee or something. Wanna come?"

I notice she hasn't invited Justin. It'll be a triple date, only I'm not being asked to bring my date.

"Can I get back to you?" I ask.

Rebecca's not stupid. She knows why I'm not committing.

"Whenever," she tells me. "We'll be there either way. Although it would be great to have some time with you. I feel I haven't seen you in ages."

Now it's clear that Justin's being deliberately excluded. Because Rebecca sees me all the time. It's just that he's always by my side when she does.

I find him right before lunch.

"What are you doing?" I ask.

"What does it look like I'm doing?" he asks back.

It looks like he is switching his books in his locker. It looks like he's about to head to lunch.

"What do you want to be doing?" I ask.

He slams the locker shut. "I want to be playing video games," he says. "That work for you?"

"Wanna get out of here and do something? There's that assembly seventh and eighth period. Nobody will notice we're gone."

I am looking for that spark. If it's gone out, I am trying to relight it. Because I have a spark inside of me, too. And right now it wants to be bright.

"What the fuck has gotten into you?" he asks. "If we could just leave, don't you think I would've done it by now? Jesus. It's bad enough to be here. Why do you have to keep pointing it out?"

"That's not what I meant," I tell him. "I just thought it could be like last week."

"Last week? I don't even know what you're talking about."

"The beach? The ocean?"

He shakes his head, like I'm making things up. "Enough, okay? Just *stop*."

So I stop. I swallow the spark and feel it scratch as it goes down.

We eat with our friends. Preston asks about the party, and Justin tells him it sucked. In his version, skank girls kept crowding the kitchen. Stephanie yelled at him for putting his feet on a table. Then the police came, because the police clearly have nothing better to do.

Preston then asks me how my night was. I tell him that my night sucked, too. I don't tell him about the basement, or about the dancing. No, my version transforms itself into Justin's version. He doesn't even notice, but I do it anyway.

I am disappearing. This is the thought that occurs to me: *I am disappearing*. Like nothing I say or do matters. My life has become so tiny that it's completely unseen.

The only way I can think to fight this is to text Rebecca and tell her I'm free to hang out after school.

• • •

He doesn't care. I tell him I made plans for during the assembly, and he genuinely doesn't care. He doesn't ask to be invited along. He doesn't even ask me what the plans are. He'll go home and play video games. He won't text me unless I text him first. I know all this—but why do I still feel surprised, as if it isn't meant to be this way?

Rebecca decides she's in the mood for ice cream, and convinces the rest of us we're in the mood for ice cream, too, even though it's not summer and the nearest good ice cream place is about twenty minutes away. It is, as we expected, surprisingly easy to get out of the assembly—we figure the visiting author won't miss us too much, since none of us have ever heard of him. Rebecca, Ben, and I pile into her car, and Stephanie and Steve meet us there. Steve is wearing the effects of the weekend more obviously than Stephanie is; she looks like she spent the past two days at the gym.

We get our cones and head for a table. When we start talking, it's not about the party, but everything that happened after—all the cleanup that had to be done, all of the bullshit with the police, who didn't end up arresting anyone. They just wanted to break up the party and they did a good job of it.

Stephanie admits she was a little relieved. "There are *some people*," she says, "who will never leave a party unless the police come." From the sound of her voice, I know I'm supposed to know who she's talking about. I have no idea.

"I really liked your cousin," I tell Steve. "He kinda saved the night for me."

Steve looks confused. "My cousin? When did you meet my cousin?"

"At the party. Nathan." I almost add *your gay cousin*, but then I realize I have no idea if Steve knows.

Now Steve laughs. "At my party? I don't think so. All my cousins are, like, eight. And none of them are named Nathan."

I don't understand what he's saying.

"But I met him," I say lamely.

"Oh dear," Rebecca jumps in, patting my hand. "It sounds like you met someone who said he was Steve's cousin."

"But why would he say that?"

Stephanie shrugs. "Who knows? Guys are weird."

What's hurting me is how honest he seemed. How real. Now it's like I've made him up.

"He was wearing a tie," I say. "I think he was the only guy wearing a tie."

"That dude!" Steve laughs. "I totally saw him. He's not my cousin, but he was definitely there."

I wonder if Nathan is really his name. I wonder if he's really gay. I wonder why the universe is doing this to me.

"I can't believe he lied," I say.

"Again," Stephanie chimes in. "Guys are weird."

"And certainly you're used to a little lying?" Rebecca adds. "This guy probably liked you and didn't know how to deal with it. That happens. It's not the worst kind of lie."

I think she's trying to make me feel better, but I'm stuck on that first part—*certainly you're used to a little lying*.

"Justin never lies to me," I say.

Rebecca plays dumb. "Who said anything about Justin?"

"I know what you meant. And I'm telling you—Justin can ignore me and say the wrong things and go into his moods, but he never, ever lies to me. I know you don't think we have much, but we do have that."

Rebecca and Stephanie shoot a look at each other, clearly not believing me. Ben is checking his phone. Steve still seems amused that some guy crashed his party pretending to be his cousin.

I hate this feeling—my so-called friends thinking they know my life better than I do. And I hate it even more this time because I thought I'd had the opposite with Nathan. Stupid, for sure, after one conversation and one email exchange. But still. Whether it was real or an illusion, it makes a rip when it goes.

Steve starts to argue with Stephanie about who was the most wasted guest at the party, and my questions about Nathan seem to have been quickly forgotten. We finish our ice cream and then don't know what to do—we've only been hanging out for about fifteen minutes, but the reason we're here no longer exists. Stephanie proposes a trip to the secondhand store down the street, and even though Ben and Steve protest, nobody can think of anything better to do.

I am disappearing again, this time into silence. As Stephanie and Rebecca try things on and Steve looks through old records, Ben and I hover on the sidelines. He keeps checking his phone, but then, as Stephanie and Rebecca argue over who looks better in a fifties sundress, he says to me, "I know it probably doesn't matter, but I'd bet good money that the guy who said he was Steve's cousin had a reason for doing it. Guys act weird, sure. But it's usually for a reason. And it's rarely to be mean. It's much more likely that he liked you." Then he goes back to his phone and writes another text.

I go onto my own phone, wanting there to be an email from Nathan explaining everything. But there isn't. So I write to him instead.

Nathan,

Apparently, Steve doesn't have a cousin Nathan, and none of his cousins were at his party. Care to explain?

Rhiannon

Almost immediately, I get a reply.

Rhiannon,

I can, indeed, explain. Can we meet up? It's the kind of explanation that needs to be done in person.

Love,
Nathan

That "Love" hits me. I know it could be a taunt or a tease. And I also know it isn't a taunt or a tease.

Rebecca is calling me over to decide who gets the dress. Ben is pulling himself farther into the background, not wanting to get involved. Steve is holding up a Led Zeppelin record and asking Stephanie if he already has it.

I don't reply to the email. Not yet. I need to think.

• • •

Rebecca gets the dress. Steve gets the record. Stephanie finds another dress that she says she likes more than the one Rebecca has. Ben spots a dictionary and starts talking about whether or not dictionaries, physical dictionaries, will exist in twenty years.

When everyone's done shopping, they make some noises about hanging out more and eventually getting dinner.

I tell them I have to go home.

Chapter Seven

I don't owe Nathan anything. He lied to me. Because of this, I should let it go.

But even if I don't owe him anything, I feel I owe myself the explanation. I want to know.

I stay awake half the night, trying to figure it out. Then I get up and write him back.

Nathan,

This better be a good explanation. I'll meet you in the coffee shop at the Clover Bookstore at 5.

Rhiannon

The bookstore seems like a good, safe place to meet. It's in public, but it's also a place Justin would never, ever go.

I already know I'm not going to tell him about this.

If I spent most of the night awake with my thoughts, Justin seems to have gotten plenty of sleep. It's almost a good morning with him. When I see him, he doesn't look like he wants to run away. He asks me how hanging out with Rebecca and the others went; I'm impressed because I didn't expect him to remember what I was doing. He even listens to my response for about a minute. Then he grows bored—but I don't blame him, because it's pretty boring. It's not what's really playing in my mind. It's not what I'm really thinking about.

Waiting. I can't stand the feeling of waiting. Knowing I'm stranded for a few hours in the boring parts.

I check my email at lunch and find something new from Nathan.

Rhiannon,

I'll be there. Although not in a way you might expect.
Bear with me and hear me out.

A

My immediate reaction is that he's not gay at all. And that his name must start with an A. He was hitting on me, and when I caught him hitting on me, he made up that he was gay. It explains the connection I felt a little more. Both magnets were working. I know I should be offended, but part of me doesn't mind if he was hitting on me, especially because he was too sweet to do it all the way. It's still a lie, and I'm still angry about that. But at least it's a flattering lie.

I know Rebecca would love it if I talked to her about this. I know she is perpetually ready for that kind of conversation—she thinks friendships are built out of that kind of conversation.

I sit across from her at lunch and I can see the question marks darting out of her eyes—does she know something is going on, or is she just hoping? Justin is right next to me, so it's not like I can say anything. But even if it was just me and Rebecca, safely alone in her car, I'm not sure I would tell her. I like that it's mine, and mine alone.

I get to the bookstore early and take a table by the window in the café. I'm nervous, like this is a first date. I know I shouldn't be feeling this way—I'm only here for answers, not to get a boyfriend. I already have a boyfriend.

It's amazing how many people will walk into a café area when you're waiting for someone else. At least I already know what he looks like. I wonder if he'll still be wearing a tie. Maybe that's his thing. Maybe he's really that much of a dork. I could be friends with that kind of behavior.

I try to distract myself with an *Us Weekly*, but my mind doesn't even want to look at the pictures. A girl comes in and I don't really notice her until she's right in front of me, at my table, sitting down.

Rude. "I'm sorry," I say. "That seat's taken."

I'm expecting her to tell me she's sorry and move on. But instead she says, "It's okay. Nathan sent me."

Weird. I take a good look at the girl—her Anthropologie top, her Banana Republic pants—and figure she's not evil. But her presence is still confusing.

"He sent you?" I say. "Where is he?" Was he so scared that I'd be pissed that he brought reinforcements? *Total* dork move.

I look to see if he's watching us, if he's waiting to see if it's safe to show his face. But he's nowhere in sight.

"Rhiannon," the girl says. I turn back to her and she's looking right at me. Unsettling. There's something big she's not telling me. She's both excited and terrified to tell me. It's all there in her eyes.

I don't look away.

I am not ready for this, whatever it is.

"Yes?" I whisper.

Her voice is calm. "I need to tell you something. It's going to sound very, very strange. What I need is for you to listen to the whole story. You will probably want to leave. You might want to laugh. But I need you to take this seriously. I know it will sound unbelievable, but it's the truth. Do you understand?"

What have I gotten myself into? What's going on here? It doesn't even occur to me to leave. No. This is now my life. Whatever she's about to say is going to be my life.

It's all there in her eyes.

We hold there for one very careful moment. Then she breaks it with her words.

"Every morning, I wake up in a different body. It's been happening since I was born. This morning, I woke up as Megan Powell, who you see right in front of you. Three days ago, last Saturday, it was Nathan Daldry. Two days before that, it was Amy Tran, who visited your school and spent the day with you. And last Monday, it was Justin, your boyfriend. You thought you went to the ocean with him, but it was really me. That was the first time we ever met, and I haven't been able to forget you since."

No. That's all my mind can come up with. No. This is not happening. This is not what I want. I came here to find something real. And now I'm being served bullshit.

It's the punch of the punch line. I am the butt of the joke.

"You're kidding me, right?" I'm so angry, so mad. "You have to be kidding."

This girl is good. She doesn't laugh. She doesn't let down her guard at all. No. She keeps going, more urgent now, like I need to believe her, like I need to fall for it even worse.

"When we were on the beach, you told me about the mother-daughter fashion show that you and your mother were in, and how it was probably the last time you ever saw her in makeup. When Amy asked you to tell her about something you'd never told anyone else, you told her about trying to pierce your own ear when you were ten, and she told you about reading Judy Blume's *Forever*. Nathan came over to you as you were sorting through CDs, and he sang a song that you and Justin sang during the car ride to the ocean. He told you he was Steve's cousin, but he was really there to see you. He talked to you about being in a relationship for over a year, and you told him that deep down Justin cares a lot about you, and he said that deep down isn't good enough. What I'm saying is that . . . all of these people were me. For a day. And now I'm Megan Powell, and I want to tell you the truth before I switch again. Because I think you're remarkable. Because I don't want to keep meeting you as different people. I want to meet you as myself."

I feel stalked. I feel tricked. I feel like everything good that's happened in the past eight days has just been pissed on. The beach. The dancing. Even taking that girl around the school. It's all just someone else's joke. And there's only one person who could have done this. Only one person who could've known.

"Did Justin put you up to this?" I can't believe this. I truly can't believe this. "Do you really think this is funny?"

"No, it's not funny," she says—and the way she says it, there isn't anything funny in there at all. "It's true. I don't expect you to understand right away. I know how crazy it sounds. But it's true. I swear, it's true."

She really wants me to believe it. I guess that would make it even funnier.

What's strange is that she doesn't seem like a bitch. She doesn't seem like someone who'd get off on torturing me. But isn't that what she's doing?

"I don't understand why you're doing this," I tell her, my voice shaking. "I don't even know you!"

She can see she's lost me, and it's making her more desperate. "Listen to me," she begs, her voice shedding some calm. "Please. You know it wasn't Justin with you that day. In your heart, you know. He didn't act like Justin. He didn't do things Justin does. That's because it was me. I didn't mean to do it. I didn't mean to fall in love with you. But it happened. And I can't erase it. I can't ignore it. I have lived my whole life like this, and you're the thing that has made me wish it could stop."

I want to stop listening. I want to stop myself from driving over here. From wanting to know what was going on. I should have left it unknown. Because now it's still unknown, but it's a much worse unknown.

And the awful part is: She's right. Justin didn't act like Justin. I know that. But that doesn't mean it wasn't Justin. It just means it was a better day than usual. I have to believe that. Because this story can't be true. I mean, why not just say he was taken over by aliens? Bitten by a vampire? And—wait—then there's the most unbelievable part of all. According to this story, I am The Girl. I am worth all that.

"But why me?" I ask, as if I've finally found the flaw, finally proven her wrong. "That makes no sense."

But she doesn't give in. She launches back with, "Because you're amazing. Because you're kind to a random girl who just shows up at your school. Because you also want to be on the other side of the window, living life instead of just thinking about it. Because you're beautiful. Because when I was dancing with you in Steve's basement on Saturday night, it felt like fireworks. And when I was lying on the beach next to you, it felt like perfect calm. I know you think that Justin loves you deep down, but I love you through and through."

"Enough!" Oh God, now I'm the girl yelling in the café. Now I'm losing it. "It's just—enough, okay? I think I understand what you're saying to me, even though it makes *no sense whatsoever.*"

"You know it wasn't him that day, don't you?"

I want her to stop. I don't want to know any of this. I don't want to be thinking about this. I don't want to be thinking about all the ways Justin has avoided talking about that day. About how my love for him made so much sense then, but hasn't since. About how I haven't found any of the him from that day in the him afterward. I don't want to think about how

77

I felt when I was dancing with Nathan. About how it felt when he sang that song. About the real reason I came here today. About what I really wanted.

"*I don't know anything!*" I insist. Again, I'm too loud. People are watching. Whatever story they're playing out in their minds, it's not going to be this one. I lower my voice—I don't want them to hear more. I don't want to do this. "I don't know," I say. "I really don't know."

Why? Why is this happening to me? Why can't I stand up and leave? Why am I thinking for even a second that it might not be a lie?

Her. This girl. I look at her. Her heart is breaking. She is looking at me and her heart is breaking. I don't understand. I don't understand why. Her hand is moving onto mine. She is holding my hand. She is trying to get me through this. She is trying to take me through.

"I know it's a lot." Her voice is hurt. Her voice is comfort. "Believe me, I know."

I can barely get the words out. "It's not possible."

"It is," she says. "I'm the proof."

Proof. Proof is a fact. None of this is a fact. This is a feeling. All of this is a feeling.

No. It's thousands of feelings. So many of them yes. So many of them no.

She wants me to believe—what? That she was Justin. That she was Nathan. That girl in school. Other people.

How can I believe that? Who would ever believe that?

It cannot be a fact.

But it's still a feeling. The yes. It's there.

How can I let myself feel that? How?

"Look," she says, "what if we met here again tomorrow at the same time? I won't be in the same body, but I'll be the same person. Would that make it easier to understand?"

Like it's that simple. Like that couldn't be a trick.

"But couldn't you just tell someone else to come here?" I point out. If I can be suckered by one person, why not another?

"Yes, but why would I? This isn't a prank. This isn't a joke. It's my life."

The way she says it—*It's my life.*

Not a feeling. Fact.

"You're insane," I tell her. If she actually believes what she's saying, how could she not be?

But she doesn't seem at all insane when she tells me, "You're just saying that. You know I'm not. You can sense that much."

I look at her again. I search for the lie in her eyes. The flaw. And when I don't see it, I decide, *Fine, it's time for me to ask some questions.*

I start by asking her what her name is.

"Today I'm Megan Powell."

"No," I say. "I mean your real name." Because if she's really jumping from body to body, there has to be a name for the person inside.

I've thrown her. She wasn't expecting this question. I wait for her to back away from what she's said. I wait for her to laugh and say I've got her.

But she doesn't laugh. She hesitates, but she doesn't laugh.

"A," she finally says.

At first I don't get it. Then I realize—she's telling me that this is her name.

"Just A?" I ask.

"Just A. I came up with it when I was a little kid. It was a way of keeping myself whole, even as I went from body to body, life to life. I needed something pure. So I went with the letter A."

I don't want to believe this.

"What do you think about my name?" I challenge.

"I told you the other night. I think it's beautiful, even if you once found it hard to spell."

True. That is true.

But I can't.

I can't.

I'm sure there are other questions, but I'm out of them. I'm sure there could be plenty more time, but I'm out of time. I can't do this. I can't allow this to be real. I can't start believing her. Because that will make me an even bigger fool.

I stand up. She stands up, too.

There are still people looking at us. Imagining we're having a fight. Or imagining we're a couple. Or imagining this is a first date that's been a total bust.

Fact: It is none of these things.

Feeling: It is all of these things.

"Rhiannon," she says. And it's in there. It's in the way she says my name. Every now and then, Justin says my name like that. Like it's the most precious thing in the world.

Forget about everyone else laughing. Now I want to laugh. This can't be happening. It can't.

She's going to tell me more. She's going to push it further. She's going to say my name like that again, and I am going to hear music in it I shouldn't hear.

I hold up my hand. "No more," I insist. "Not now." And then it's there—the answer I don't want, the benefit against the doubt. "Tomorrow. I'll give you tomorrow. Because that's one way to know, isn't it? If what you say is happening is really happening—I mean, I need more than a day."

I'm waiting for her to put up a fight. I'm waiting for her to argue it some more. Or maybe this is the part where the camera crew comes out and I discover my humiliation has all been filmed for some cruel TV show.

But no.

None of that happens.

All that happens is that she thanks me. Genuine thanks. Thankful thanks.

"Don't thank me until I show up," I warn her. "This is all really confusing."

"I know," she says.

It's my life.

I have to go. But then I turn back one last time to look at her, and I see how she's on the border between hope and devastation. It's that visible to me. And even though the alarms are loud and clear in my head, I feel I can't leave her like this. I want to push her a little closer to hope and a little farther from devastation.

"The thing is," I say, "I didn't really feel it was him that day. Not completely. And ever since then, it's like he wasn't there. He has no memory of it. There are a million possible explanations for that, but there it is."

"There it is," she echoes. There's no bragging in her voice. No trickery.

It can't be real, but it's real to her.

81

Fact. Feeling.

I shake my head.

"Tomorrow," she says.

Now it's my turn to echo. "Tomorrow," I tell her, committing myself to something I feel like I became committed to a long time ago. Tomorrow. A word I've used for as long as I knew what it meant.

But now . . . now it feels like it means something different.

Now it feels like it means something slightly new.

I don't text Justin. I don't call him.

No, I go straight to his house and pound on the door.

His parents are still at work. I know he's the only one home. It takes him a couple of minutes, but he opens the door. He's surprised to see me.

"We weren't supposed to be doing something, were we?" he asks.

"No," I tell him. "I just need to talk to you for a second."

"Um . . . okay. Do you want to come in?"

"Sure."

He takes me into the den, where his warfare game is paused. I have to move the controller to clear a seat next to him.

"What's up?" he asks.

"It's about last week. I need to talk to you about it."

He looks confused. Or maybe just impatient.

"What about last week?"

"When we went to the beach. Do you remember that?"

"Of course I remember that."

"What songs played as we drove there?"

He looks at me like I've just asked him about rocket science. "How the fuck am I supposed to remember what songs were playing?"

"Was it cold or warm?"

"You were there. Don't you know?"

"You told me a story about climbing a tree when you were eleven. Do you remember that?"

He snorts. "I could barely climb a ladder when I was eleven—I don't think I was climbing any trees. Why are you asking me this?"

"But you remember being there, right?"

"Sure. There was sand. There was water. It was a beach."

I don't understand. He has some memory. But not all of it.

I decide to try a lie.

"You were so nice to me when I was stung by that jellyfish. God, that hurt. But I liked the way you carried me back to the car."

"I wasn't going to leave you there!" he says. "You're easy to carry."

He wasn't there. He was there—but he wasn't there.

I am so confused.

His hand is brushing over my knee, up my leg.

"I can carry you somewhere now, if you want."

He's coming in for a kiss. His lips are against mine. His body is starting to press.

This is not what I want, and he has no idea.

And I don't know how to explain, so I kiss him back.

Acceleration. His hand going under my shirt. His tongue in my mouth. The cigarette taste of him. The sweat and grit on his hand from the controller.

I know it's really bad to pull away. That it will hurt him if I pull away. But I pull away. Not far. But enough.

He pulls back in reaction. "What? I figure, if you came all this way . . ."

"I can't," I tell him. "I've got too much going on in my head. I'm not in the mood."

He moves his thumb slowly against my breast. "I believe I know ways to put you in the mood."

Usually my body reaches out for this.

"Stop," I say.

He's not a jerk. When I say stop, he stops. But he doesn't look happy about it.

"Are you getting tired of me?" he asks.

He wants it to sound like he's joking. And I could point out that if he'd stayed sober on Saturday night, we could have done something then. But is that really true? After dancing with Nathan, would I really have had sex with Justin?

I know what I'm supposed to say, and I say it: "No, I could never get tired of you." I kiss him again, but it's clearly a good-bye kiss. "I'm tired, yes. But not of you."

I stand up, and he doesn't get up to walk me out. Instead, he grabs the controller, unpausing his game.

I've hurt him. I didn't mean to, but I have.

"I'll see you tomorrow," he says.

Tomorrow. The version he's offering isn't the same as the one the girl—A—offered.

I guess I'm not going to know which tomorrow I'm stepping into until I actually get there.

Chapter Eight

I fall asleep right after dinner and wake up right before midnight. And in that waking moment, I think: *I want to go back there. I want to go back to that day when everything was perfect, and Justin was everything I want him to be.*

Even if it wasn't Justin.

I can't believe I am allowing myself to think this. I can't believe I'm opening my email. I can't believe I am typing.

A,

I want to believe you, but I don't know how.

Rhiannon

I can't believe I am hitting send.
But I do.
And I guess this means there is a part of me that believes.

• • •

I check my email again at lunch.

Rhiannon,

You don't need to know how. You just make up your
mind and it happens.

I am in Laurel right now, over an hour away. I am in the
body of a football player named James. I know how
strange that sounds. But, like everything I've told you,
it's the truth.

Love,
A

A football player named James. Either this is the most elaborate prank ever pulled on a stupid girl or it's real. These are
the only two options. Trick or truth. I am trying hard to think
of another explanation, but there's nothing in the middle.
   The only way to know is to play along.

A,

Do you have a car? If not, I can come to you. There's
a Starbucks in Laurel. I'm told that nothing bad ever
happens in a Starbucks. Let me know if you want to
meet there.

Rhiannon

• • •

A few minutes later, a reply:

Rhiannon,

I would appreciate it if you could come here. Thank
you.

A

I have to excuse myself to go to the girls' room because I
can see Rebecca's wondering who I'm emailing in the middle
of lunch. The answer is so ridiculous that I can't even think of
a good lie to cover for it.

Safe in a stall, I type back:

A,

I'll be there at 5. Can't wait to see what you look like
today.

(Still not believing this.)

Rhiannon

And then I am standing there, the girl in the stall with the
phone out, staring at the screen that doesn't even hold the
message she typed, since it's already flown away, into the hands
of someone she doesn't really know. There is nothing that can
make you feel quite so dumb as wanting something good to be
true. That's the horrifying part—that I want this to be true. I
want him—her? him?—to exist.

87

I promise myself I won't think about it until five o'clock, and then I break that promise a thousand times.

Even Justin can tell I'm distracted. The moment when I least need him to pay attention, he finds me after school and is concerned.

"I missed you today," he says. His hands move to my back and he starts to work the tension from the muscles there. It feels good. And he's doing it in the middle of the hall, right by our lockers, which isn't something he usually does.

"I missed you, too," I say, even though it doesn't feel entirely true.

"Let's go find a Girl Scout and get some cookies," he says.

I laugh, then realize he means it.

"And where will you find a Girl Scout?" I ask.

"Three doors down from me. I swear, she has a vault full of Thin Mints. Sometimes there are lines on her porch. She's like a dealer."

I have time for this. It's not even three yet. If I get on the road by four, I should be fine to get to the Starbucks in Laurel by five.

"Does she have Samoas, too?"

"Are those the coconut ones or the peanut butter ones?"

"Coconut."

"I'm sure she has them all. Seriously. She's a cartel."

I can tell he's excited. Usually I can find complaints waiting in the corners of his words or gestures. But right now, they're nowhere in sight.

He's happy, and part of the reason he's happy is because he's happy to see me.

"Let's go," I say.

• • •

We park our cars in his driveway and then walk three doors down. He doesn't hold my hand or anything, but it still feels like we're together.

The girl who answers the door can't be older than eleven, and she's so small that I'm amazed her mom lets her answer the door at all.

"Have you placed a preorder?" she asks, pulling out an iPad.

This cracks Justin up. "No. This is more of a drive-by."

"Then I can't promise availability," the girl states. "That's why we encourage preorders." She reaches for a table next to the door and hands us a cookie listing, as well as a business card with a website address on it. "But since you're here, I am happy to see what I can do. Just note that the prerefrigerated Thin Mints are preorder only."

Justin doesn't even look at the paper. "We'd like a box of Samosas," he says. "The coconut ones."

"I believe you mean *Samoas*," the girl corrects. "I am going to have to close and lock the door while I check inventory. Are you sure you only want one box? A lot of people say they only want one, and then they're back the next day for more."

"Mia, you know I live down the street. Just get us the box."

Mia is clearly considering a harder sell, then thinks better of it. "One moment," she says, then shuts the door in our faces.

"Her parents once got so desperate that they asked me to babysit," Justin tells me. "And I was so desperate for cash that I said yes. She offered me cookies, then left a note for her

89

mother to take the cost of the cookies out of my pay. I set the note on fire and dropped it in the sink. I don't think she appreciated that."

I can't imagine asking Justin to babysit. And I can also imagine him being the most fun babysitter ever, if you didn't try to bill him.

Mia returns with our box of Samoas. Justin takes the box from her hand and starts to walk away without paying, which makes Mia turn purple in outrage. Then Justin says, "Just kidding," turns back, and gives her the cash in singles.

"Next time, *preorder*," she tells both of us before slamming the door again.

"Not the sweetest girl," Justin comments as we head back to his house. "But she gives good cookie."

Instead of going inside, Justin leads me to the backyard. His mom has a small garden with a bench. He takes me there.

"Samoa for your thoughts," he says, pulling open the box and the plastic.

"My only thought is: *I want a Samoa*," I tell him.

"Here," he says, putting one between his teeth. I lean in and snatch it up.

"Yum," I say, mouth full.

He pops one into his own mouth. "Yeah, yum," he agrees, some coconut falling into the air between us. After he swallows, he says, "I imagine we taste the same right now."

I smile. "I imagine we're both pretty coconutty. And chocolatey. And caramelly."

"There's only one way to know for sure."

He goes in for the kiss and I let him take it. I tell myself this is what I want. Just like the ocean. Just like a couple.

He pulls away. "Yum."

"Give me another."

He presses in for another kiss. I push him away and say, "I meant another cookie." He laughs. I appreciate the laugh.

Instead of insisting on the kiss, he passes me the box of cookies. I take two.

They're really good, much better than I remembered them being. Sweet and rough.

"Don't get too hooked," Justin warns. "That's how Mia gets you. Before you know it, you're preordering by the dozens. And then, even worse, you're insisting that they be *refrigerated*."

"You speak like someone who knows. I'll bet your fridge is full of Thin Mints."

"Oh, no. It's worse than that. I only eat the fat mints now."

Why are you in such a good mood? I want to ask him. And then I want to ask myself, *Why do you have to question this?*

"Wanna see my stash?" he asks.

"I've already seen your stash."

"And what do you think?"

"It's *huge*."

We're being silly, but that's nice. Even though we've been together for a while, it's still nice to flirt, and to feel the lightness of flirting.

I don't want to tell him I can't stay long. I know that will make it less exciting than it was a minute ago.

So I don't say anything. But I also don't make a move to go inside. I kiss him here, on the bench. I kiss him here and feel awful because one of the reasons I am kissing him here is because I know it'll be easier to leave if we're already outside.

He doesn't sense it, though. He is kissing me back. He is

happy. He is sure to move the precious box of cookies out of our way as we crash into each other.

I begin to convince myself that this is what I want. This is where I am meant to be. I am only going to see A in order to get the explanation. But that is not my life. This is my life. Justin is my life.

I get there late. I've had an hour to straighten myself out, calm myself down, make myself appear to be a girl who has not just spent an hour making out with her boyfriend. I've also been thinking of questions to ask, ways to know whether what A is saying is true. I mean, it can't be true. But I'm looking for ways to prove that.

When I get to the Starbucks, I'm expecting the girl from yesterday to be there. Or Nathan. Someone to tell me, ha ha, it was a joke. But neither of them is there. Instead, there's this guy—a big football player of a guy. Not my type. Almost scary in his size. But he looks gentle when he waves to me.

Again, my perspective changes when I look into his eyes. All the assumptions fall away.

I take a deep breath. I know I need to settle this. I try to remember my plan.

"Okay," I say as soon as I get to his table and sit down. "Before we say another word, I want to see your phone. I want to see every single call you've made in the past week, and every single call you received. If this isn't some big joke, then you have nothing to hide."

I can't imagine that after being with me so sweetly, Justin

would have set this up. But I want to make sure his number isn't on the phone. I want to see if there are any texts or calls on there from yesterday.

I search around. I look at the contacts. I don't find any phone calls from yesterday. The two texts are from friends of his. There's nothing about me anywhere.

So there's that.

I hand back the phone and tell him it's time for me to quiz him. I start by asking what I was wearing that day on the beach.

Worry flashes in his eyes.

"I don't know," he says after half a minute. "Do you remember what Justin was wearing?"

I try to remember. But what I remember instead is the feeling, the wonder of it all. Not the clothes.

"Good point," I say. "Did we make out?"

He shakes his head. "We used the make-out blanket, but we didn't make out. We kissed. And that was enough."

I note his use of the phrase *make-out blanket*. And the fact that he doesn't make too much of a deal of it.

"And what did I say to you before I left the car?" I ask.

" 'That's the nice note.' "

"Correct. Quick, what's Steve's girlfriend's name?"

"Stephanie."

"And what time did the party end?"

"Eleven-fifteen."

"And when you were in the body of that girl who I took to all of my classes, what did the note you passed me say?"

"Something like, *The classes here are just as boring as in the school I'm going to now.*"

"And what were the buttons on your backpack that day?"

"Anime kittens."

I try to think of a way he could know all this, from all those different people. Short of him being able to read my mind, I can't explain it.

"Well," I say, "either you're an excellent liar, or you switch bodies every day. I have no idea which one is true."

"It's the second one," he assures me. Then he looks concerned again. "Let's go outside," he whispers. "I feel we may be getting an unintended audience."

I can't see the person he's talking about, but I can see other people who could easily be listening to us. Still, his proposal is a little too step-into-my-van for my taste.

"Maybe if you were a petite cheerleader again," I tell him. "But—I'm not sure if you fully realize this—you're a big, threatening dude today. My mother's voice is very loud and clear in my head: *No dark corners.*"

He points out the window, to a bench along the road. "Totally public, only without people listening in."

"Fine," I say.

I'm trying to think of new questions as we walk outside. I haven't even gotten any coffee, but it doesn't seem like the right time to stop for a latte.

He seems nervous. And if I'm honest, I know it's not a serial-killer nervousness. It feels like the only thing that could be killed here are his hopes. I have never seen a boy hope so visibly. I wonder if he knows he's doing it.

Distance. I let him sit down first so I can keep a little distance. So I can look into those eyes without falling into them. So I can keep some judgment.

I want to know more, so I need to ask more. If he's going to convince me, he's going to have to tell me much more.

"So," I resume, "you say you've been like this since the day you were born?"

He hesitates for a brief moment. I get a sense that he doesn't have conversations like this very often.

Well, I don't, either.

"Yes," he says quietly. "I can't remember it being any different."

"So how did that work? Weren't you confused?"

Again, he thinks about it for a second, then answers. "I guess I got used to it. I'm sure that, at first, I figured it was just how everybody's lives worked. I mean, when you're a baby, you don't really care much about who's taking care of you, as long as someone's taking care of you. And as a little kid, I thought it was some kind of a game, and my mind learned how to access—you know, look at the body's memories—naturally. So I always knew what my name was, and where I was. It wasn't until I was six or seven that I started to realize I was different, and it wasn't until I was nine or ten that I really wanted it to stop."

"You did?" I ask. The idea of leaving your body sounds almost fun to me. A relief.

"Of course," he says. "Imagine being homesick, but without having a home. That's what it was like. I wanted friends, a mom, a dad, a dog—but I couldn't hold on to any of them more than a single day. It was brutal. There are nights I remember screaming and crying, begging my parents not to make me go to bed. They could never figure out what I was afraid of. They thought it was a monster under the bed, or a ploy to get a few more bedtime stories. I could never really explain, not in a way that made sense to them. I'd tell them I didn't want to say goodbye, and they'd assure me it wasn't goodbye. It was just good night. I'd tell them it was the same thing, but they thought I was being silly."

Now it doesn't sound fun at all. It sounds lonely.

He goes on. "Eventually I came to peace with it. I had to. I realized that this was my life, and there was nothing I could do about it. I couldn't fight the tide, so I decided to float along."

I can't get my mind around it. No friends. No people in your life from day to day.

So lonely.

"How many times have you told this story?" I ask him.

"None. I swear. You're the first."

There's only you. Why am I thinking of Justin right now? Why am I thinking of the time, drunk on wine in the passenger seat of my car, he said those words to me? I wasn't even mad. I didn't mind driving. Instead of *Thank you,* that's what he said. And he was so grateful when he said it. So damn grateful.

But I can't think about that. Instead, I go back to A's story. "You have to have parents, don't you?" I say. "I mean, we all have parents."

He shrugs. "I have no idea. I would think so. But it's not like there's anyone I can ask. I've never met anyone else like me. Not that I would necessarily know."

I don't always get along with my parents, but I am still glad they're around.

I think he's going to tell me more about not having parents, about not having roots. But he surprises me.

"I've glimpsed things," he says.

I expect him to say more. To tell me what this means, what he's seen. But I have to remember: He's new at this. He's still very unsure.

"Go on," I prompt.

Permission. He smiles, happy for it. I want to hug him, if only for that smile. "It's just—I know it sounds like an awful way to live, but I've seen so many things. It's so hard when you're in one body to get a sense of what life is really like. You're so grounded in who you are. But when who you are changes every day—you get to touch the universal more. Even the most mundane details. You see how cherries taste different to different people. Blue looks different. You see all the strange rituals boys have to show affection without admitting it. You learn that if a parent reads to you at the end of the day, it's a good sign that it's a good parent, because you've seen so many other parents who don't make the time. You learn how much a day is truly worth, because they're all so different. If you ask most people what the difference was between Monday and Tuesday, they might tell you what they had for dinner each night. Not me. By seeing the world from so many angles, I get more of a sense of its dimensionality."

"But you never get to see things over time, do you?" I ask. "I don't mean to cancel out what you just said. I think I understand that. But you've never had a friend that you've known day in and day out for ten years. You've never watched a pet grow older. You've never seen how messed up a parent's love can be over time. And you've never been in a relationship for more than a day, not to mention for more than a year."

"But I've seen things," he says. "I've observed. I know how it works."

"From the outside?" I'm really trying to get my mind around this, but it's hard. *Blue looks different.* "I don't think you can know from the outside."

"I think you underestimate how predictable some things can be in a relationship."

I should've known we'd get here. I should've known this would come up. He met me as Justin, after all. He knows the deal. Or thinks he does.

I need to make it clear. "I love him," I say. "I know you don't understand, but I do."

"You shouldn't. I've seen him from the inside. I know."

"For a day," I point out. "You saw him for a day."

"And for a day, you saw who he could be. You fell more in love with him when he was me."

This is very hard to hear. I don't know if it's true or not. If you'd asked me yesterday, maybe yes. If you ask me now, after Girl Scout cookies, maybe no.

He goes for my hand. But I can't do it. It's committing too much. "No," I say. "Don't."

He doesn't.

"I have a boyfriend," I go on. "I know you don't like him, and I'm sure there are moments when I don't like him, either. But that's the reality. Now, I'll admit, you have me actually thinking that you are, in fact, the same person who I've now met in five different bodies. All this means is that I'm probably as insane as you are. I know you say you love me, but you don't really know me. You've known me a week. And I need a little more than that."

"But didn't you feel it that day? On the beach? Didn't every-thing seem right?"

Yes. Everything within me jumps to that one word: *yes*. It did seem right. But that was feeling. All feeling. I still cannot speak to any fact.

But I cannot withhold my answer, either. So I tell him, "Yes. But I don't know who I was feeling that for. Even if I believe it was you, you have to understand that my history with Justin plays into it. I wouldn't have felt that way with a stranger. It wouldn't have been so perfect."

"How do you know?"

"That's my point. I don't."

I shouldn't have left Justin. I shouldn't have made an ex-cuse to go. This is too dangerous, because none of it can be fact.

I look down at my phone. I haven't been here long, but it's getting close to too long.

"I have to make it back for dinner," I tell him. Technically correct. If I want to get back in time, I should be leaving now.

I'm thinking he'll put up a fight. Justin would put up a fight. He'd make it clear he wanted me to stay.

But A lets me go.

"Thanks for driving all this way," he says.

Should I tell him he's welcome? What does that even mean? Welcome to what?

"Will I see you again?" he asks.

I don't have the heart to say no. Because there's a part of my heart that wants to stay, and will stay with him until I come to get it back.

I nod.

"I'm going to prove it to you," he tells me. "I'm going to show you what it really means."

"What?"

"Love."

No. I am scared of that.

I am scared of all of this.

But I don't tell him that. I tell him goodbye instead—the kind of goodbye that's never, ever final.

Chapter Nine

I remember the way everyone reacted when I got together with Justin, when we became a thing. They didn't think I was paying attention, but I was.

Rebecca told me I could do better. She told me Justin could never really care about anyone because he didn't really care about himself. She said I deserved to be with someone who had his shit together. I told her I didn't know anyone who had their shit together, including her. She told me she was going to pretend I hadn't said that. She told me I was smarter than I thought I was, but I always liked to prove myself stupid by making bad decisions. I told her I loved him anyway, and my use of the word *love* surprised us both. I held up; she backed down.

Preston said he was happy for me, and when I asked him why, he told me it was because I had found something meaningful. He didn't think Justin was unworthy of my love, because he believed everyone was worthy of love. "He needs you, and that's not a bad thing," he told me. "We all need somewhere to put our love." I remember liking this thought—that I had this certain amount of love that I needed to store someplace, and I'd decided to keep some of it in Justin.

Steve said Justin was decent.

Stephanie said she wasn't sure.

I don't think any of them—even Preston—expected it to last longer than a month. Any love I stored in Justin would ultimately be given away, lost in a fire, left by the side of the road.

And if this was their reaction to Justin, I couldn't imagine what they would say if I told them about A.

The thought will not leave my head:

If this is possible, what else is possible?

I get to school and walk to my locker, and it's only when I'm at my locker that I realize I haven't stopped to look for Justin.

And then, even stranger: I don't go looking for him.

I wait to see how long it'll take him to come looking for me.

Not between first and second periods.

Not before lunch.

Even at lunch, I sit between Preston and Rebecca, and instead of taking the spot across from me, he sits farther down.

It isn't until the end of lunch that he says something to me.

And what he says is, "I'm so tired."
I know I'm not the one who's going to wake him up.

I find myself wondering who A is today. Where A is.

And at the same time, I wonder if all the A's I've met are in a room together, laughing at me. Not believing how a girl could be so stupid. Looking at the video of my face over and over again. Daring each other to push it further.

That's not it, I tell myself.

But what else is possible?

I check my email after lunch and find word from him (her?).

> Rhiannon,
>
> You'd actually recognize me today. I woke up as James's twin. I thought this might help me figure things out, but so far, no luck.
>
> I want to see you again.
>
> A

I don't know what to say to this.
Trick or truth?
Yes, I want to see A again.
Yes, I'm afraid.
No, it doesn't make sense.

But what does? I'm asking myself this all afternoon. Does it makes sense that Preston is seen as The Gay One when none of the rest of us are seen as The Straight One? Does it make sense that Stephanie's father freaked out when she (briefly) dated Aaron because Aaron is black? Does it make sense that Justin and I can get as close as two people can be, and still can't figure out anything to say to each other when we're separate and walking the halls of school? Does it make sense that I am sitting here learning about the gestation cycle of a frog when there is no way that this knowledge is going to matter to me as soon as the next test is over? Does it make sense that Mr. Myers is spending his life teaching the gestation cycle of a frog to kids who mostly don't care?

Does it make sense that some people get everything they want because they're pretty? Would it make all of us nicer—or at least a little more humble—if we had to switch every day?

"What are you thinking about?"

Justin's caught me at my locker, in a daze.

"It's nothing," I tell him. "Just daydreaming."

He lets it go.

"Look," he says. "What're you doing now?"

It's the end of the day. I have no idea what I'm doing. I could've driven back to the Starbucks and met the twin of the guy from yesterday. Although how would I have known it was really a twin? What if it was the same guy again? It's not like I could really tell.

Suddenly I'm suspicious.

Really suspicious.

I wonder if tomorrow he'll say he's a triplet.

Or that he's stayed in the same body after all.

Alarm. I'm starting to get pissed off. Irrationally pissed off. Or maybe rationally pissed off.

"Are you even listening to me?"

I am not listening to him. I need to listen to him. Because he is my boyfriend, and he has no idea what's going on inside my head.

"No plans," I say.

We both know what's next. But he's not going to say it. He wants me to say it.

So I do.

"Wanna hang out?"

"Yeah. Sure. Whatever."

We go to his house. He wants to watch an old episode of *Game of Thrones*.

"Is this the one where someone dies?" I ask as it starts. I'm joking. They're all the one where someone dies.

"Smart-ass," he says.

I check my email. Nothing new from A.

Like my silence might push him into confessing.

"Put that away," Justin says. "It's distracting."

I put it away. I sit there. Someone's head gets smashed in. We do not make out.

It's only when three episodes are over and I'm getting ready to leave that he tells me something is on his mind.

"I fucking hate doctors," he says. I'm a little confused. There hasn't been a doctor in sight on *Game of Thrones*—it would have been much better if there had been.

"Is there any particular reason you hate doctors right now?" I ask.

"Yeah, because they're going to let my grandma die. They're going to put her through hell, and make all of us pay for it, and at the very end, she's going to die anyway. That's always what they do. Hospitals wouldn't make money without sick people, right? They just love this shit."

"Your grandmother's sick?" I ask.

"Yeah. Grandpa called us last night. Says it's serious cancer."

"Are you okay?"

"What do you mean, am I okay? I'm not the one with cancer."

I want to ask, *Do you want to talk about it?* But the answer is pretty obvious. He doesn't want my sympathy. He doesn't want to tell me he's sad. He just wants me to be there as he vents his rage. So I do that. I let him yell about doctors, and about how his grandfather is the one who smokes, but look at which one of them ended up with cancer. I let him criticize his parents' reaction. He's mad at them for not dropping everything to go see her, when what he really means is that *he* wants to drop everything to go see her. But he won't say that. Not to me. Not to himself.

I stay until he wears himself out. I stay until he changes the subject. I stay until he decides to watch a fourth episode.

I'll be there when he wants to deal with it. He knows that, and right now that's the best I can do.

• • •

When I get home, Mom is sitting in her usual spot, watching the news on her usual channel. If the story is really sad—a girl gone missing, a boy trapped in a well—she'll talk back to the screen, little murmurs of sympathy, *Oh, that's too bad* or *Goodness, how awful.*

I imagine the pretty newscaster looking into this room, looking at my mother sitting in that chair, and saying the same things. Because hasn't she fallen down her own kind of well? Hasn't she found her own way of being missing? Liza used to push her—telling her she needed to go out more, once even telling her she needed to get some friends. But now that it's my turn, I find I've given up. It's probably the only way I can make her happy, to leave her alone. That's what my dad has done all these years, and it seems to have worked out fine for him.

I think about calling Liza, about telling her what's going on.

You're as crazy as she is. That's probably what she'd say.

But Mom isn't crazy. She just doesn't care anymore.

She enjoys her shows, I think.

I want to see you again.

I don't think Justin's ever said that to me. But he hasn't really needed to, has he? There's never any doubt that he'll see me again. Never any need to want it.

• • •

107

I start another email.

A,

I only want to see you again if this is real.

Rhiannon

But I don't send it.

Chapter Ten

I wake up and write another email.

A,

So, who are you today?

What a strange question to ask. But I guess it makes sense. If any of this makes sense.

Yesterday was a hard day. Justin's grandmother is sick, but instead of admitting he's upset about it, he just lashes out at the world more. I'm trying to help him, but it's hard.

I don't know if you want to hear this or not. I know how you feel about Justin. If you want me to keep that part of my life hidden from you, I can. But I don't think that's what you want.

Tell me how your day is going.

Rhiannon

This one I do send. I try to act like it's a normal email that I'd send to a normal friend. Then I try to have a normal day, partly to figure out what a normal day really is. At first it works. I go to school. I go to classes. I go to lunch and sit next to Justin. He won't commit to any emotion.

When lunch is over, I check my email.

Rhiannon,

Today is a hard day for me, too. The girl whose body I'm in is in a bad place. Hates the world. Hates herself. Is up against a lot, mostly from the inside. That's really hard.

When it comes to you and Justin, or anything, I want you to be honest with me. Even if it hurts. Although I would prefer for it not to hurt.

Love,
A

I try to return to normal. I try not to imagine where A is, what that body looks like. Justin has work, so I'm on my own after school. I check my email again and find a cry for help.

I really need to speak to you right now. The girl whose body I'm in wants to kill herself. This is not a joke.

There's a phone number. I call it right away.

I know it's not a joke. I'm sure there are people who could joke about a thing like this, but I know A isn't one of them.

I just know.

The voice that answers is a girl's. "Hello?" She sounds a little like me.

"Is that you?" I ask.

"Yeah. It's me."

"I got your email. Wow."

"Yeah, wow."

"How do you know?"

"It's all in her journal—all these ways to kill herself. It's really . . . graphic. And methodical. I can't even get into it—there are just so many ways to die, and it's like she's researched each and every one. And she's set herself a deadline. In six days."

I feel the dredging inside me. I feel the girl I once was reaching out to connect with that. I try to focus on the present.

"That poor girl," I tell A. "What are you going to do?"

"I have no idea."

She sounds so lost. So overwhelmed.

"Don't you have to tell someone?" I suggest.

"There was no training for this, Rhiannon. I really don't know."

I've been there, I want to tell her. But it's too scary.

"Where are you?" I ask.

A tells me where she is, and it's not that far. I tell her I can be there in a little while.

"Are you alone?" I ask.

"Yeah. Her father doesn't get home until around seven."

"Give me the address," I say. After she does, I say, "I'll be right there."

• • •

I don't know this girl. A hasn't told me much. But maybe that's why it's easier to fill in the blanks with myself.

I shouldn't think it, but I think it anyway: *This is the girl I'd be if I hadn't met Justin.*

That's how bad it was. Or maybe that's just how bad it seemed. I don't know now. I can't tell the difference. All I know is I was convinced that nobody would care if I died. I had elaborate fantasies about my very simple funeral—no one but my relatives there. No boy in tears in the front row. No one who could get up and talk about me as if they really knew me.

I knew I wasn't going to do it. But I also knew I could. I treasured that thought. That I could.

Most of the time when we think we're looking for death, we're really looking for love.

That was definitely the case with me. Because Justin came in and gave me the meaning I was looking for. Justin became the mourner I wanted, and that led to other friends, other mourners. I populated my funeral until I didn't want one anymore.

But I realize that's not always the case.

I realize there are girls who don't have that.

I realize I am driving toward one of them right now. Not because of what A told me, but because of the sound of her voice. The fear.

I recognize that.

It's a short drive, but I try to come up with a plan.

I'm not really thinking about A at all. I am not wondering

why A, who's lived in so many bodies, doesn't know what to do. I am not amazed that I know more than A does.

I'm just driving and thinking as fast as I can.

I find the house. It's a normal house. I ring the doorbell. It sounds like a normal doorbell.

She answers, and from the moment I see her, I know that she's another disappearing girl, that she's desperately trying to disappear. The signs of it tattoo her body—the wear and tear. It is hard for unhealthy people to masquerade as healthy ones, especially once they've stopped caring if other people notice.

The only difference is her eyes. Her eyes are still alive.

I know that's not her.

I know for sure now that this is actually happening. No trick. Just truth. Plenty of feeling, but at the center of it—fact.

"Thank you for coming," A says.

She leads me up to the girl's room. It's a pit, like she lashed out against it and left herself the wreckage to live in. Her clothes are all over the place, and there's no way of telling the difference between the clean and the dirty. She's broken her mirror. Everything on the walls is on its way to being torn down. She might as well cut her wrist and rub FUCK YOU across the walls.

It's not a mess. It's anger.

There's a notebook on the bed. I open it. I know what I'm going to find, but still it hits me in the gut.

This is how to stab yourself.

This is how to bleed.

This is how to choke.

This is how to fall.

This is how to burn.

This is how to poison.

This is how to die.

These aren't hypotheticals. This isn't her being dramatic. This is her finding the facts to match the feelings. To end the feelings.

It is all so wrong. I want to shake her. I want to tell her to step away from the funeral.

And there's the deadline at the end. Practically tomorrow.

A's been quiet as I've been reading. Now I look up at her.

"This is serious," I say. "I've had . . . thoughts. But nothing like this."

I've been standing this whole time, the notebook in my hand. Now I put it down. And then I put myself down, too. I need to sit down. I place myself on the edge of the bed. A sits down next to me.

"You have to stop her," I say. I, who am certain of so few things, am certain of this.

"But how can I?" A asks. "And is that really my right? Shouldn't she decide that for herself?"

This is not what I am expecting A to say. It's so ridiculous. Offensive.

"So, what?" I say, not bothering to keep the anger out of my voice. "You just let her die? Because you didn't want to get involved?"

She takes my hand. Tries to calm me down.

"We don't know for sure that the deadline's real. This could just be her way of getting rid of the thoughts. Putting them on paper so she doesn't do them."

No. That's an excuse. This is not the time for excuses. I throw it back at her: "But you don't believe that, do you? You wouldn't have called me if you believed that."

She's silent in response, so I know I'm right.

I look down and see her hand in mine. I let myself feel it, let it mean more than just support.

"This is weird," I say.

"What?"

I squeeze once, then pull my hand away. "This."

She doesn't get it. "What do you mean?"

Even though it's a different situation, even though we're in an emergency situation right now, she's still looking at me that way. I can feel her feeling things for me. I am receiving that.

I try to explain. "It's not like the other day. I mean, it's a different hand. You're different."

"But I'm not."

I wish I could believe that was true. "You can't say that," I tell her. "Yes, you're the same person inside. But the outside matters, too."

"You look the same, no matter what eyes I'm seeing you through. I feel the same."

If this is possible, what else is possible?

I can't imagine what it must be like to live like that.

A is asking me to imagine it. I know she (he?) is. But it's hard.

I go back to her argument about this girl, about not interfering. "You never get involved in the people's lives?" I ask. "The ones you're inhabiting."

She shakes her head.

But there's a contradiction here, isn't there? "You try to leave the lives the way you found them," I say.

"Yeah."

"But what about Justin? What made that so different?"

"You."

I cannot wear that answer. It can't possibly fit.

"That makes no sense," I say.

Then, as if to answer my thoughts, she leans in and kisses me. I am not expecting it. I am not expecting the feel of her lips, the chapped roughness. I am not expecting her fingers light against my neck.

I am not sure who I'm kissing.

I'm really not sure.

Because if it's A, the person who kissed me on the beach, it's one thing. But if it's this girl, that's another. This girl doesn't want to be kissed by me. This girl isn't a fairy-tale character who can be cured by a kiss. This girl needs much more help than that. I know.

After a minute of letting it happen, I pull back, even more confused than before.

"This is definitely weird," I say.

"Why?"

I feel it should be obvious. "Because you're a girl? Because I still have a boyfriend? Because we're talking about someone else's suicide?"

"In your heart, does any of that matter?"

I know the answer she wants. But it's not the truth.

"Yes," I tell her. "It does."

"Which part?"

"All of it. When I kiss you, I'm not actually kissing you, you

116

know. You're inside there somewhere. But I'm kissing the outside part. And right now, although I can feel you underneath, all I'm getting is the sadness. I'm kissing her, and I want to cry."

"That's not what I want."

"I know. But that's what there is."

I can't stay on the bed. I can't stay in this conversation. I didn't come here to talk about us. I came here because we need to save this girl's life.

I stand up and try to push us back on course.

"If she were bleeding in the street, what would you do?" I ask.

A seems disappointed. I can't tell whether it's because I've changed the conversation back, or because she knows she has to make the call.

"That's not the same situation," she says.

Not good enough. "If she were going to kill someone else?" I challenge.

"I would turn her in."

Aha. "So how is this different?"

"It's her own life. Not anyone else's."

"But it's still killing."

"If she really wants to do it, there's nothing I can do to stop it."

If A weren't in someone else's body, I might try to slap some sense into her, this logic is so damaged. You can't cry for help, then claim to be a bystander.

"Okay," she says before I can go on, "putting up obstacles can help. Getting other people involved can help. Getting her to the proper doctors can help."

"Just like if she had cancer, or were bleeding in the street."

I see it's all sinking in. It's still amazing to me that she's never had to deal with this before.

"So who do I tell?" she asks.

"A guidance counselor, maybe?" I offer.

She looks at the clock. "School's closed. And we only have until midnight, remember."

"Who's her best friend?" I ask.

But that's the problem, isn't it? It's what A confirms—there's no one.

"Boyfriend? Girlfriend?" I try.

"No."

"A suicide hotline?"

"If we call one, they'd only be giving me advice, not her. We have no way of knowing if she'll remember it tomorrow, or if it will have any effect. Believe me, I've thought about these options."

"So it has to be her father. Right?"

"I think he checked out a while ago."

I've always felt like the expert on checked-out parents. What's interesting is that now I discover another truth underneath: Even if they seem that far gone, they're rarely all the way gone. If they were already gone, they would've left.

"Well," I say, "you need to get him to check back in."

Because that has to be possible. Maybe not easy. But possible.

"What do I say?" A asks.

"You say, 'Dad, I want to kill myself.' Just come right out and say it."

That would wake my parents up. I know it would.

"And if he asks me why?"

"You tell him you don't know why. Don't commit to anything. She'll have to work that out starting tomorrow."

"You've thought this through, haven't you?"

"It was a busy drive over," I tell her, even though the truth is that most of it is just appearing to me now.

"What if he doesn't care? What if he doesn't believe her?"

"Then you grab his keys and drive to the nearest hospital. Bring the journal with you."

I know it's asking a lot.

But I also know she's going to do it.

She's still there on the bed. Looking lost. Looking worried.

"Come here," I say, sitting back down next to her. I give her the biggest hug I can. To look at her, you'd think her body would break from the embrace. But it's stronger than it seems.

"I don't know if I can do this," she whispers.

"You can," I tell her. "Of course you can."

We go through it one more time. Then we both know it's time for me to go. If her father comes home while I'm there, it will only make things more confusing.

It's hard to leave. It's hard to be a part of this girl's story and then walk away from it.

I realize as I'm leaving that I don't even know her name. So I ask A.

"Kelsea," she tells me.

"Well, Kelsea," I say, imagining she can hear me, "it's good to meet you. And I really, really hope you'll be okay."

But there's no way to know for sure, is there?

Chapter Eleven

When I get home, I need to distract myself. I get on the computer and binge on all the stupid websites I like to look at when my brain can't take anything deeper. I am not expecting to find anything that has to do with me. So when I see it, I'm shocked.

Just one new window. One click. And there he is—Steve's fake cousin Nathan—staring back at me.

THE DEVIL AMONG US!

At first I think it's a prank. But how? This isn't some high school website. This is a Baltimore newspaper. Not a good one, but still.

It's definitely Nathan. If I was unsure about the photo, his name is right there in the article: *Nathan Daldry, age 16*. He claims to have been possessed by the devil six nights ago. He woke up after midnight, at the side of the road. He has no idea what happened to him.

But I do. That's the night I danced with him.

I read the article with a strange numbness. He's not the only person who claims to have been "taken over." Other people say the devil went into their bodies and made them do evil things.

Only, Nathan doesn't really specify what evil things he was made to do. He just assumes that anything he can't remember is bad.

The devil. They are saying A is the devil.

But the devil wouldn't have helped Kelsea. The devil wouldn't have been so scared.

I don't know what A is, but A is not the devil.

I think about Nathan in his tie. Awkwardly standing around the party. I wonder how much of that was A and how much of it was Nathan. I wonder what would make him think he'd been possessed. It sounds like people are making a big deal of it, and that there's even a reverend acting as his spokesman. Is Nathan out for the attention? Or does he genuinely not know?

After dinner, I search some more. Nathan's story has gotten out there. If A left his body right before midnight, he must have woken up without any memory of me or the party. Or did he remember the party and have to make an excuse to the police officer who found him asleep at the side of the road?

I wish I knew Kelsea's last name so I could look her up, too. Not that I think she'll be updating her online status tonight to say *Everything's okay!* I can't really imagine what A is going through. What A has to do. But I'm certain that A is doing it.

Because A is not the devil. And A is not an angel, either.

A is just a person.

I guess I know that. A is just a person.

• • •

Justin texts me when he's off work.

Wanna hang out?

I don't. So I tell him I'm tired.

He doesn't text back.

I keep thinking about Kelsea all night, wondering what happens after A is gone.

In the morning, I can't stand it. I realize I still have the phone number at their house. I can call and make sure she's okay. I can pretend it's a wrong number. I just want to hear someone's voice. I want to be able to tell from the sound of her voice, or her father's.

It's nine in the morning. Nobody answers.

I call again. They can't be sleeping. This would have woken them.

So they're not there.

I email A:

A,

I hope it went well yesterday. I called her house just now and no one was home—do you think they're getting help? I'm trying to take it as a good sign.

Meanwhile, here's a link you need to see. It's out of control.

Where are you today?

R

I think he needs to know what Nathan is saying, and the fact that people are listening to it.

I wonder if he's dealt with this kind of thing before.

And then I step back and acknowledge how weird it is that I've accepted all this. I mean, I still want more proof. Which is where the idea comes from for what I'm going to do next.

I start searching the Internet again.

About an hour later, there's a new email from A.

Rhiannon,

I think it's a good sign. Kelsea's father is now aware of what's going on, and before I left, he was figuring out what to do. So if they're not home, they are probably getting help. Thank you for being there—I would have done the wrong things without you.

I am sure you know this, but I am going to say it anyway: I am not the devil. Nathan had a very bad reaction to me leaving him—they weren't the best circumstances, and I feel bad about that. But he has leaped—or been pushed—to the wrong conclusion.

Today I am a boy named Hugo. I'm going to a parade in Annapolis with some of his friends. Can you meet me there? I'm sure there will be some way for me to get away for a little bit, and I would of course love to see you. Let me know if you can make it. Or if you can't reach me—I'm not sure I'll be able to check here—look for a Brazilian boy with a "vintage" Avril Lavigne T-shirt on. It is, I imagine, the T-shirt of his that is least likely to be worn by anyone else.

Hoping to see you.

Love,
A

Annapolis is far. Not too far, but far. Especially if there's no way to know if I'll get to see him.

I do not have the energy to chase around after someone else.

And I have something else I want to do.

Justin texts around eleven. I'm guessing he's just woken up. And I'm scared that he hasn't, because then he might have seen me close to his house.

What are you doing? he asks now.

Just some things, I type back. *See you later?*

He lets that hang for a good ten minutes before answering, *Sure*.

Awesome, I reply.

I have to be careful here.

• • •

Annapolis, I keep thinking as I drive.

But I take a different turn.

It's as I'm walking up the front steps that I realize how ridiculous I must look. It seemed like a good idea when it was just an idea. As an actual thing that I am doing, it's on the sillier side of sane.

There aren't camera crews or anything outside. No reporters. No one to notice the girl with the bag over her shoulder as she heads to the front door.

I just need to know. It will only take a minute. I'm sure of it.

He has to be the one to answer the door. It's a Saturday, so anyone could be home.

I ring the bell and take a breath. I keep rehearsing in my head.

Then the door opens and it's him.

Same awkward body. Same messy black hair. No tie.

And no recognition in his eyes.

"Can I help you?" he asks.

I give him a second to look at me. Really look at me.

I am the girl you danced with.

I am the girl who was with you that night.

You sang for me.

But he didn't do any of these things, did he? He's looking at me like he's never seen me before. Because he's never seen me before.

"I'm helping my sister out and selling Girl Scout cookies," I say, nodding toward the bag on my shoulder. "Can I interest you in any?"

"Who is it?" a voice behind Nathan asks. His mother—it has to be his mother—shuffles into the frame, suspicious.

"Girl Scout cookies," I say. "I have Thin Mints, Samoas, and Tagalongs."

"Aren't you old to be a Girl Scout?" Mrs. Daldry asks.

"It's for her sister," Nathan mumbles.

Don't you know me? I want to ask.

But when he says no, what will I say next? How can I begin to explain?

Nathan's mother softens a little. "Do you want a box?" she asks her son. "We haven't had any since the Hayes girl moved away."

"Maybe the peanut butter ones?" he says.

His mom nods, then tells me, "Let me get my wallet."

I expect Nathan to ask me something—where I'm from, where my sister is, anything. But instead he looks embarrassed to be stuck with me. Not because he remembers the time we had together. But because I'm a girl in his house.

I start to hum "Carry On" to myself. I look one last time for recognition.

Nothing.

The difference is also there in his eyes. Not physically. But in the way he's using them. In what they are saying to me. There's no excitement. No longing. No connection.

His mom comes back and pays me. I hand over a box and that's it—we're done. She thanks me. I thank her.

Nathan goes back to his life. I imagine he's already forgotten I was there.

• • •

I get back in the car.

Pizza? Justin texts.

Annapolis? my mind asks.

I check my email before turning the ignition.

Nothing from A.

I am not going to run around a city looking for an Avril Lavigne T-shirt.

I tell Justin I'll pick him up.

"What took you so long?" he asks as soon as I get there.

I realize I didn't tell him how far away I was.

"Just running around for my mom," I say. Running around *with* my mom, he won't believe. Running around *for* my mom, he probably will.

He looks like he didn't get much sleep. But, I figure, maybe he always looks like that. I try to remember the last time I saw him fully awake. Then I think, *Duh, it was at the ocean.*

Of course it was.

"Hello?" he says. Shit, I've missed something.

"Sorry," I tell him. "Just tired. A little spacy."

"I've heard that before," he says gruffly. And I realize that, yeah, I pretty much said that to him last night. "Why so tired?"

"Life," I tell him.

He gives me a look.

He's not buying it.

We go for pizza. Once he's got food in him, he talks.

"I don't give a fuck what you're doing," he says, "but at least

127

have the decency to let me know how long it's going to take. It's just *rude*."

I tell him I'm sorry.

"Yeah, yeah. I know you're sorry, but what does that really mean? When it all comes down to it, isn't that word just one short excuse? It's like, my dad can be King Asshole to my mom and tell her that she and I are a complete waste of his time, and then he'll come back and say, 'Sorry, I didn't really mean it,' like now everything's fine, now everything's erased. And she'll accept it. She'll tell him that *she's* sorry. So we're this big, sorry family, and I get all the shit because I refuse to play along. I get it enough from them, and now you're doing it, too. Don't turn us into Steve and Stephanie, because you know we're better than that. You and I don't play games and we don't cover things up with *sorry* this and *sorry* that. If you don't want to tell me what you're doing—fine. But if you say you're coming over, come the fuck over. Don't make me wait like you know I don't have anything better to do. I just sat there like a dumbfuck waiting for you."

I almost say *Sorry* again. Almost.

"In case you were curious, my father finally got off his ass to see my grandmother. I told him I wanted to come and he said it wasn't the right time. And I was like, 'When's the right time, after she's dead?' That really pissed him off. And I wanted to say, *What's it like, Dad, to be a failure as both a son and a father? How do you account for that?* But he had his give-me-one-reason-to-belt-you face on. He never does it, but man, he wants to."

"Is she getting any better?" I ask.

"No. She's not 'getting any better.' Jesus."

Fair. I need to focus. And when I focus, I see the pain he's in. His grandmother is the one person in his family he really loves. Hers is the only blood he wants in his veins. I know this. He's told me this. I have to stop treating it like he has no reason to be angry.

"You should call her," I say. "They can't stop you from calling her. Is your dad there yet?"

He shakes his head. "He's probably still on the plane."

I reach across the table and pick up the phone.

"So beat him to it."

A lot of the time, love feels like it's about figuring out what the other person wants and giving it over. Sometimes that's impossible. But sometimes it's pretty simple. Like right now. He doesn't have the words to thank me, but when I hand him the phone, he holds on for a moment, lets me know I've gotten it right.

Right after he dials, I tell him I can go. Give him some privacy.

"No," he says. "I want you here." Then: "I *need* you here."

So I stay, and watch him talk to his grandmother like it's all going to be fine. Not going near *goodbye*, even though it's probably the word most on his mind.

After he's done, he puts the phone back on the table and says, "Wow, that was hard."

I wish I were sitting next to him, not across from him. I press my knees against his knees.

"It's alright," he says. Then he picks up a slice of pizza and keeps eating.

I'm about to ask him what his grandmother said, but then the phone rings and it's Steve, telling us about a party at Yonni Pfister's house.

"We're there," Justin says. Then, after he hangs up, he tells me where we're going.

Annapolis, I can't help thinking. But we're going nowhere near Annapolis.

Say any city enough times, it starts to sound like a made-up place.

Rebecca is at the party. She searches me out.

"I think our boyfriends are getting pretty baked," she tells me.

"Lucky us," I say.

She looks at me in surprise and laughs. "Did you really just say that? Good for you!"

Don't tell Justin, I want to say. But I know she won't. She might tell Ben, but he won't tell Justin, either.

Am I the only one who actually likes Justin?

"What's been going on?" Rebecca asks me.

"I'm just tired," I say.

"Yeah, but tired of what?"

She's genuinely interested. She genuinely cares. She is my friend.

I don't tell her a thing.

I duck out of the party before it's too late to call Kelsea's house.

This time someone answers.

"Hello?" His voice is rough. Tired.

"Hi, is Kelsea there?" I ask. I just want to hear her voice. I just want to know she's okay.

"Who is this?"

I try to think of a name that isn't mine. "It's Mia. I'm a friend of hers?"

"Well, Kelsea isn't here right now. And she won't be using her phone for a few days. If you leave a message there, though, I'm sure she'll get back to you. Just give it some time."

I risk it and ask, "Is she okay? I'm just a little . . . concerned."

"She's somewhere getting help," he says. "It's going to be okay." He pauses; this is new ground for him. "I know it'll mean a lot to hear from her friends. It's good of you to call."

He's not going to tell me more, and that's fine. This is enough to know.

"Thank you," I say. I want to tell him he did the right thing. But I don't want to make too much of an impression.

I'm already the friend who isn't really there.

I'm home late. I have to walk Justin to his door because he's so out of it. I wonder if his mom is awake.

"Thank you," he says quietly. "My grandmother is an amazing lady, and you're not too bad yourself."

"Don't give your mom a hard time," I tell him.

He raises his fingers in a salute. "Yes, ma'am." Then he leans over and kisses me good night. I'm surprised, and he can tell I'm surprised.

"Night, ma'am," he says. Then he disappears inside.

• • •

131

I email A when I get back to my house.

A,

Sorry I couldn't make it to Annapolis—there were some things I had to do.

Maybe tomorrow?

R

Chapter Twelve

It's Sunday. Justin won't be up for a while. We haven't made plans. My parents won't leave the house.

I'm free.

I tell my mom I have errands to run, then email A and ask if he wants to be one of my errands.

Yes, he writes back. *A million times yes.*

I am just going to do this, I tell myself as I make all the arrangements, as I come up with plans.

I am not going to think about it.

I am not going to think about what it means.

I am just going to do it, and be with A, and see what it means as it happens.

A's told me he (she?) is a girl named Ashley today. I've gotten directions to her house. I know she'll be waiting when I pull up.

I guess I'm picturing the girl A was when I first met her (him?). Pretty, but not overwhelmingly so. Someone I could be friends with. Someone I could be.

But holy shit, not this girl.

She comes out of the house and I'm like, *What kind of music video am I living in?* Because this girl is smoking hot. She looks like she should travel with backup singers. And photographers. And three stylists. And a small dog. And Jay-Z.

This is the kind of girl you never see in real life. You can almost pretend girls like this don't really exist. They're computer-generated by fashion magazines to make you feel lame.

Only this girl is *real*.

And I know I shouldn't care—this isn't a contest. But really? I already feel fat, and she isn't even at the car yet.

The one thing she doesn't have is a *walk*. A girl like this should have a walk. But I guess that's A inside. Stomping when he should sashay.

When she gets in the car and I see her up close, I have to laugh. Even her skin is perfect. All I'm asking for is a simple fucking pimple.

"You've got to be kidding me," I say.

She makes putting a seat belt on look sexy. Jesus.

She sees me laughing and asks, "What?"

She doesn't get it.

"*What?*" I repeat. Like A doesn't realize how amazing she is today.

She holds up her hand, defending her reaction. "You have to understand—you're the first person to ever know me in more than one body. I'm not used to this. I don't know how you're going to react."

Okay. I may have forgotten that. But still.

"I'm sorry," I say. "It's just that you're this super hot black girl. It makes it very hard for me to have a mental image of you. I keep having to change it."

"Picture me however you want to picture me. Because odds are, that'll be more true than any of the bodies you see me in."

She makes it sound easy. It's not easy. Especially with a pretty girl.

"I think my imagination needs a little more time to catch up to the situation, okay?" I say.

She nods. Even her nod is stunning. Not fair at all. "Okay. Now, where to?"

I've given this some thought. And I am not going to change the plan just because of the body in my passenger seat.

"Since we've already been to the ocean," I say, "I figured today we'd go to a forest."

So much for not thinking about it.

As we're driving, all I can do is think about it. About her. About A inside her body. We're talking—I'm telling her about the phone call with Kelsea's father and the party last night, and she's telling me about the parade she went to yesterday, in the body of a gay boy with a boyfriend. But even as we're talking, my mind is racing with all kinds of thoughts. And the pathetic thing is that I know if A looked like Nathan today, I wouldn't be having any of these thoughts. It would feel normal, because I'd be out with a normal boy.

But this is so different. Too different. Even though when she looks at me, I can feel A inside, it's not easy to separate the two. And it's not easy to realize this is part of the lottery. Some days, A is going to be like this.

I don't see where I could possibly fit into a life like that.

I don't want to kiss her. I could never kiss her.

So there's that.

But I can talk to her and not worry that I'm talking too much, or talking too little, or saying the wrong thing. It's like my life is usually lived behind this veil of judgment, and A manages to pull back the veil, seeing me more truthfully than anyone else.

I tell myself to notice that. To remember it. To not get so caught up in how attractive she is that I forget everything else.

I take us to this national park that I know has picnic benches. I've planned a picnic for two—and even if Ashley looks like she eats half a meal a day, I'm hoping A will find a way to eat like the rest of us. There are a few other people in the park, but I try to avoid them. This day is meant to be ours.

My phone is off. I am here, now.

"I love this place," A tells me.

"You've never been here before?" I ask.

She shakes her head. "Not that I can remember. Although it's possible. At a certain point, it all blurs together. There are a lot of days when I haven't really paid attention."

I know she's paying attention now. She smiles at me as I turn off the car. She watches as I head to the trunk. She seems delighted when I pull out the picnic hamper.

The hamper came with a blanket, and I put it over the picnic table like a tablecloth—because, when it all comes down to it, I don't like sitting on the ground if a table is an option. Then I put out all the food I bought—nothing big, just a lot of small things, like chips and salsa and cheese and bread and hummus and olives.

"Are you a vegetarian?" A asks.

I nod.

"Why?"

I am so tired of this question. Shouldn't it be the meat eaters who are asked why? And it's always like they're expecting this crazy answer. So I decide to give the craziest answer I can think of.

I keep a straight face and say, "Because I have this theory that when we die, every animal that we've eaten has a chance at eating us back. So if you're a carnivore and you add up all the animals you've eaten—well, that's a long time in purgatory, being chewed."

It's funny to see Ashley's perfect features contort into a grimace. "Really?" she asks.

I laugh. "No. I'm just sick of the question. I mean, I'm vegetarian because I think it's wrong to eat other sentient creatures. And it sucks for the environment."

"Fair enough," she says.

I'm not sure I've persuaded her.

Maybe over time I can, I think.

Then I think, *What?*

I shouldn't be thinking of anything over time. It's just one day plus another day plus another day. Maybe.

When things get bad with Justin, the question I find myself asking is: What's the point? Like, why put ourselves through all this? Why try to squeeze two people into the shape of a couple? Are the things you gain really worth the things you lose?

Now I'm asking myself the same things about A. We're talking about favorite foods, and the best meals we've ever had, and the foods we hate the most—when she asks me all these questions, I enjoy answering, and when I ask her questions back, I enjoy the answers she gives me. If this were a date, it would be going really well. But there's a part of me that's standing outside of it, that's looking at it as it happens, and that part is asking, *What is this? What's the point?*

When we're done eating, we pack the leftovers in the hamper and return it to the trunk. Then, without discussing what we're going to do next, we walk into the woods. The paths aren't obvious—we find our way through the trees by heading into them, looking for the widest distances, the clearest ground.

When we're alone, when we're walking like this, all of the conversation that's been happening on the outside moves to the center of our minds. *What is this?* I know I can't answer it alone.

"I need to know what you want," I say.

She doesn't seem surprised by the request. If it were Justin, I know I'd get a *What's gotten into you?* But A answers without missing a beat.

"I want us to be together," she (he?) tells me.

She says it like it's easy. But there's no way my mind can turn it into something easy. Not when she's in a different body every day. I can have a conversation with any of them, I'm sure. But when it comes to chemistry, when it comes to making that part of me come alive—I know some days are going to work and some aren't. Like now. She has to see that.

"But we can't be together," I say. I'm amazed by how calm I sound. "You realize that, don't you?"

"No," she says. "I don't realize that."

Frustrating. It's like talking to a child who still believes that proclaiming something out loud can make it real. I wish I could believe like that.

I stop walking and put my hand on her shoulder. The truth hurts to say, especially because she looks so unready to hear it.

"You need to realize it," I tell her. "I can care about you. You can care about me. But we can't be together."

"Why?"

"Why?" It's exasperating to have to spell it out. "Because one morning you could wake up on the other side of the country. Because I feel like I'm meeting a new person every time I see you. Because you can't be there for me. Because I don't think I can like you no matter what. Not like this."

"Why can't you like me like this?"

"It's too much. You're too perfect right now. I can't imagine being with someone like . . . you."

"But don't look at her—look at me."

I am. I *am* looking at her.

"I can't see beyond her, okay?" I say. "And there's also Justin. I have to think of Justin."

"No, you don't."

This makes me angry. Whatever Justin and I have, it can't be dismissed in a single sentence.

"You don't know, okay? How many waking hours were you

in there? Fourteen? Fifteen? Did you really get to know every-thing about him while you were in there? Everything about me?"

"You like him because he's a lost boy. Believe me, I've seen it happen before. But do you know what happens to girls who love lost boys? They become lost themselves. Without fail."

I don't want to hear this. "You don't know me—"

"But I know how this works!" Her voice is loud, certain. "I know what he's like. He doesn't care about you nearly as much as you care about him. He doesn't care about you nearly as much as I care about you."

I can't hear this. What good is hearing this?

"Stop! Just stop."

But she won't. "What do you think would happen if he met me in this body? What if the three of us went out? How much attention do you think he'd pay you? Because he doesn't care about who you are. I happen to think you are about a thousand times more attractive than Ashley is. But do you really think he'd be able to keep his hands to himself if he had a chance?"

"He's not like that," I say. Because he's not.

"Are you sure? Are you really sure?"

"Fine," I say. "Let me call him."

I don't know why I'm doing this, but I'm doing it. I take out my phone. Turn it on. Call him.

"Hullo," he answers.

"Hi!" I'm too cheery. I take it down a notch. "I don't know what you're up to tonight, but I have this friend in town I'd love for you to meet. Maybe we could all get dinner?"

"Dinner? What time is it?"

"It's only two now. Maybe at six? At the Clam Casino? I'll treat."

"Okay. Sounds good."

"Great! I'll see you then!"

I hang up before he can ask me who my friend is. I'll have to think of a story.

"Happy?" I ask A.

"I have no idea," she replies.

"Me either." Because now that I'm thinking about it, I'm wondering what I've just done.

"When are we meeting him?"

"Six."

"Okay," she says. "In the meantime, I want to tell you everything, and I want you to tell me everything in return."

Everything.

I start when I was born. My father was away for business and my mother was all alone in the hospital. She knew I was going to be a girl. One night my father, after a few beers, told me the story of how she called my name as I was being born. As if I would hear her calling. As if he were there in the room to know what she said.

We moved around a lot when I was really young, but I don't remember much of it. My first memory is actually of Liza hiding with me under our parents' bed. I remember her telling me to be quiet. I remember seeing their feet, hearing their voices looking for us. I don't remember being found.

I give A all these little Lego-like details, and don't have any idea what they build. But I can see A building something—a story—as I hand them over. I can see A putting it together, and wanting to.

I ask her when she first knew about being the way she is. She tells me that until she was four or five, she just assumed she was normal—she assumed everyone woke up every day with new parents, in a new house, with a new body. Because when you're young, people are willing to reintroduce the world to you each day. If you get something wrong, they'll correct you. If there's a blank, they'll fill it in for you. You're not expected to know that much about your life.

"There was never that big a disturbance," she tells me. "I didn't think of myself as a boy or a girl—I never have. I would just think of myself as a boy or a girl for a day. It was like a different set of clothes. The thing that ended up tripping me up was the concept of tomorrow. Because after a while, I started to notice—people kept talking about doing things tomorrow. Together. And if I argued, I would get strange looks. For everyone else, there always seemed to be a tomorrow together. But not for me. I'd say, *You won't be there*, and they'd say, *Of course I'll be there*. And then I'd wake up, and they wouldn't be. And my new parents would have no idea why I was so upset."

I try to imagine going through that, but I can't really. I don't think I could ever get used to it.

A continues. "There were only two options—something was wrong with everyone else, or something was wrong with me. Because either they were tricking themselves into thinking there was a tomorrow together, or I was the only person who was leaving."

"Did you try to hold on?" I ask.

"I'm sure I did. But I don't remember it now. I remember crying and protesting—I told you about that. But the rest? I'm not sure. I mean, do you remember a lot about when you were five?"

I see her point. "Not really. I remember my mom bringing me and my sister to the shoe store to get new shoes before kindergarten started. I remember learning that a green light meant go and red meant stop. I remember coloring them in, and the teacher being a little confused about how to explain yellow. I think she told us to treat it the same as red."

"I learned my letters quickly. I remember the teachers being surprised that I knew them. I imagine they were just as surprised the next day, when I'd forgotten them."

"A five-year-old probably wouldn't notice taking a day off."

"Probably. I don't know."

I can't help wondering about the people whose body A takes for a day. I wonder what they feel the next day. I think about Nathan staring at me so blankly. But mostly I think about Justin.

"I keep asking Justin about it, you know," I say. "The day you were him. And it's amazing how clear his fake memories are. He doesn't disagree when I say we went to the beach, but he doesn't really remember it, either."

"James, the twin, was like that, too. He didn't notice anything wrong. But when I asked him about meeting you for coffee, he didn't remember it at all. He remembered he was at Starbucks—his mind accounted for the time. But not what actually happened."

"Maybe they remember what you want them to remember."

"I've thought about that. I wish I knew for sure."

We walk in silence for a minute, then stop at a tree with a ladder of knots. I can't help but touch one. A touches the other side, and works her hand around to mine. But I keep moving, too. Circling.

"What about love?" I ask. "Have you ever been in love?"

Which is my way of asking: Is it possible? Is any of this possible?

"I don't know that you'd call it love," A tells me. "I've had crushes, for sure. And there have been days where I've really regretted leaving. There were even one or two people I tried to find, but that didn't work out. The closest was this guy Brennan."

A stops. Looks again at the tree, at the knots.

"Tell me about him," I say.

"It was about a year ago. I was working at a movie theater, and he was in town, visiting his cousins, and when he went to get some popcorn, we flirted a little, and it just became this . . . spark. It was this small one-screen movie theater, and when the movie was running, my job was pretty slow. I think he missed the second half of the movie, because he came back out and started talking to me more. I ended up having to tell him what happened so he could pretend he'd been in there most of the time. At the end, he asked for my email, and I made up an email address."

"Like you did for me," I point out. So Nathan knew what he was doing a little more than I'd thought.

"Exactly like I did for you. And he emailed me later that

144

night, and left the next day to go back home to Maine, and that proved to be ideal, because then the rest of our relationship could be online. I'd been wearing a name tag, so I had to give him that first name, but I made up a last name, and then I made up an online profile using some of the photos from the real guy's profile. I think his name was Ian."

This surprises me, that A was a boy in love with a boy. Maybe because it's a girl's voice telling me this story. Or maybe because I assume *girl* when I hear *boyfriend*. Which I know isn't right, but it's where my mind goes.

After I express my surprise, she asks me if it matters. I tell her it doesn't. And while she tells me the rest of the story— she tried to keep it going online, but he wanted to meet, and she knew they never could, so she ended it—I try to convince myself that it really *doesn't* matter. And I guess it doesn't matter, in terms of her (him). But it still matters in terms of me. At least a little.

As she wraps up the Brennan story, A tells me, "I promised myself I wouldn't get into any more virtual entanglements, as easy as they might seem to be. Because what's the point of something virtual if it doesn't end up being real? And I could never give anyone something real. I could only give them deception."

"Like impersonating their boyfriends," I can't help but say.

"Yeah. But you have to understand—you were the exception to the rule. And I didn't want it to be based on deception. Which is why you're the first person I've ever told."

I know this is meant as the highest compliment A can give me. But I want to know what I did to earn it. I want to know

145

how A knows I'm the right person to tell. I want to know what that means.

I tell her, "The funny thing is, you say it like it's so unusual that you've only done it once. But I bet a whole lot of people go through their lives without ever telling the truth, not really. And they wake up in the same body and the same life every single morning."

Now she's curious. "Why? What aren't you telling me?"

I have known you less than two weeks, I think. I wish I could disarm myself so completely in such a short time. But even if A thinks I've earned that, I am not even close to believing she's earned it. Not because of who she is or what she is. Because it's so soon.

I get that her life has a special set of rules. But my life has rules, too.

I look her right in the eye. I am not angry—I want to be sure she knows I'm not angry. But I *am* serious. "If I'm not telling you something, it's for a reason. Just because you trust me, it doesn't mean I have to automatically trust you. Trust doesn't work like that."

"That's fair," she says. Although I can tell she's also a little disappointed.

"I know it is," I tell her. "But enough of that. Tell me about—I don't know—third grade."

There is no point in talking more about us. We need to talk about ourselves separately for a little while longer.

It's not entirely separate, of course. We've both been afraid of teachers. We've both gotten lost at theme parks. We've both fallen into hair-pulling, teeth-kicking fights with siblings. We've grown up on the same TV shows, being the same

146

age. Only, while we both had dreams of waking up in Hannah Montana's body and Hannah Montana's life, A actually believed that the dream could come true.

I ask about all those lives, all those days, and what A can remember. The result is like a series of snapshots—a slideshow of bits and pieces with the faces always changing. All of the firsts—first snow, first Pixar movie, first evil pet, first bully. And other things I wouldn't have even realized were things— the size of bedrooms, the strange diets parents put their kids on, the need to sing in church even if you don't know any of the tunes or any of the words. Discovering allergies, illnesses, learning problems, stutters. And living the day with them. Always living another day.

I try to keep up. I try to offer some of my firsts, some of my surprises. But they don't seem as first or as surprising.

We talk about family. She asks me if I hate my mother.

"No," I tell her. "That's not it. I love her, but I also want her to be better. I want her to stop giving up."

"I can't even imagine what that's like. To come home to the same parents every day."

"There's no one who can make you angrier, but you also can't really love anyone more. I know that doesn't make sense, but it's true. She disappoints me every day she just sits there. But I know she would do anything for me, if she had to."

It's strange to say this out loud. It's not something I'd ever say to my mother, or even think in her presence. But maybe I should. I don't know.

Even though I'm afraid of the answer, I ask A if she's always been around here, or if she jumps to bodies in much farther places. In other words, I want to know if one day she'll be too far away to see, if she could wake up on the other side of the world.

"It doesn't work like that," she tells me. "I honestly don't know why it works the way it does, but I know that I never wake up that far from where I was yesterday. It's like there's a method to it—but I couldn't tell you what it is. Once I tried to chart it out—the distances between bodies. I tried to see if it made mathematical sense. But it was mathematical gibberish. Random, but in a limited way."

"So you won't leave?" I ask.

"Not by waking up. But if the body I'm in goes somewhere else—I go with it. That becomes my new starting point. That's how I got here, to Maryland. This one girl had a field trip to DC, and the group she was in was cheap, so they stayed outside the city. The next morning, I didn't wake up back in Minnesota. I was still in Bethesda."

"Well, don't take any field trips soon, okay?" I make it sound like a joke, but I mean it.

"No field trips," she agrees. Then she asks me about my own travels, and I tell her all about how I haven't really been anywhere since we settled down in Maryland. Even DC is a stretch. My parents like to stay put.

She asks me where I want to go. I tell her Paris. Which is such a silly answer, because I feel like it would be any girl's answer.

"I've always wanted to go there, too," A says. "And London."

"And Greece!"

"And Amsterdam."

"Yes, Amsterdam."

We walk round and round the forest, planning to travel the world. We walk past tree after tree and all the years we've lived seem to be there to be reached for. We return to the car and take more chips, more olives. Then we walk a little farther, talk a little further. I can't believe how many stories there are—but they keep appearing because our stories are talking to each other; one of mine leading to one of A's, then one of A's leading to one of mine.

I never talk like this, I think. And then I realize this is very close to what A was saying before. *You're the first person I've ever told.*

Yes, A is the first person I've ever told most of these stories to. Because A is the first person who has listened and heard and wanted to know.

Which might not be fair to Justin. Because how much have I actually tried to tell these things to Justin?

Only on the beach. Only that day.

Thinking of Justin makes me think of the stupid dinner plans we've made. I look at my phone and find that hours have passed. It's five-fifteen.

There isn't even time to cancel.

"We better get going," I tell A. "Justin will be waiting for us."

Neither of us wants to do this now. We want to stay here, keep this.

I feel like I've made a mistake.

I feel like what we're about to do is a big mistake.

Chapter Thirteen

She tries to talk to me on the car ride over, and I try to talk to her, but I think we're both lost in what we're about to do. It's awful that we're going to trick him like this. And it's even more awful that I'm dying to know what he'll do.

I've gotten used to how Ashley looks, so it throws me to see the reaction when we hit the Clam Casino. The greeter is Chrissy B, this guy I went to high school with. He graduated last year, wanting to do musical theater. The closest he's come so far is when someone orders the Happy Clamday to You special, and he and the other staff members have to sing the "Happy Clamday" song while someone blows out a candle that's sitting on a half shell. It's a pretty scary place, but the food is good.

Chrissy B takes one look at Ashley and it's like he's projecting all of his runways onto her. I've never seen him snap to attention so fast, or handle the menus so self-consciously. It's like I'm not even there, not until I say hi and ask him if Justin's already around. Chrissy B seems annoyed to have to answer me. But he tells me no, and I say we'll wait. Justin doesn't like it when I sit down before he does—I think because then we're committing to staying, and sometimes he changes his mind.

As we wait for him, I can sense other people looking at Ashley. If A notices, she keeps her cool. I don't like it. Some of the guys are looking so openly, so hungrily—what right do they have to do that? Some of the women are admiring, and others are resentful. Whatever their feelings, they have a reaction. If I were Ashley, I would feel like a bug trapped in a jar.

Justin walks in about ten minutes after we do, which is only five minutes late.

He sees me first, and starts to head over. Then he sees Ashley and stops for a second. He's not immediately predatory, like the other guys. He's floored. Completely floored.

"Hi," I say. It's awkward because usually I'd kiss him hello. But I don't want to do that in front of A. "Ashley," I say, "this is Justin. Justin, this is Ashley."

Ashley puts out her hand to shake—it's a very not-Ashley gesture, and I almost laugh from nervousness. Justin shakes. He's looking at her whole body when he does.

"Let me get you a table!" Chrissy B chirps, as if his stage time in this amateur production has finally come.

As we walk over, more people look. If they're thinking there's a couple here, it's Ashley and Justin. I'm the third wheel.

I don't know what to say or do. I have no idea how to explain Ashley to Justin. And now that we're here, I don't want them to get along. I don't want him to fall for her. I don't want him to look at her in a way he'd never look at me. I don't want to be humiliated like that.

"So," Justin says once Chrissy B has fanned out the menus and left us to our choices. "How do you two know each other?"

I can't think of a single thing but the truth, which isn't nearly good enough.

But A doesn't hesitate. "Oh, it's a funny story!" she says, and it's like her voice already believes it's a funny story, and is sure we'll agree in about ten seconds. "My mom and her mom were best friends in high school. Then we moved away when I was eight. Mom couldn't stand the cold, so we went to LA. My dad got a job working on movie sets, and Mom became a librarian at the downtown library. I didn't think I'd get into the LA thing, but I totally did. When I was ten, I told my mom I wanted to do commercials—not that I wanted to be an *actress*, but that I wanted to do *commercials*! And from there I've done some bit parts and auditioned for a lot of TV shows. Nothing yet, but I've come close. And every few years, Mom and I make a trip back here, to see some family and old friends. Rhiannon and I see each other every couple of years—but it's been a while this time, hasn't it? Like, three or four years?"

"Yeah," I say, because I sense I'm supposed to say something here. "I think it's three."

A is really getting into it. And she's also really getting into Justin. I can see her leg brushing up against his. He doesn't move into it, but he doesn't move away.

This isn't happening, I tell myself.

I knew I couldn't compete with Ashley. So what did I do? I put myself in a competition.

I have no one to blame but myself.

"So have you been on any shows I would've seen?" Justin asks.

She starts to tell him about being a corpse on a medical investigation show, and being in a party scene on a "reality" show. And the stupid thing is—I'm believing it. I'm actually imagining her on that coroner's slab, or joking with a D-list celebrity over a keg.

"But LA's such a fake place," Ashley confesses when she's through with her résumé. "That's why I'm glad I have real friends like Rhiannon."

She gives my hand a little squeeze. I find that reassuring.

Our dinner arrives, and Ashley starts to talk about guys, including this one time she "shared a moment" with Jake Gyllenhaal at some château. As she's talking about this encounter, she keeps touching Justin's hand. I do not find that reassuring.

Luckily, Justin pulls away to get back to his lobster roll. I ask Ashley how her parents are doing. She answers flawlessly. Justin isn't so interested in parents, which is good.

But then the food is done, and Justin's hands are free, and Ashley goes full throttle again. Defensively, I reach for Justin's hand myself. It feels like lobster roll. He doesn't shake me off, but it's clear he doesn't understand why I'm holding it, either. I try to move my leg against his, but I'm at the wrong angle. It looks like I'm trying to get a napkin from under the table.

"How's everything going?" Chrissy B comes over to ask, his eyes full of Ashley.

"Wonnnnnderful!" she purrs.

Who are you? I think.

Chrissy B bounces away, happy.

I want to ask for the check. I do not want any more courses of this. Justin isn't looking at me. He's not seeing me. He's not getting the SOS I'm sending.

I need to calm down. If I start acting needy or emotional, it will only make Ashley more attractive.

"I'm going to the ladies' room," I announce. I touch Justin on the arm. He gives me a look like, *You do not need my permission to go to the bathroom, Rhiannon.*

I don't need to pee. I need to stare at myself in the mirror and ask myself what I really want. I need to splash water on my face and wake myself up . . . but I'm afraid someone will come in and see me doing it, so I stick with staring at myself in the mirror. I see a girl who isn't ugly, but who will never, ever be Ashley. I see the girl Justin has grown used to. I see a girl who is deeply unexciting, and who dared her boyfriend to find someone better.

I am so stupid. So, so stupid.

And I am especially stupid for leaving them alone together.

I wash my hands even though I haven't touched anything. Then I push myself back to the table. I can see their conversation has gotten real intense. Something is happening.

I interrupt. I don't even wait until I've sat back down. I stand there and tell A, "I don't want this. Stop."

"I'm not doing anything!" Justin yells. But he looks guilty. "Your friend here is a little out of control."

"I don't want this," I repeat, this time to both of them.

"It's okay," Ashley says. "I'm sorry."

"You should be!" Justin tells her. "God, I don't know how they do things in California, but here, you don't act like that."

He's up now. I want to ask what happened. I don't want to know what happened.

"I'm gonna go," he says. Then, out of the blue, he kisses me. I want to believe it's for me, but it's for her. I know it's for her.

154

I don't want it.

"Thanks, baby," he says. "I'll see you tomorrow."

That's it. He's not turning back. I watch him even after he's gone.

I have done this. This was all me. Setting the trap, then getting caught in it.

I look at Ashley as I sit back down. She looks like she's witnessed a car accident. Or maybe she was the driver.

"I'm sorry," she tells me again.

"No," I say, "it's my fault. I should've known. I told you that you don't understand. You can't understand us."

The waitress is back, asking if we want dessert. I say no, just the check. She has it ready.

"I'll get it," A says.

"It's not your money," I point out. "I'll pay."

I text Justin to say I'm sorry. I tell him I'll call him as soon as I'm home. It's awful, but I wish Ashley had driven herself. I wish we could stop the night here. I am grateful that A will wake up in another body tomorrow. I am grateful I'll never have to see Ashley again.

It's only by separating them that I can hold on to A, and everything that happened before we got to this restaurant. But even still—we've done some damage. A hasn't hurt me . . . but she's allowed me to hurt myself. Which is almost the same thing.

When we get back to my car, she tells me again that she's sorry. I see why Justin gets sick of it when I say it so much.

After a while, she gives up. She realizes I need her to be quiet.

Finally, we get to her house.

"I had a great time," she says. "Until."

"Yeah," I say. "Until."

"He'll be fine. I'm sure he just thinks I'm this crazy California girl. Don't worry about it."

Pointless. What a pointless thing to say.

"I'll talk to you," she tells me.

If we'd come here straight from the woods, I wonder what would be happening now. Whether I'd kiss her even though she's Ashley. Whether we'd feel invincible.

"I'll talk to you," I echo. Even though I have no idea what we'll have to say.

I can't worry about A now.

I have to get Justin back.

Chapter Fourteen

I don't wait until I get home. I drive away from Ashley's house, turn a few corners, then pull over by the side of the road and call him.

He hasn't texted me back, and I'm worried he won't pick up. But he does.

"What's up?" he says. I can hear the TV loud in the background.

"I'm really sorry about that," I say.

"Not your fault. I have no idea where you picked up that black bitch, but let me tell you, she is *not* your friend. At all."

"I know. It was stupid of me to invite you along. I should've just dealt with her."

"She was out of control. Completely out of control."

"I guess looking like that can do that to you."

"It's no excuse. Seriously. What a *bitch*."

It wasn't really her, I want to say. *You didn't meet her at all.*

"I'll see you in the morning," Justin says. This is his way of saying we're not going to talk about this anymore.

"See you in the morning," I tell him. "And sorry again."

"Stop. It's fine."

No, it isn't.

I wonder if maybe it isn't only Ashley's life that has been hi-jacked. Maybe mine has been hijacked, too. Maybe I need to focus on the real things, not the fantasy things. Even if A is real, A will never be constant. Justin is my constant.

I'm worried that Justin will be pissed at me for what happened, but mostly he's pissed at Ashley. When we bump into our friends in the hall before homeroom, he can't wait to tell everyone what happened.

"Rhiannon has this total slut friend from California who *totally* made the moves on me last night—with Rhiannon right there! It was wild. She was totally hot, and she could not keep her hands off me. Finally I was like, 'Hey, what do you think you're doing?' And Rhiannon came right in and told her to get the hell off. I swear to you, it was out of control."

"Dude!" Steve says.

"Yeah. That's what I'm saying."

I know this is how guys talk. I know that the point of the story is that he chose me. But it still feels like he's bragging. It still feels like the point was that this hot, slutty girl wanted to sleep with him.

I'm not going to say anything—I'm just going to let the story be over. But Rebecca picks it up and won't let it go.

"What exactly is it that makes her a slut?" she asks. "What if she was just flirty?"

"Oh, give it a rest, Rebecca," Justin spits out. "You weren't there. You didn't see this black bitch in action—it was price-less."

"Now she's a 'black bitch'? Really, Justin?" Even though I don't want her to look at me at all, she turns my way. "Can you tell the rest of us what really happened?"

"He's right," I say. "She was out of control."

Now Rebecca's not just angry at Justin; she's disappointed in me.

"Cute, Rhiannon. Real cute."

Justin tries to level her with a look. "Rebecca, you weren't there. And I can call someone a black bitch if she was black and acted like a bitch. That's just a fact."

"Bullshit! Her being black has nothing to do with your story, you asshole. And I'll bet if she were telling her side of the story, she wouldn't be a bitch, either."

"So it's okay all of a sudden to call me an asshole?"

"One, I've been calling you an asshole for years. And two, please note that I'm not calling you a white asshole—because even though I'm sure your whiteness adds to your sense of en-titlement, I'm willing to let it slide so we can focus on the fact that you're a *universal* asshole right now."

"Okay," I interrupt. "You've made your point. Enough."

"Yeah, man," Justin says to Ben. "Turn your girlfriend off, okay?"

I know he's saying this to make Rebecca extra mad.

"She's right," Ben says. "You're being an asshole."

I feel bad because now Justin is feeling attacked, and even though his choice of words is wrong, the story he's telling isn't a lie. Ashley *did* come on to him. And even though she did it with my permission, he doesn't know that. He thinks one of my friends tried to steal him from me—and that *is* being a bitch. A universal bitch.

"If you don't change the subject right now, I am going to unleash the biggest fart this school has ever seen," Steve tells us. "You have been warned."

Rebecca pulls back and lets it look like she's dropping the conversation. But from the way she looks at me, I know she's filing it away for later.

In art class, she launches right into me.

"Why do you let him talk like that? How can you just sit there and let him shit all over everyone?"

"Rebecca, you have to understand—"

"No. Don't defend him. I don't know who this California friend of yours is, but maybe *she's* the one you should be defending. Because if you think of her as some slutty black bitch, then you're not all that great a friend to have."

Wait. What? What are we fighting about?

"Rebecca, why are you mad? I don't understand why you're mad."

"I'm mad because my best friend is dating an asshole. And no matter how many times I point it out to her, she looks at me like I'm the one saying the world is round, and she's like, *No no no—flat.*"

"It wasn't his fault," I insist. "She was trying to trap him into doing something. He was right to be mad."

"That must have been so hard on him, to have a hot girl

flirt in his direction. I don't know how he could stand it. Poor victim."

"It wasn't like that." There's no way I can explain.

"Well, in his version, it was. You know, the racist, sexist version he gave us in the hall? Or maybe you don't even notice those parts anymore."

"I do, but . . . that's not him. That's just him being mad."

"Oh, like it doesn't count if you're pissed off? I wish there were an Olympic competition where you could show off all the contortions you do in order to justify your relationship with him."

I hate it when she uses her smartness to *contort* things about me, to make me feel so dumb.

"Why do you have such a problem with me and Justin?" I challenge. "*Why?* It's not like he hits me. It's not like he abuses me. It's not like he cheats on me. Why can't you just accept that I see things in him that you might not see. And that you might not see them because you're a bitch to him all the time."

"So I get to be the bitch now? Fine. Then you, my friend, are the scary girl. *He doesn't hit me. He doesn't abuse me. He doesn't cheat on me.* Can you hear yourself? If those are the standards you have—*Hey, he hasn't punched me, so everything must be okay!*—that scares me. That makes me think that at some point you've used these justifications. *Oh, it's really bad right now, and he's being awful . . . but at least he's not hitting me.* Have a little more respect for yourself than that, okay?"

We are in the middle of art class. We are supposed to be drawing a sleeping turtle that Mr. K has brought in. Other people can probably hear us.

"Can we please not have this conversation here?" I ask her. When it comes out of my mouth, it sounds a little like pleading.

Rebecca sighs. "I don't know why I bother." Then she shakes her head, correcting herself. "No, I do know. Because you are my friend, Rhiannon. And because it kills me to see you twist yourself around to be with him. I know you're not really hearing me right now, but one day, these words might come in handy. They might help. Which is why I'm putting them out there. So they'll be there when you need them, and you'll know that I'm here when you need me."

It's perfectly said. Too perfectly said. I want to tell her that I already have one guidance counselor and don't really need another. I want to tell her that I can tell she enjoys seeing me suffer, because if I'm the patient, then she gets to be the nurse, the doctor, the guardian angel. Part of me appreciates it, but mostly I resent it.

She returns to her drawing and I return to mine. The turtle wakes up and tries to run away. Mr. K catches it every time it attempts to escape. The first time this happens, the class laughs. The fourth time, it's just inconvenient.

When I hang out with Justin after school, he doesn't mention Ashley or even Rebecca. We go back to his place and play some video games—I lose in an early round and have to watch until he's done. Then he moves his hands on me and we start to make out, and without us talking about it, I know we're going to go all the way this afternoon. I try to get into it, but I keep wondering if he'd like it better if I had a different body—if I had Ashley's body. Then as we're getting naked and more intense, I think about being in his body and having sex with Ashley. Would I like it? Do I want that? I can't feel that way, and then I start thinking the opposite—what if A were in Justin's body right now? What if it were A inside of me, A covered in sweat, A kissing me? I know it would be different. I know he'd be looking at me more. Feeling me more. Here more. I feel so fucked up for thinking these things. For imagining A here, A with me. I am cheating on Justin in my head, even if it's still his body that I'm cheating with.

It finishes before I've really gotten anywhere. Justin asks me if I want him to keep going with me, but I tell him no, I'm fine. I'm good. I'm great.

Chapter Fifteen

I check my email before I go to sleep that night. No emails from Justin. No word from Rebecca. Just something from A.

I have to see you again.

A

I wonder what body A is in right now. I wonder if I would've wanted to sleep with it. I wonder if I'm wrong to wonder that. I wonder what the hell I'm doing.

I don't answer. I want to see A—of course I do.

But I still don't see the point.

Justin is in a dire mood when I catch him in the morning. Another long-distance lecture from his dad. Another test he's not ready for. Another day he doesn't want to be here.

I try to plant myself firmly at his side. I complain about my own history test coming up today. I tell him that hanging out with him yesterday was much more fun than studying, anyway. I don't tell him that I studied when I got home.

"I fucking hate this place," he tells me. I must remind myself I am not a part of the place. He is not talking about me.

It's hard to be supportive when you have no idea what you're supporting. It's hard to be there for someone when he won't let you know where he is.

I tell him I'll see him at lunch. He doesn't react. And why should he?—I'm only stating the obvious. We always know how our day will go.

I walk to my classes. I talk to the people I always talk to. I am barely paying attention to my own life.

I go to Spanish and I listen to people talk about the glories of Madrid. I go to art and I can barely lift a brush.

Then I'm walking into math and something inside me wakes up. Alert. Instead of going into the classroom, I glance back at the hall and see someone looking at me. In an instant I know A has come back. A is here.

It's in the eyes. This boy with his swoopy hair and his polo shirt and his jeans could be any boy. But those eyes, that way of looking at me, could only belong to A.

I walk away from class, from the way the day was supposed to go. Everyone around me rushes to get to class as the second bell rings. But not him. Not me. Not us.

Us. I should not be thinking of us as *us*. But it feels like *us*. Here in this hallway, before we've said a word, we're *us*.

I don't know if I want it to be true, but it doesn't seem to care what I want. It exists beyond me.

Classes start, and we're alone together. I map out where Justin is at this moment, and know he's nowhere near.

We're safe. From what, I don't know.

"Hey," I say.

"Hey," he says.

"I thought you might come."

"Are you mad?"

"No, I'm not mad," I tell him. "Although Lord knows you're not good for my attendance record."

He smiles. "I'm not good for anybody's attendance record."

"What's your name today?" I ask.

"A. For you, it's always A."

"Okay," I say.

And it works. By not knowing this boy's name, I can think of him as A.

There isn't any question of us running away. I have that history test, and things with Justin are tense enough without me disappearing and having to lie about it. I can miss math, but that's all I can miss.

It's so strange to walk the halls with him. I'm worried we'll bump into someone. I guess I'll have to pretend he's a new student. That I'm showing him around.

"Is Justin in class?" he asks as we hit the English wing.

"Yeah. If he decided to go."

I don't want to stay in the halls. I lead him into one of the English rooms, and we sit down in the back so no one will be able to see us from the door.

It's weird being in desks. It's hard to face each other. But we turn and find a way.

"How did you know it was me?" he asks.

"The way you looked at me. It couldn't have been anyone else."

Taken. I don't know my hand is waiting to be taken until he takes it, holds it. Hands so different from Ashley's, from Nathan's. Different even from Justin's, even though this guy is about Justin's size. Our hands fit differently.

"I'm sorry about the other night," he says.

I don't want to do this again. But I tell him, "I deserve part of the blame. I never should have called him."

"What did he say? Afterward?"

Honest. I feel I have to be honest.

"He kept calling you 'that black bitch.'"

I watch A grimace. "Charming."

Again I feel the need to defend Justin. "I think he sensed it was a trap. I don't know. He just knew something was off."

"Which is probably why he passed the test."

He won't give up. The way he wants Justin to be a bad guy—it reminds me of Justin.

I pull my hand away. "That's not fair."

"I'm sorry."

Sorry. He's sorry. I'm sorry. We're all so sorry.

He asks me, "What do you want to do?"

That look again. Those eyes. Not sorry. Yearning.

I do not turn away. I try to be a fact, not a feeling.

"What do you want me to do?" I ask.

"I want you to do whatever you feel is best for you."

Too perfect, too scripted, too out of touch with that yearning.

"That's the wrong answer," I say.

167

"Why is it the wrong answer?"

He doesn't get it. "Because it's a lie."

He blinks. "Let's go back to my original question. What do you want to do?"

How can I tell him that what I *want* isn't the point. It's never the point. I want a million dollars. I want to never return to school and to get a good job anyway. I want to be prettier. I want to be in Hawaii. Want costs you nothing, unless you try to spend it. *What do you want to do?* isn't what he should be asking. He should be asking me what I *can* do.

How can I make him see this? I say, "I don't want to throw everything away for something uncertain."

"What about me is uncertain?"

Kidding. He has to be kidding.

"Really?" I say. "Do I have to explain it to you?"

He waves his hand dismissively. "Besides that. You know you are the most important person I've ever had in my life. That's certain."

"In just two weeks," I point out. "That's uncertain."

"You know more about me than anyone else does."

"But I can't say the same for you. Not yet."

"You can't deny that there's something between us."

I can't deny it—that's true. But I can deny that it means what he thinks it means.

"No," I say. "There is. When I saw you today—I didn't know I'd been waiting for you until you were there. And then all of that waiting rushed through me in a second. That's some-thing . . . but I don't know if it's certainty."

Fourth period isn't over, but I was planning on studying for history during math, and I still need to do that now. I have to remind myself that here is where my life is, and I can't afford to screw it up.

"I have to get ready for my test," I tell A. "And you have another life to get back to."

Hurt. It crosses his face and dims his eyes. "Don't you want to see me?" he asks.

Want. Everything about him is want.

"I do," I say. "And I don't. You would think it would make things easier, but it actually makes them harder."

"So I shouldn't just show up here?"

Is this helping? No, it's not helping. This is the disruption, because it makes everything else seem lesser.

Instinctively, I know: I can't show up to school every morning wondering if he'll be here. I can't be looking into the eyes of every stranger hoping it will be him.

So I tell him, "Let's stick to email for now. Okay?"

I can sense all the want pulsing beneath his skin. I can see how badly he's trying to keep himself together. But there it is. He doesn't get to choose. I don't get to choose.

The classroom door opens and a teacher I don't know comes in. She takes one look at us and says, "You can't be here. Shouldn't you be in class?"

I mumble something about a free period. I pick up my bag. A doesn't have one, and I hope the teacher doesn't notice.

We say goodbye in the hallway. I know I'm not going to see him like this again. I will see him as someone else. But not like this. Not with him as hopeful as he was when he saw me this morning.

I can still feel the connection between us, even as I walk away.

I go to Justin's locker after school, but he's already gone.

I spend the rest of the day and night alone. My parents don't count.

Chapter Sixteen

Something is off the next day. Justin barely speaks to me. Rebecca looks at me curiously. Even my teachers seem more aware that I'm in the room, and won't stop calling on me. I have an English report I have to finish during lunch, so I spend it in the library.

After sixth period, Preston texts to see if I want to do something after school. I feel like I haven't talked to him in a while—and I'm grateful that someone is actually trying to make plans with me.

We decide to drive to the outlet mall—Preston has a cousin at Burberry who's let him know the coat he's been crushing on is getting marked down today. He still can't afford it, but at least he can try it on one more time before it's sold.

I think the coat's going to be the top priority in our conversation, but then Preston jumps in my car, plugs in his iPod to blast some Robyn, and says, "So . . . spill!"

"What am I supposed to be spilling?" I ask as I pull out of the parking lot.

Preston sighs theatrically. "Must I spell it out for you? I have it from *very* reliable sources that you were walking the halls yesterday with a rather attractive gentleman who nobody's ever seen before. You may have even sequestered yourself in an empty classroom with him—although when you emerged, there was no evidence of untoward behavior. Apparently his hair is very swoopy, which has led at least fifty-eight percent of my reliable sources to believe he may play for my team. Which would be the most exciting news to hit my world in about a decade. Every night I pray for a lovely, swoopy-haired homosexual to come to our school, in the same way that Margaret prayed for boobs and my grandfather prays for my eternal salvation."

I remind myself I need to keep driving. I need to focus or I know I'm going to swerve.

Caution. My first instinct is to say, *I have no idea what you're talking about*. But clearly someone saw me. Many people saw me.

My second instinct is to think, *Justin's heard. Justin knows.*

My third instinct is to scream.

My fourth instinct is to cry.

My fifth instinct is to deny all these other instincts and say, lightly, "I'm sorry, Preston—I have no idea if he swoops your way. He was just a prospective student—I've started showing them around, like Tiffany does. He lives in California—he's not even sure his dad is going to get the job here. And even if he did . . . the whole question of straightness or gayness didn't come up."

"Oh." Poor Preston looks so disappointed.

"Sorry."

"It's okay. A boy can dream, can't he?"

I want to tell him maybe it's better that way. Maybe real life is never going to live up to his daydreamy kind of love.

"So who saw me?" I ask delicately. "I mean, us."

"Kara Wallace and her group. Lindsay Craig thought you were macking on him—but then they saw you leave and said everything was in the right place, if you know what I mean. Kara was all excited, because her gaydar was really going off."

"Do you really believe in that gaydar stuff?"

Preston nods. "You can tell. There's an energy that travels between you. I can't say whether it's body language or if there's an actual chemical reaction. But you can feel it. He puts it out there, you put it out there, and you can feel it."

I think about A. About the way I knew it was him.

Then I put that thought away.

"And has word of this spread? I mean, should I be worried about Justin hearing the gossip?"

"Does Justin even *do* gossip? He doesn't strike me as the type."

No, but I can imagine Lindsay going up to him and sharing her theories—*I just thought you should know,* she'd say, gossip's good little helper.

It could explain his noncommunication today. But a thousand other things could also explain it. And calling him and making a big deal of some rumor could seriously backfire if he hasn't heard anything.

"Really," Preston says, "don't worry about it. The only reason I brought it up was . . . well, for selfish reasons. Woe is me. I am woe."

He's only kind-of joking, and it's only kind-of convincing.

"Are you okay?" I ask.

He smiles ruefully. "I'm fine. Although I'd be much more fine if you'd said you'd already given the swoopy-haired boy my number."

"What happened with Alec?"

"Not swoopy-haired."

"And that guy in Massachusetts you were chatting with?"

"Not swoopy-haired. And not local."

"So swoopy hair is the thing? You can't be with a guy unless his hair swoops?"

"If there's an exception, I haven't met him yet."

"I'm serious. Do you really believe that much in a 'type'? Is there really only one kind of person for you? Couldn't you be open to someone outside your type if he or she was great enough?"

"*Or she?*"

"I'm just saying—if you loved someone enough, would it really matter?"

"I know you want me to say no, but let's be real here. We're all wired to like certain things and to hate certain things. A lot of these things are negotiable, but some of them are fundamental. Don't ask me why—I'd need a PhD and a really powerful microscope to begin to tell you why. Could I love a guy without swoopy hair? Yeah, sure. Could I love a guy with a mullet? Much harder. Could I love a girl with a mullet? As a friend, sure. But—how to put this?—would I want to have *relations* with her? No. Not interested. At all. Nuh-uh."

"But don't you wish it were possible? I mean, don't you wish anything were possible?"

"Do I wish it? Sure. I mean, why not? But do I think it's true? Nope. Sorry. Not by a long shot. I have two years of being

174

in love with our mutual friend Ben to show for that. Not everything is possible. Falling for a straight boy is thus inadvisable."

I don't steer to the side of the road at the breaking of this
news, but I do turn down the radio to focus in on it more.
"Wait—you're in love with Ben?"

"I *was* in love with Ben. The torture chamber kind of love.
Oh, Lord, what I would have done for, to, or with that boy.
This was before he was with Rebecca. Well, the beginning of it
was before he was with Rebecca."

I picture Ben two years ago. His swoopy hair.

"But you knew he wasn't gay, right?" I ask. "I mean, he
wasn't, was he? I'm not missing that, too?"

"No, you're not." Preston stares out the window. "It was
just something I tried to convince myself could happen. It was
easier for me to come out if I thought there was someone to
be in love with. A destination for my trajectory. I know that's
silly, and I know he did nothing to deserve it—but I had to
picture some kind of future, and while I was at it, I decided to
cut him out from reality and paste him into my fantasy. I felt a
lot of things at that moment, and I needed to feel every single
one of them. Then I had to tell myself I was done. He wasn't
going to suddenly like boys, any more than I was going to suddenly like girls."

I know Preston won't understand where the question's coming from, yet I have to ask. "But what if he could've changed? I
mean, what if Ben could've changed into a girl, and you could
have been with him that way?"

"Rhiannon, if I'd wanted to fall for a girl, there were *plenty*
of awesome girls around to fall for. That's not how it works."

Silly. I feel silly.

175

"I know, I know," I say. "Sorry."

"It's okay." Then he takes a good look at me. "What's on your mind?"

I can't tell him the real reason, but I wonder if I can try to keep it vague and still have a conversation.

"I'm just wondering why people stay together," I say. "Why they connect in the first place, and what keeps that connection strong. I want it to be all the things inside—who you are, what you believe. But what if the things on the outside are just as important? When I was little, I was always worried I'd fall in love with someone ugly. Like Shrek. Then I figured that love would make anyone beautiful to me, if I loved them enough. I want to believe in that. I want to believe that you can love someone so strongly that none of that will matter. But what if it does?"

We're at the mall now. I pull into a parking space. Neither of us makes a move to leave the car.

Preston is looking really concerned.

"Is this about Justin?" he asks. "Are you no longer attracted to him?"

"No!"

"Is it about . . . someone else?"

"NO!"

Preston holds up his hands. "Okay, okay! Just checking."

"It was just something I was thinking about. That's all."

I'm letting him down. I'm letting myself down. Because I'm shutting down this conversation. I'm making it clear we're done.

We get out of the car and head to the Burberry outlet.

Preston tries on the coat and I tell him it looks amazing. We talk about clothes and classes and our friends. But we don't talk about what's really on my mind. Preston knows this. I know this.

I keep waiting for a text from Justin. Either he's heard the gossip and is going to want to know who the guy was, or he hasn't, and he'll text to see what I'm doing.

One of the two.

Or, in the end, neither.

I think about writing to A, but I convince myself not to. I don't want to encourage him too much. I can't have him show up again. I need to figure things out. But how can you figure out something that doesn't have a shape? It's the shapeless things—like love, like attraction—that are the hardest to map.

I give in and text Justin as midnight nears. I'm sleepy and vulnerable. The night won't let me settle down until I get rid of at least one thing that's unsettling me. I decide to keep it simple.

Missed you today.

He doesn't write back to me until the next morning.

Did you?

Chapter Seventeen

I get the message while I'm already waiting at his locker. The tide of emotions rises in me too fast. When he shows up a minute later, it crashes over all of the walls I've put up.

I hold up the phone. "What do you mean, 'Did you?'"

He doesn't look mad. He looks bothered. I am just this girl who's in the way right now.

"If you missed me so much, then why avoid me all day?" he asks. "I feel if you were actually missing me, you would have made some effort."

"I was with Preston! We went to the mall! Are you saying you wanted to go shopping with me and Preston? Really?"

I don't know why I'm yelling at him, why I sound like I'm fighting when I don't want to be fighting.

"I'm not talking about your *shopping trip*." (He says *shopping trip* the same way he'd say *gay*.) "I'm talking about everything. You're not here."

Is he still mad at me for Ashley? Or has he heard about the mystery guy and the empty classroom?

"I've been around," I tell him. "I've been here." Then I

decide to address things sideways. "I've been busy, for sure. Tests and showing new students around and everything. But I've been here, and if you've wanted to see me, all you had to do was call."

He slams his locker door so hard it hits the locker next to his. I startle back—more at the movement than the noise.

"Can you hear yourself? All I have to do is call? Is that how it's going to be? Should I start making *appointments* with you? Jesus."

People are looking at us now. We are that couple fighting in the hall.

"I'm sorry," I say. I'm not sure what for. I'm just sorry.

"Do you even care that I had a shit day? Did it even occur to you to ask?" he challenges.

"What's wrong?" I ask now.

"This conversation," he says, this time slamming his locker in the direction of closed. "That's what's wrong."

It's not just this conversation. I have done a hundred things wrong. I have become the kind of person who worries about being caught, not about what she's done.

I don't want to be that kind of person.

"Can we talk about this?" I ask quietly.

"I'll see you later" is Justin's response. Which is something, but not very much.

The bell rings and people start to hurry. A few take a moment to look at me, to see if I'm going to give them a meltdown worth talking about.

I disappoint them in the same way I disappoint everyone else.

• • •

Lunch is tense.

I missed Justin between first and second periods—I don't know if this was deliberate on his side, or if my timing was just off. When I saw Preston between third and fourth, I asked if he'd managed to contain all the rumors. I made it sound like I was joking, but he saw right through me. He assured me that the gossip had moved on, as gossip tends to do. I know this is true, but it would be just my luck to be the exception.

I want to save the seat next to me for Justin, but when Rebecca brings over her tray and sits there, I can't think of how to ask her to move down without sounding weak. When Justin comes over, I can see him looking at that taken space as if it's evidence. He sits a couple of seats away.

At the very least, I want a hello from him.

Our friends notice this. They notice it, but they don't say a word.

I should be figuring out a way to save things, to make him feel better about me. But instead I have the stupid, unhelpful thought: *A would never do this to me*. Even if we disagreed. Even if we fought. A would never ignore me. A would never make me feel like I no longer exist. Whatever body A is in, A would always find a way to acknowledge me.

There's no way for me to know this as a fact. But I'm certain of it as a feeling.

"Rhiannon?"

It's Rebecca's voice. She's asked me something.

I leave my thoughts for a second, return to the table. I look over to Justin and see that he's paying attention to me now. He saw me drift off. Once upon a time, he would have assumed I was thinking about him. But I don't see any of that in his face now. He lowers his eyes back to his lunch.

"I'm sorry," I say again. But this time it's to Rebecca, for not listening to whatever it is she has to say.

You have to fix this.

That's what I'm telling myself all through the rest of the day.

A is going to leave me. A will never be mine. A will never be able to be a normal part of my life.

Justin is here. Justin loves me. Justin is a part of me. I cannot ignore that.

He is angry, but he is angry because he's confused, because I'm making him miserable. He knows something is off. He knows me well enough to know that.

He is not making things up. I am really doing this to him.

Which is why I have to stop.

Which is why I have to fix it.

He doesn't seem surprised to find me at his locker at the end of the day.

"I know I've been out of it," I say before he can dismiss me. "I know I haven't been paying attention a hundred percent. That has nothing to do with you, I swear. And I'm grateful to you for calling me on it, because sometimes I'm so out of it I don't even realize I'm out of it, you know? But I'm back. I'm here now. I want to know what's going on with you. I want to be a part of it. I want us to take as much time as we need to get back on track."

"It's fine," he says.

I watch as he puts his books in his locker. The back of his neck taunts me. His shoulders draw me in.

"Do you want to do something?" I ask.

He closes the locker. Turns back to me.

"Sure," he says. And in his eyes, in his voice—I sense it. Relief.

I ask him where he wants to go.

He says his house.

I know makeup sex is supposed to mean making it up to each other after having a fight. But right now I feel like it's makeup sex because I'm making it all up. I have transformed myself into such a devoted, pretend girl that even I can believe the imitation is real. I know actions speak loudly to Justin, and he is speaking loudly back. I am grateful for the communication, for the way the intensity makes my body feel. But my mind is in another room.

In the heat of it, in the rush of it, he feels safe enough to say, "Don't leave me."

And I promise. I recognize how vulnerable he is, and I swear.

• • •

Afterward, I ask him about his shit day yesterday, and he barely remembers why it was so bad. Just the usual reasons, and the weight of them feeling so usual. He doesn't mention me with another guy, and I don't find it underneath his words, either. I think I'm in the clear.

He asks me to stay for dinner. I call my mother, who seems irritated but doesn't say no. Justin's mother also seems irritated when she comes home and Justin tells her I'm staying—but that irritation is directed at him, not me. I tell her I don't have to stay, that I know it's last-minute, but she says she's happy to have me here, and that it's been too long since she's seen me. When Justin and I first started dating, she treated me like this stray he'd picked up. Now that we've been dating awhile, I've been upgraded to pet status—part of the family, but not really a member.

Justin's father likes me more, or at least wants more for me to like him. He manages to come home exactly five minutes before dinner is ready, then acts like he's at the head of the table even though the table is square. Justin and I are perpendicular, and we answer his father's questions like it's a joint interview. Our bland answers about school and homework go unchallenged by his bland responses. I risk asking about Justin's grandmother, and am told she's doing as well as can be expected. Everyone tenses up, so I change the subject and compliment the food. Justin's mom tells me she's sorry that there won't be enough for seconds, since she wasn't planning on cooking for four.

In the beginning, I'd wanted Justin's house to become my second house, and Justin's family to become my second family. But I only made it halfway. This makes sense, because Justin barely wants his family for himself. Part of me was disappointed that my second chance at a decent mom fell short. But mostly I decided to claim the absence in Justin's life. I can remember thinking that if he didn't feel like he had a family, I would be his family. If he didn't feel like he had a home, I would make our space together a home. I believed love could do this. I believed this was what love was for.

Now I'm not sure what we have. What kind of family we are. I used to imagine us in the future—getting married, having kids—and then play it backward until it reached us now. But I haven't done that in a while.

Justin is uncomfortable all through dinner. And I know I am the comfortable part—I know that I am the person at the table who brings him the most happiness, who he feels closest to. When dinner's over and I've helped his mother do the dishes, I find him back in his room, playing a video game. He pauses it when I come in, then pats the space next to him, beckoning me over.

"Sorry to put you through all that," he says, kissing me.

"Dinner was good," I tell him, even though it wasn't really.

I know we're not going to go beyond kissing with his parents in the house. It's like every move we make is amplified straight to their ears.

He passes me a controller and we play awhile. If we were different kids, we'd be doing our homework together. Instead, we avoid our homework together. I realize how irresponsible this is. I don't think it occurs to Justin at all.

I'm glad we're back to normal. I don't know if I've missed this, but it feels right for right now. It's like A has never existed. A is a story I told myself.

Justin is better at this game than I am, which is true of most of the games we play. I keep dying, and he keeps passing me new lives.

At nine, I finally beg off, tell him I have to get my bio work done so I don't fail out. I'm bringing it up partly because it's true and partly because I want him to remember to do his work, too. He's much more at risk of failing out than I am.

"Okay—I'll see you tomorrow," he says. His eyes don't leave the screen.

I make sure to say goodbye to his parents on my way out. His mom says again that it was good to see me. His father walks me to the door.

When I step outside, I don't feel I've lost anything by leaving. Like when I leave my own house, there's always a part of me that stays behind, waiting for me to get back. That's what makes it my home—that feeling that a part of me is always waiting for me there.

As I walk to my car, I don't turn back to see if Justin's at the window, watching me go. I know he isn't.

The part of him that waits for me isn't that strong. Not when he knows he has me.

When I get back to my room, I'm not worried about our fight anymore. This morning seems like ancient history.

It's A I'm worried about. It's A who I think is waiting for me. I haven't sent word all day, and it's feeling, now that I acknowledge it, like an abandonment. Which is wrong—it's A who abandons me in the jump from place to place, body to body.

But I know I'm guilty here, too.

I check my email and am almost relieved to find that there

isn't anything new. This excuses some of my silence, if A is be-ing silent, too. Although if A is being silent, it may very well be because I told A to stop.

I get ready for bed, then sleep for eight hours. When I wake up, the first obligation I feel is to end the silence. So I write:

> A,
>
> I'm sorry I didn't get to write to you yesterday. I meant to, but then all these other things happened (none of them important, just time-consuming). Even though it was hard to see you, it was good to see you. I mean it. But taking a break and thinking things out makes sense.
>
> How was your day? What did you do?
>
> R

I know this is in two different places at once—*I meant to write to you, but let's keep taking a break.* But it's an accurate reflection of where I am. Or where I think I am.

Even though I know it's impossible, and I know it won't help, I still want to know where A is.

Does this mean I'm waiting for A?

I don't know.

At the very least, I'm waiting to see what happens next.

Chapter Eighteen

I get a rushed email from A as I'm driving to school. I read it in my car, before I go inside. A tells me he (she?) spent yesterday in the body of an immigrant girl who had to clean toilets to make a living, and the day before A wasn't feeling well, so he stayed home at this other girl's house and watched TV. Today A's another girl who has this big track meet, so she has to stay where she is. Even though I told him not to come here, I'm disappointed.

I want to contradict myself. I want to overrule my hesitations. I want A to be here.

But I can't steal that girl from her track meet. And when I picture A as some runner girl, I slow myself down. What if she's another Ashley? Or even just normal-looking. What would we do then?

I think about writing back to A, but if I'm not telling him (her?) to drop everything to see me, I don't have much else to say. I am not going to tell A about Justin—not about the fight, not about the making up. And what else do I have in my life that's worth talking about?

I turn off my phone and head into school.

• • •

I go through the motions. I try not to talk in class, but talk
when I have to. I say hello to friends, but not much more.
I give Justin what he wants—enough distance to be himself,
but enough closeness to know I haven't gone far. I eat lunch
without tasting it.

I find myself thinking of Kelsea, about her notebook con-
taining all those ways to die. Not because I want to kill myself.
I am nowhere near wanting to kill myself. But I can understand
feeling so detached from your own life. To feel that your connection to everyone else is so thin that all it would take is one
decisive snip to be separated completely. If I don't cling, I drift.
I feel that no one is holding me. In my life, I am the only one
who holds.

Except for A. But A is not here.

Rebecca and Preston try to reach me. They see the thin
thread and tie messages to it, sliding them my way. Preston
invites me to another round of buyless shopping. Rebecca tries
to bribe me into a coffee excursion after school. Both of them
remind me that Daren Johnston is having a party tomorrow
night. I'm sure I'll end up going.

Plans. I realize I'm not making plans because I want to see
where A is living tomorrow, if A will be free. It's the weekend.
I can drive far if I have to.

No. I see Justin and I think, Stop it. He asks me if I want to
go to a movie. He even lets me choose.

Once upon a time, this would have made me happy.

• • •

I can't be bothered to tell my mother I'm not coming home for dinner. This will make it two nights in a row, and she's going to give me hell for it. So I figure I might as well do what I'm going to do and get the hell after, instead of getting the hell before and not being able to go.

We drive around for a while, then get some Taco Bell and head to an earlyish movie. As we're waiting for the coming attractions, I find myself looking at all the other people in the theater. Most of them are my age, and I can't help but wonder if one of them might be A. Her track meet would be over by now. Maybe she decided to go to a movie with friends afterward. It's not impossible.

A few girls catch me watching. Most turn away. A couple confront me, staring back to make me feel uncomfortable.

Justin is fidgety, maybe sensing how my attention is wandering. I lean into him, hold his hand. He shifts the popcorn in his lap so this can happen. But when the previews start, he pulls away.

I don't think the movie is what he expected it to be. The posters promised it was a horror movie set in space. But soon it's clear that the most horrific thing the astronaut is fighting is the endlessness of his boredom and the pointlessness of his life. Justin's eyelids start to flutter. I want to use his shoulder as a pillow, but he told me once that if I lean there for too long, it kills his circulation. So I go back to looking at the audience as much as I can, picking out which person I'd be most attracted to, if A were inside.

I know the answer should be *all of them*.

It is not *all of them*.

It's not as simple as saying all the guys are yes and all the girls are no. It's more complicated than that. Although mostly it's the guys I consider.

The answer—the real A I want—is sitting right next to me.

When I get home, it's my father who's waiting in the kitchen, looking disappointed. He tells me Mom's already gone to bed, and that it was inconsiderate of me to ditch dinner without a call. I lie and say I told Mom ages ago that this was going to be a date night with Justin. I call it a "date night" so my dad will imagine we went for ice cream sodas and gazed lovingly into each other's eyes the whole time.

He falls for it completely.

I check for a new email from A, but don't find anything. And I don't write back, since I still don't have anything interesting to say.

The next morning, my mother says she isn't speaking to me. I know I'm supposed to feel bad, but mostly I'm happy not to deal with her.

I'm worried that they won't let me go to the party tonight, so I make a big production of doing my homework and completing some random chores. It's very easy to win my father over this way.

Before I leave the house, I consider emailing A and letting him (her?) know where I'm going to be. Then I remember what happened to that poor guy Nathan the last time this happened, and I decide to stay silent. Still, I wonder where he (she?) is. I also wonder why I haven't heard anything.

I pick Justin up, because I know he's planning on drinking. I ask him what he did all day and he barely remembers. I think maybe his life is as uneventful as mine, and that's why we're together. To be each other's eventfulness.

Or maybe that's why we go to parties, to find some eventfulness there. Or wastedness. Or both. Preston's also driven, so he and I sip Diet Cokes as I tell him about the movie, which is more interesting to make fun of than it was to watch. While I'm talking, Preston keeps his eye on the door, waiting for his gaydar to go off. It stays silent for a while until this James Dean wannabe strides in. Preston comes to attention like a hunting dog that's spotted the prettiest duck to ever fall from the sky.

"Really?" I say. "Him?"

Preston nods once. Twice.

"Do you want me to find out who he is?" I ask.

Preston shakes his head once. Twice.

A minute later, Dirk Nielson bounds in, car keys dangling in his hand. He looks around, spots James Dean, heads over, and kisses him hello.

"Shit," Preston says.

"Sorry," I tell him.

"Well, it was nice for the five seconds it lasted."

James Dean looks over at us—looks over at me. For a brief second, I feel connection. But then I really look into his eyes and I know: It's not A. It's nothing.

I talk to Preston some more, then Rebecca and Ben come

join us. I'm telling them about the movie when Stephanie comes tearing out of the kitchen, looking like she's on fire. Steve follows her for a few feet before stopping and yelling "WHAT THE FUCK?" at least three times at her back.

"Who wants to take this one?" Rebecca asks. When no one else makes a move, she sighs and bolts after Stephanie. Ben and Preston head over to Steve.

I walk around them and find Justin doing shots with Kara Wallace and Lindsay Craig, the girl who was so certain I was up to no good with the guy I was taking around school.

I steel myself and walk over. "So what happened with Steve and Stephanie?" I ask.

I am clearly asking Justin, but Lindsay answers. "She saw him eating pepperoni and said it was really rude of him because she's been vegetarian for, like, the past three minutes."

Kara finds this funny. Justin just shrugs at me, like he stopped trying to figure Stephanie and Steve out years ago.

Lindsay's staring at me in a way that makes me wonder whether I wore the wrong thing, said the wrong thing, or am just the wrong person. I decide not to ask.

Justin seems taken care of, so I head back out of the kitchen. Once again, I find myself wandering around all of the conversations, avoiding all of my friends. *I am this body,* I think. When my friends see this body, they assume they know a lot about the person inside of it. And when people I don't know see it, they also make assumptions. No one ever really questions these assumptions. They are this layer of how we live our lives. And I'm no different from them. When I saw James Dean walk in, I felt I knew as much about him as I'm sure he felt he knew about me when he looked my way. It's like an instant form of reading, the way we define each other.

The house isn't that big. There's no dance floor in the basement—I'm not even sure there is a basement. There's a line for the bathroom off the living room, so I walk upstairs, hoping to find a bathroom there. And also because it's quieter upstairs.

All of the doors on the hallway are closed. I open the first and see it's a bedroom. I'm about to close it when a voice says, "Hello? Can I help you?"

I poke my head in and see Daren Johnston cross-legged on his bed, reading *The Outsiders*.

"Oh, hi, Rhiannon," he says. "The bathroom's the second door on the right. I left it open, but I guess someone closed it. I mean, there might be someone in there, so you should probably knock."

"Thanks," I say. But I don't leave. "Why are you up here reading? I mean, it's your party."

Daren smiles slightly. "I guess I like thinking about throwing a party more than I actually like having people over. Lesson learned."

"Why don't you tell everyone to go home?"

"Because they're enjoying themselves, I think. They shouldn't have to suffer just because I'm feeling antisocial. I needed to leave, so I allowed myself to leave."

I nod to the book. "First time?"

"Nah. More like my twelfth."

I remember when I read it—Justin and I were in the same English class last year, and we read it together one Sunday afternoon, lying in his bed. It was a race to see who would finish first, but I slowed myself down because I loved the feeling of us turning the pages at the same time, being in the same part of the story. When we were done, he said how he was blown away by the line "Nothing gold can stay"—he really felt it was true. Then he smiled and said, "So I guess we'll have to be silver," and he called me Silver for days after.

"Do you think gold can stay?" I ask Daren now.

His smile is different from Justin's—a little more knowing, a little less eager. "I don't think anything can stay," he tells me. "Good or bad. So I think the important part is to not get caught up in worrying about whether something will stay, and instead enjoy it for the time it's here."

A door opens in the hallway and a guy calls out, "Daren! Where are you hiding?" He sounds like a construction foreman calling workers back from lunch.

Daren doesn't move. "For the record," he says to me, "I'm not hiding."

"DARRRRRREN!" the voice bellows. Then the door to the bedroom opens wider and James Dean walks in. I had imagined his voice would be . . . sexier.

"There you are!"

"Here I am," Daren admits.

"Come party!"

"I will when I'm finished with this book. I only have a hundred pages left."

James makes a move to manhandle Daren up. Then another voice calls, "Charles! Where are you, Charles?"

"It was so much more enjoyable when people used telegraphs," Daren says with a sigh.

"I guess Dirk wants me," Charles/James says. "I'll see you when your book is done." Then he turns to the door and hollers, "COMING!"

Daren hasn't put down the book.

"You see, Rhiannon," he says after Charles has left. "Nothing dumb can stay."

After using the bathroom (which Charles has left surprisingly tidy, even putting down both seat and cover), I return to the kitchen. When I walk in, I find Kara's disappeared and only Lindsay is with Justin now. He looks drunk and she looks determined. As if she can sense me coming, she reaches out and puts her hand on his shoulder, then moves it down to his chest. His reaction is so fast you could almost call it instinct—in one smooth move, he's removed her hand and pushed her away. There's no way for her to save face, the rejection is so complete. And the best part is I know he hasn't seen me yet. He didn't do it because I was watching.

He did it because he's true to me.

I let a minute pass, and let Lindsay slither off. Then I make my presence known. Justin doesn't exactly light up to see me, but he doesn't dim, either.

I tell him how I found Daren reading *The Outsiders* upstairs.

"I love that book!" Justin says.

"Remember when we read it?" I ask.

He's probably had too many shots to know what I'm talking about. Or at least that's what I figure. Then he calls out, "Heigh-ho, Silver!"

Not quite as romantic as its origin. But I'm happy he remembers.

He steps away from the kitchen counter. "Let's see what's going on," he says.

I follow. We find our friends, we shoot the shit, and I no longer feel like the hidden girl in the visible body. Now I am Justin's version of me—that's who I am, and that's who people see. And it's okay. It helps me navigate the party. It helps me know what to do. It helps me see who to be.

I stop looking for A. I turn back to these people, because they're my life.

Chapter Nineteen

On Sunday, I give in and write to A. I'm worried that I haven't heard anything.

> A,
>
> Just another weekend here. Went to a party. Talked to some people, but none of them were you. Got in trouble with my mom, but survived. Did some homework. Slept a lot this morning, then saw a better movie this afternoon with Rebecca than I saw on Friday night. (Warning: VAST is boring.)
>
> Where/who/how have you been?
>
> R

I hit send even though it doesn't sound right, because I can't imagine how to make it sound better. He doesn't want to hear the details about Justin, and I don't want to tell them. So I've flattened my weekend before mailing it to him. I haven't given him any reason to be interested.

Which is maybe for the best.

• • •

The next morning I wake up and feel off. At first I think it's because I fell asleep in my clothes. That doesn't happen very often, so it's weird to see my T-shirt, my jeans. But that's not the only thing. It's like I've woken up in an unfamiliar bed, even though this is my bed, in my room. I expect to look at my clock and find it's four in the morning, to explain the disorientation. But it's the normal time to wake up. My alarm is going off.

It must be because it's Monday, I think.

But then I correct myself.

No, it's Tuesday.

When I go to hit off the alarm, I find a folded piece of paper on top of it. Even before I open it, I have a vague idea it's a letter I wrote. But I don't remember what it says.

Dear Rhiannon,

Before I say anything, or explain anything, I want you to stop reading and try to remember everything you did yesterday.

It's my handwriting—but I know immediately that I didn't write this.

I know immediately.

A.

Here.

A.

Me.

I start to shiver uncontrollably. I want to yell out, but I'm afraid my parents will hear.

I cannot believe this.

But I *can* believe this.

I know I will only have one chance to remember what happened before whatever is written on this piece of paper colors my memories or fills in the blanks. So I put the letter down. I sit back in bed.

Yesterday, I tell myself. *What was yesterday?*

I remember climbing. I'm outside, on my own. And I am climbing up a mountain. I am looking out over all of these trees.

It's peaceful.

I didn't skip school. I was in school before that. I had lunch with Justin. He called me Silver again. He ate pizza and complained about Stephanie and Steve. I remember that Stephanie and Steve had a fight—but that was Saturday night, at the party. It was not yesterday. I don't think I saw Stephanie or Steve yesterday. I can't remember.

I also can't remember what I said to Justin. I can remember him talking to me. But nothing that I said.

Maybe I didn't say anything.

I remember leaving dinner early. Coming up here.

I remember writing the letter.

But it's not me writing the letter. I remember the pen in my hand. The paper underneath. But I can't remember deciding what to say.

I don't remember thinking. But I also don't remember someone else thinking for me.

I pick up the letter again.

I would have never chosen to do this. I hope you know that. I had no idea it would happen until I woke up and opened your eyes.

I have tried to respect your day as much as I know how. I could have stayed in bed, stayed at home—but that would have driven me crazy, to be alone with you like that. I had to go out into the day like it was any other day.

I hope I have not changed anything for you. I hope that I did not alter your life in any way. If I did, please know it was not my intention. I have done the best I can.

I have tried to leave your memories alone. I have tried not to learn anything you would not want me to know.

I hope this doesn't scare you. The last thing I want is to scare you.

I must say to you again: This was not my choice. If it had been my choice, it would be unforgivable.

What do you remember? I am about to tell you the course of your day. This is the last chance for you to have memories uninformed by this account.

When I woke up, I was in shock. In all of my years, I've never woken up in the body of someone I care so much about. I wanted to respect your privacy as much as possible, so you are wearing yesterday's underwear, and in moments when anything I had not seen already was exposed, I kept my eyes closed.

I met your parents over breakfast, then drove to school. Since I had been there before, it was not hard to navigate. I don't think anyone knew something was wrong. I went to class and kept my head down. I tried to take good notes for you. If you want details about classes, you can find them in your notebooks.

I tried to avoid Justin. I knew you would have wanted me to avoid him. This was effective until lunch, when he suggested we go for pizza. I couldn't find a way out of it. Nothing more than conversation happened. He is annoyed with Stephanie and Steven for fighting.

I did not see him again until after school. He wanted to do something but I told him I had to pick up your mother from a doctor's appointment. Just in case he mentions it.

(I realize it is strange that I keep saying "I" here—by "I," I of course mean "you." You have to understand: As I did these things, it didn't feel like you were doing them. It felt to me like I was doing them. I wonder if you will feel the same.)

Because we had already been to an ocean and a forest together, I felt it would be best to head to a mountain. I also wanted us to be alone . . . and we were very alone as we climbed. (If you want to know where we were, the search should still be on your phone. I haven't erased anything.) It felt good to be solitary, to feel an exertion that was purely physical. I wanted you to remember that, and to remember me there with you. I don't know if this is possible. But—and I know this sounds strange—I felt like I was feeling it for both of us.

Not wanting to get you in trouble, I made it back in time for a very cordial dinner with your parents. Then

I retreated to your room, attempted as much of your homework as possible, and decided to write you this note.

I have no way to know how you will react to this, nor would I presume to say there is a right or wrong way to react. Even if I haven't caused any damage, I know this breach may still be irreparable. I will understand if you never want to see or speak or write to me again. But I will also hope desperately that you will want me to remain in your life. I leave that up to you.

I know it is neither my fault nor my choice, but still I am sorry. I know it must be as hard to read this as it has been to write it.

Yours,

A

My mother knocks on the door, making sure I'm awake. Do I remember telling Justin I was taking her to the doctor? Yes, I do. I remember saying that, and when I think harder about it, I even remember telling him it was an appointment for a sleep doctor. He joked to me about stealing some of her pills.

How can I know this, if I wasn't there?

I can only know this because A left it for me. It doesn't matter which of us was in control of my body, as long as the memory was made and stored away.

I want to be angry. I want to be freaked out. I want to be

able to laugh at this, to find it ridiculous. These would all be rational responses. But instead I feel . . . sad. Sad that A had to go through this. Sad that there was no way it could be avoided. Sad that it complicates things even more. I know with all my heart that A isn't lying to me—my body and my life were safe when he was in control of them. I know A wouldn't have done anything to hurt me.

I also realize—in a way I couldn't have realized before—how easy it would have been for A to destroy everything. A could have made me do anything. Break up with Justin. Take naked photos of myself and email them to A's account. Run away.

But nothing like that happened. I know nothing like that happened.

Still, it can't all go back to normal. No, this thing has happened to me. I can't just shrug it off like all the other people whose bodies A inhabits. They don't know how they missed a day. But I know. I can't help knowing.

I imagine A waiting to see if I will ever be in touch again, if this is enough to make me walk away.

I write:

A,

I think I remember everything. Where are you today? Instead of writing a long email, I want to talk.

R

Almost immediately, I get a response.

R,

I am so relieved to hear from you. I am about two
hours away, a boy named Dylan. But I will go wherever
you want me to go.

A

I don't want to wait. But I know I have to go to school to
see if A did any damage without realizing it. So I tell A to meet
me back at the bookstore, after school. We'll have to wait until
then.

His response is a simple

Thank you.

I don't say anything back. I don't need to. All I have to do
is be there later on—and prepare to see what happened with
everyone else on the yesterday I missed. I am expecting it to be
a minefield—to have to account for something I said or didn't
say, someplace I went or didn't go. I'm ready for the people
in my life to be angry with me or upset with me or confused
by me.

What happens instead is even worse:

Nobody seems to have noticed I was gone. Or wasn't myself.

It starts with my mother, sitting in her usual chair. I ask her
if I seemed off yesterday.

"No, you were perfectly pleasant," she says. "We had a nice
dinner."

I don't point out that a "nice dinner" should have seemed
odd to her. Suspicious.

But she lives in her own world. I'm not surprised she didn't notice.

My friends, though—I think they would have noticed something. Maybe not everything. But at least something.

I don't feel them treating me any differently, though. I don't feel any daylong gap in my friendship with them.

So I ask.

"Was I weird yesterday? Different?"

Rebecca tells me I was fine.

Preston says he didn't really see me.

Ben pretends he didn't hear the question.

Stephanie says, "Do you want to know who's different? *Steve's* different."

And Justin—Justin says, "Yeah, you were weird, but that's not exactly *different*."

He's joking. I can tell he's joking. And I can tell from his joking that it was a good day, that we had a good time, that he didn't mind me going to my mom's doctor's appointment instead of going home with him. A didn't do anything to make things worse between us. If anything, A made it a little better.

I am relieved to have avoided being caught. And I'm pissed that no one noticed the difference.

I leave school a little early. Before anyone can stop me and ask me where I'm going. Before no one can stop me and ask me where I'm going.

As I drive to the bookstore, I reach for more of yesterday. Mostly I see the trees beneath me. I feel what it was like to be standing on that mountain. I breathe in as I remember breathing it in.

I feel better.

A hasn't told me anything about Dylan, the boy whose body I'm about to meet. But when I step into the bookstore's café, there's no question who I'm looking for, because it's so clear he's looking for me. Our eyes meet, and our eyes have already met. I head over.

"Hey," I say.

"Hey," he says back. He's chosen the same table as last time. And this, of all things, overwhelms me. Everything that's happened since last time—it's like I'm feeling it all at once.

"I need coffee," I say to him. I need to gather my thoughts. And I really do need coffee.

He doesn't seem to mind. "Yeah, of course," he says. He's really geeky today, with a geeky voice. Like something from *Big Bang Theory*. His T-shirt doesn't have anything on it—it's just a blue T-shirt. I wonder how hard A had to look to find one without a joke on it. Then I yell at myself for jumping to so many conclusions just because the guy looks like a geek.

"Do you want anything?" I offer.

"Sure."

He doesn't try to come with me, and I'm glad to have the two minutes of waiting and ordering and waiting. I stare at my hands and think of him staring at my hands yesterday. Did they look like the same hands? Or does familiarity somehow alter them? The girl behind the counter calls out my order and hands it over. I carry our drinks to the table and for a few seconds—a few too many seconds—we sit there awkwardly. He's waiting for me to say something. I'm waiting for him to say something. We're not saying anything.

I break the silence and tell him, "It feels like the morning after."

He looks at me kindly, nervously. "I know."

The morning after. I can't believe I said that. Because what does he know about a morning after? Isn't he always somewhere else?

He's looking at me—at all of me. My hands. My face. My eyes. Even though I do it every day, I wonder what it was like to be inside me, to see the world like this when you're not already used to it.

Calm. What I feel right now is a strange calm. A and I have just done something it's possible that nobody else has ever done. I am sitting across from someone who has seen through my eyes. And A is sitting across from someone who can tell him what it was like to have vanished for a day.

"I woke up and I knew something was different," I tell him. "Even before I saw your letter. It wasn't the usual disorientation. But I didn't feel like I'd missed a day. It was like I woke up and something had been . . . added. Then I saw your letter and started reading, and immediately I knew it was true. It had actually happened. I stopped when you told me to stop, and tried to remember everything about yesterday. It was all there. Not the things I'd usually forget, like waking up or brushing my teeth. But climbing that mountain. Having lunch with Justin. Dinner with my parents. Even writing the letter itself—I had a memory of that. It shouldn't make sense—why would I write a letter to myself for the next morning? But in my mind, it makes sense."

Gently, he asks, "Do you feel me there? In your memories."

I shake my head. "Not in the way you'd think. I don't feel you in control of things, or in my body, or anything. I feel like you were with me. Like, I can feel your presence there, but it's outside of me."

Listen to me. If I turned the TV on at one in the morning and heard a girl saying the things I'm saying, I would think she was a total nutjob. "It's insane that we're having this conversation," I point out.

But of course that's not how A is going to see it or feel it. *This is normal to him,* I remind myself.

"I wanted you to remember everything," he says. "And it sounds like your mind went along with that. Or maybe it wanted you to remember everything, too."

"I don't know. I'm just glad I do."

"And do you remember feelings? Or is it just the scene you see?"

"What do you mean?"

"Like, if I asked what was going through your mind when you had lunch with Justin, could you?"

I close my eyes and try to go back there. I see him eating pizza. I don't really remember what he said, only that he's talking a lot. But I can't remember being happy or annoyed or angry or anything. I just remember that I was there.

"Nothing," I say, my eyes still closed. "You know when you're really pissed at someone and then, a few days later, you remember that you were pissed but can't remember what it was about? Well, this is the opposite of that."

I open my eyes and see him taking in what I'm saying. I think I'm confirming something he's always suspected.

"You really don't know what it's like for us, do you?" I say.

"No," he answers quietly. "I don't."

He asks me about a few of the other things that happened yesterday—talking to Rebecca, the climbing, the dinner conversation with my parents. I tell him the only one that's vivid to me is the climbing. I do feel something when I think of that—that sense of breathing in, of freedom. Is this emotion or is this actual physical sensation that I'm remembering? We can't decide.

"It's interesting," I admit. "Really twisted and weird and crazy—but also interesting."

"You are extraordinary for understanding, and for being willing to be with me even after I . . . was where I was."

"It's not your fault. I know."

"Thank you."

It's hard to believe that I thought I could stay away from him. It's hard to believe I thought I could run away from this. Because it feels so comfortable right now.

"Thank you for not messing up my life," I say. "And for keeping my clothes on. Unless, of course, you don't want me to remember that you sneaked a peek."

"No peeks were sneaked."

"I believe you. Amazingly, I believe you about everything."

And because I believe him, I also want him to tell me more about what it was like for him—what he saw when he was me. But it also feels like a raging-ego thing to ask. What kind of girl asks for a second opinion about her own life?

A senses me holding back. Of course.

"What?" he asks.

I decide to go for it.

"It's just—do you feel you know me more now? Because the weird thing is . . . I feel I know you more. Because of what you did, and what you didn't do. Isn't that strange? I would have thought that you would've found out more about me . . . but I'm not sure that's true."

"I got to meet your parents," he says.

Oh boy. "And what was your impression?"

"I think they both care about you, in their own way."

I laugh. "Well said."

"Well, it was nice to meet them."

"I'll be sure to remember that when you really meet them. 'Mom and Dad, this is A. You think you're meeting him for the first time, but actually, you've met him before, when he was in my body.'"

"I'm sure that'll go over well."

And the stupid thing is: I'm sure they would love him. If only I could freeze him as he is, and take him home to Mom and Dad, they'd be thrilled.

But I can't tell him that. It would be unfair of me to tell him that. So I ask him something else. Just to be sure.

"It can never happen again, right?" I say. "You're never the same person twice."

He nods. "Correct. It will never happen again."

"No offense, but I'm relieved I don't have to go to sleep wondering if I'm going to wake up with you in control. Once, I guess I can deal with. But don't make a habit of it."

"I promise—I want to make a habit of being with you, but not that way."

He says it so casually, like it's no big deal. Like I might not even hear it.

But I hear it.

"You've seen my life," I say. "Tell me a way you think this can work."

"We'll find a way."

"That's not an answer," I point out. "It's a hope."

"Hope's gotten us this far. Not answers."

"Good point." I sip my coffee. "I know this is weird, but . . . I keep wondering. Are you really not a boy or a girl? I mean, when you were in my body, did you feel more . . . at home than you would in the body of a boy?"

"I'm just me," he (she?) says. "I always feel at home and I never feel at home. That's just the way it is."

I don't know why this isn't enough for me—but it's not. "And when you're kissing someone?" I press.

"Same thing."

"And during sex?"

"Is Dylan blushing? Right now, is he blushing?"

Bright red. "Yeah."

"Good. Because I know I am."

I don't know why the word *sex* would make him blush so much. But then I realize why, and I blurt out, "You've never had—?"

He sputters. "It wouldn't be fair of me to—"

"Never!"

He's as red as a strawberry now. "I am so glad you find this funny," he says.

"Sorry."

"There was this one girl."

211

Aha! "Really?"

"Yeah. Yesterday. When I was in your body. Don't you remember? I think you might have gotten her pregnant."

"That's not funny!"

"I only have eyes for you," he says. And the way he says it isn't funny at all. Or teasing. Or careless.

Sincerity. I think that's the word for this. For meaning something so much that it can't be anything other than what it is.

I'm not used to it.

"A—" I start. I have to tell him. I have to keep us in the world of reality. And in the world of reality, we cannot be together.

"Not now," he interrupts. "Let's stay on the nice note."

The nice note. That rings its own note within me. And that note is, momentarily, louder than reality.

"Okay," I say. "I can do that."

So instead of talking about tomorrow, we talk more about yesterday. I ask him what else he noticed, and he brings up all of these things that I would never, ever notice. Physical details like a small red birthmark at the base of my left thumb, and memories like this time Rebecca got gum caught in her hair. He's also pretty committed to convincing me that my parents care about me. I tell him he must've gotten them on a good day. He doesn't argue—but I can also see he doesn't completely know what I mean. Because he's never with someone through bad days and good days. He doesn't know life like that. Which again reminds me how he'd never be equipped to deal with someone as bad-good as me.

A glances at the time on his phone, and I realize I should be keeping track of time as well. Home for dinner. Home for homework. Home for bed. Home for my life.

"It's getting late," I say.

"I know."

"So we should probably . . ."

"But only if you promise we'll see each other again. Soon. Like, tomorrow if we can. And if not tomorrow, then the day after tomorrow. Two-morrow. Let's call that two-morrow."

It's starting again, and there's nothing I can do to stop it. Because I don't want to stop it. Because as long as it stays like this—two people talking over coffee—there aren't any decisions that have to be made.

"How can I say no?" I say. "I'm dying to see who you'll be next."

The sincerity returns as he tells me, "I'll always be A."

I stand up and kiss him on the forehead.

"I know," I say. "That's why I want to see you."

I imagine people looking at us as we stand up from the table, as we throw out our coffee cups and say goodbye. *That went well*, they'd think. Just two teenagers on a date. Not a first date—no, too familiar for that. And not nearly a last date. Because it went well. Because this geeky boy and this quiet girl clearly like each other. You don't have to be inside our bodies to realize that.

Chapter Twenty

The next day, A is four hours away from me, in the body of some girl. It might as well be forty hours or forty days.

I tell A there's always tomorrow. And as I type it, I want to believe it.

But I don't really believe it.

With a whole day ahead of me, I decide to do an experiment. I am going to pretend I am a stranger in my own body.

I stare in the mirror, right after my shower. How many times have I done this before? Stared at myself as the steam cleared. Tried and failed to make it seem better. Countless. But how many of these times have I actually *seen* myself? I will look at what's wrong. I will fixate on the blemishes, the bad hair, the fuzz, how uneven I am, how tired I look, how fat I'm getting, how loose. But I don't take an overall picture. I don't step back and look at the whole thing and think, *This is me*. And I certainly don't step back and look at the whole thing and ask, *Is this really me?*

I'm doing that now. How much of my body is really me? My face is me, for sure. Anyone who looked at my face would know it was me. Even with my hair wet and drawn back, it's me. But after that? If I showed myself a picture of myself from the shoulders down, would I be sure it was me? Could I identify myself that way?

I close my eyes and ask myself what my feet look like. I only kind of know. Same with my hands. I have no idea what my back looks like.

I let it define me, but I can't even define it.

If I were a stranger in my body, what would I think of it? I open my eyes and I'm not sure. A stranger wouldn't know any of the stories behind any of the small scars—the tricycle fall, the lightbulb smash. A stranger might not care if my boobs aren't identical, or if the mole on my arm has more hair than the rest of my arm. Why bother judging if you're a stranger in a body? It's almost like driving a car. Yes, you don't want the car to be a shitheap, but pretty much a car is a car. It doesn't matter what it looks like as long as it gets you where you need to go.

I know I am not a car. But as I walk through school, I imagine this smaller Rhiannon driving my body. She is my real self. The body is just a car. And I wonder. When Preston talks to me, it feels like he's talking to the driver. But when a guy I don't know looks at me in the hall, he's staring at the car. When my teacher looks out at the class as he's droning on about history, he's not seeing the drivers, he's seeing the parked cars. And when Justin kisses me—I don't know. Sometimes it feels like he's trying to kiss the driver. Other times, he's just kissing the car.

I try to imagine myself in other bodies, steering them around, experiencing how they're seen. The conclusion I reach: I don't like my body very much, but I'm not sure I'd like anyone else's body any better. They're all strange when you look at them for too long.

I know A is not here, but I want A to be inside one of the bodies I'm staring at. I want a head to turn and for me to see A inside. Because only A could understand all of the crazy places my mind is going. Because A has taken my mind there. A has made me want to reach past all the cars, to get to all the drivers.

"Are you okay?" Preston asks at lunch. "You're really out of it today."

"No," I tell him. "I'm really, really inside of it."

He laughs. I think a laugh is like the driver honking the horn, advertising pleasure.

I think that if A were in Preston's body, I'd kiss him hard.

I know this is a ridiculous thought. I have it anyway.

Preston, of course, has no idea what I'm thinking. He sees me, yes, but not in a way that would give away my thoughts.

The car can smile all it wants, but that doesn't mean you can see the driver's expression.

I receive emails from A.

He tells me:

The girl I am today is not nice. I can make her nice for a day, but what does that do?

216

He says:

I want us to be walking in the woods again.

He asks:

What are you doing?

And I don't know what to say.

I don't really talk to Justin until after school. He wants me to come over to his house and I can't. I don't have any excuse; I just know I can't.

I have loved his body for so long. I have loved it with devotion, with intensity. If I close my eyes, I can see it better than I see my own, because I have studied it, traced it, detailed it with so much more attention than I have ever spent on myself. It still attracts me. I still feel attachment to it. But it's also just a body. Only a body.

If I kiss him now, I will be thinking this. If we have sex now, I will be thinking of this.

So I can't.

Of course he asks me why not. Of course he asks me what else I have to do.

"I just need to go home," I say.

It's not enough. He's pissed. It's one thing for me to say I'm going shopping with Preston, or have made plans with Rebecca. It might even be bearable if I said I had homework or wanted to go home and be with my mom.

But I'm telling him I'd prefer nothing, and that makes him

217

feel like less than nothing. I understand that, and feel bad about it.

But I can't. I just can't.

The next day, A is only forty-five minutes away from me. In the body of a boy.

I have a math quiz in the morning, so I can't cut out until lunch. It's not even that I care so much about math. But I realize this could be what my life is becoming, trying to go to as little school as possible to get to wherever A is. And if this is going to be my life, I am going to have to be careful about it. I am not about to flunk out because of a crush, or whatever it is. But I'm also not going to stay away any longer than I have to.

Since A is being homeschooled today, he has to come up with a plan to escape. I wait for his message, and then get it around noon—he's made a dash for the public library, and I should get there as soon as I can.

I don't waste any time. As I drive over, I picture him there—which is strange, because I don't know what he looks like today. Mostly, I'm imagining Nathan from the party. I don't even know why.

The library is very, very quiet when I arrive. The librarian asks, "Can I help you?" when I come in, and I tell her that I'm looking for someone. Before she can ask me why I'm not in school, I walk swiftly away from the desk and start to scan the aisles for A. There's a ninety-year-old man checking out the psychology section, and a woman who very well might be his wife taking a nap in a comfy chair by an old card catalog. In the kids' section, there's a mother nursing.

I'm about to give up when I see a row of desks by the window. There's a redheaded boy sitting at one of them, reading a book. He's completely lost in it, not noticing me until I'm right next to him. I notice that he's cute in an adorable way, and at the same time I get angry at myself for noticing this. It shouldn't matter. I need to think about A and not care about the body he's in.

"Ahem," I say, to lead him back from the world of the book he's reading. "I figured you were the only kid in the building, so it had to be you."

I'm expecting a smile. A glint. A relief that I'm finally here.

But instead the boy says, "Excuse me?" He seems supremely annoyed that I've interrupted his reading.

It has to be him. I've looked everywhere else.

"It's you, right?" I ask.

I am not ringing any bells in this boy. "Do I know you?" he asks back.

Okay. Maybe not. Maybe A's in the men's room. Maybe I'm at the wrong library. Maybe I need to stop walking up to strangers and assuming they're not strangers.

"Oh, I'm sorry," I apologize. "I just, uh, am supposed to meet somebody."

"What does he look like?"

Now I'm going to seem like an idiot. Because I should know the answer to that question, but I don't.

"I don't, um, know," I tell the boy. "It's, like, an on-line thing."

"Shouldn't you be in school?"

There's no way this boy is over eighteen, so I shoot back, "Shouldn't *you* be in school?"

"I can't," he says. "There's this really amazing girl I'm supposed to meet."

I've already told myself to start walking away, so it takes a second for me to get what he means.

I've been played. By the one person I didn't think would play me.

"You jerk," I say.

"Sorry, it was just—"

No. I will not let him apologize. "You jerky . . . jerk."

I'm going to start walking away. I'm going to go. We've never had rules, but he's broken one anyway.

A's standing up now. "Rhiannon, I'm sorry."

He's reaching out, but I don't want it.

"You can't do that," I tell him. "It's not fair."

He will always know what I look like. I will never know what he looks like.

"I will never do it again. I promise."

It's not enough. "I can't believe you just did that," I say. "Look me in the eyes and say it again. That you promise."

He looks me in the eyes. We hold there for a second.

Now I can see him. Not literally. It's not like there's a little person waving inside his eyes. I just know he's there.

"I promise," he says.

He means it. I know he means it. He is in the clear—but I'm not about to let him feel like he's there yet.

"I believe you," I tell him. "But you're still a jerk until you prove otherwise."

• • •

Neither of us has had lunch yet, so we decide to go eat. A tells me the boy's mother is coming back in two hours to pick him up. We don't have much time.

We go to the first restaurant we find, a Chinese restaurant that smells like it's just been mopped.

- "So, how was your morning?" A asks.

"It was a morning," I tell him. "I had a math test. That can't possibly be worth talking about. Steve and Stephanie got into another fight on their way to school—apparently, Stephanie wanted to stop at Starbucks and Steve didn't, and because of that she called him completely self-centered and he called her a caffeine-addicted bitch. So, yeah. And, of course, Steve then skipped out of first period to get her a venti hazelnut macchiato. It was sweet of him to get her coffee, but passive-aggressive because she really likes caramel macchiatos much more than hazelnut ones. At least she didn't point this out when she thanked him, so everything was back to its shaky normal by the time second period started. That's the big news."

I don't tell him that when I saw Justin, he gave me shit for ditching him yesterday (even though it's not like we had plans). He kept telling me he hoped I'd had an *amazing* night. I told him I had a really *amazing* time studying math. He acted like he didn't believe me, like I ran off to some party without him.

Instead of talking about Justin, I ask A more about the girl he was yesterday. I feel I deserve credit because I ask this as if it's the most natural question in the world. *What else did you do when you were a girl yesterday?*

"It was like being a grenade," A says. "Everyone was just

221

waiting for her to go off and do some serious damage. She had power, but it was all cultivated from fear."

I think of Lindsay Craig and her minions. "I know so many girls like that. The dangerous ones are the ones who are actually good at it."

"I suspect she's very good at it."

I picture A as Lindsay, or some other mean girl. "Well, I'm glad I didn't have to meet her." Because what would the point be? If A was like that, there's no way we could ever be like this, the way we are now. This might be a cheap Chinese restaurant with grease stains on the menus and ceramic cats guarding the soy sauce on the tables, but it's still an escape, it's still exciting. We hold hands and look at each other and not much needs to be said. I have found someone who cares about me, and right now I can accept that.

"I'm sorry for calling you a jerk," I say. "I just—this is hard enough as it is. And I was so sure I was right."

"I *was* a jerk. I'm taking for granted how normal this all feels."

"Justin sometimes does that. Pretends I didn't tell him something I just told him. Or makes up this whole story, then laughs when I fall for it. I hate that."

"I'm sorry—"

"No, it's okay. I mean, it's not like he was the first one. I guess there's something about me that people love to fool. And I'd probably do it—fool people—if it ever occurred to me."

I don't want to sound like a complainer. I don't want to sound like this weak girl who can't take care of herself. But I also want him to know—I can't stand people being mean. People playing games. I want to guard myself against it, but I make a shitty guard for my own heart. I would rather lose the game than play it. I would rather be hurt than be mean. Because I can live with myself if I'm hurt. I don't think I could live with myself if I were mean.

I'm worried A is going to try to say something to make it all better. That he's going to tell me it's all in my mind. Or, even worse, like Justin, he's going to tell me I have to learn how to take a joke. Like my lack of humor is the real offense.

But A's not saying any of that. Instead, he's emptying the chopstick holder.

"What are you doing?" I ask. The woman behind the cash register is giving us a strange look, and I don't blame her.

A doesn't answer. Instead, he works the chopsticks into the shape of a heart, covering the table. Then he takes all the Sweet'N Low packets from our table and two others in order to turn the heart a pale paper pink.

It's too much. And it's awesome at the same time.

When he's done, he points proudly to the heart. He looks like a kindergartner who's just finished a fort.

"This," he says, "is only about one-ninety-millionth of how I feel about you."

I laugh. I think he's forgotten that his heart is full of Sweet'N Low.

"I'll try not to take it personally," I tell him.

He seems a little offended. "Take what personally? You should take it very personally."

"The fact that you used artificial sweetener?"

Saccharine. Everything fake. But also real.

He takes a pink packet from the heart and throws it playfully at me.

"Not everything is a symbol!" he shouts.

I am not going to let myself sit undefended. I pull a chop-stick from the heart and use it like a sword. He takes up my challenge, and raises another chopstick in the same way. He lunges. I parry. We are happy fools.

The waiter comes over with some plates. A turns his head and I pierce his chest.

"I die!" A calls out.

"Who has the moo shu chicken?" the waiter asks.

"That's his," I say. "And the answer is, yes, we're always like this."

After the waiter leaves, A asks me, "Is that true? Are we always like this?"

"Well, it's a little too early for always," I answer. Not to ruin the moment. Just to make sure we're not carried away by it.

"But it's a good sign," he says.

"Always," I tell him.

I forget about the rest of my life. I don't even have to push it away—I've forgotten about it. It's no longer there. There is only now, there is only me and A and everything that we're sharing. It doesn't feel like amnesia as much as it feels like a sudden absence of noise.

At the end of the meal, we get our fortunes. Mine says:

YOU HAVE A NICE SMILE.

"This isn't a fortune," I say, showing it to A.

"No. *You will have a nice smile*—that would be a fortune," he tells me.

Exactly. A fortune has to tell you what's going to happen, not what already is.

And, really, who doesn't have a nice smile?

"I'm going to send it back," I say.

A looks amused. "Do you often send back fortune cookies?"

"No. This is the first time. I mean, this is a Chinese restaurant—"

"Malpractice."

"Exactly."

I wave for the waiter, who comes immediately.

"My fortune isn't really a fortune, it's just a statement," I tell him. "And it's a pretty superficial statement at that."

The waiter nods and returns with a handful of cookies, each individually wrapped.

"I only need one," I tell him. More than one would be cheating. "Wait one second."

I open a second cookie—and am relieved by what I find inside.

ADVENTURE IS AROUND THE CORNER.

"Well done, sir," A says to the waiter once I show it to them both.

"Your turn," I say. A carefully opens his cookie, and practically beams when he reads what the fortune says.

"What?" I ask.

He holds it out to me.

ADVENTURE IS AROUND THE CORNER.

I am not a superstitious person. But I'm excited to get to that corner. Wherever it may be.

I know we don't have much time left. I know that A and I are only borrowing this time from someone else, not receiving it entirely for ourselves. But I want to borrow it for as long as I can. I want him to keep talking to me. I want to keep listening to him.

Back in the library, I ask him to tell me more books to read. Because I know the answer to this question will get me to know him even more.

He shows me the book he was reading before. It's called *Feed*.

"It's about the difference between technological connection and human connection. It's about how we can have so much information that we forget who we are, or at least who we're supposed to be." He takes me farther down the shelves, to the very end of the YA section, and holds up *The Book Thief*. "Have you read this?" I shake my head, and he continues. "It's a Holocaust novel, and it's narrated by death itself. Death is separate from everything, but he can't help feeling like he's a part of it all. And when he starts seeing the story of this little girl with a very hard life, he can't look away. He has to know what will happen." He pulls me back to an earlier shelf. "And on a lighter note, there's this book, *Destroy All Cars*. It's about how caring about something deeply can also make you hate the world, because the world can be really, really disappointing. But don't worry—it's also funny, too. Because that's how you get through all the disappointments, right? You have to find it all funny."

I agree. And I'd talk to him more about that, but he doesn't want to stop. I've asked him the right question, and he wants to answer it fully. He shows me a book called *First Day on Earth*. "I know this will sound weird, but it's about a boy in a support group for people who feel they were abducted by aliens. And he meets this other guy who may or may not be an alien. But it's really about what it means to be human. And I read it a lot, whenever I find it in a library. Partly because I find new things every time I read it, but also because these books are always there for me. All of them are there for me. My life changes all the time, but books don't change. My reading of them changes—I can bring new things to them each time. But the words are familiar words. The world is a place you've been before, and it welcomes you back."

He shakes his head. "I've never said that to anyone, you know. I've never even said it to myself. But there it is. The truth."

I want to take out all the books, want to start sharing those worlds with him. Then I remember: This isn't my library. This isn't my town.

"What about you?" A asks. "What do you think I should read next?"

I know I should show him something really smart and sophisticated, but I know he's asking me the question in the same

227

way I asked him—to see me in the answers, to know more about me after the answers than he did before them. So instead of pretending that *Jane Eyre* is the story of my life, or that *Johnny Tremain* changed me completely when I read it, I lead him over to the kids' section. I'm looking for *Harold and the Purple Crayon,* because when I was a kid, that appealed to me so much—the power to draw your own world, and to draw it in purple. I see it on display at the front of the section and go to get it.

As I lean over to pick it up, A surprises me by calling out, "No! Not that one!"

"What could you possibly have against *Harold and the Purple Crayon?*" I ask. As far as I'm concerned, this is a dealbreaker.

A looks relieved. "I'm sorry," he says. "I thought you were heading for *The Giving Tree.*"

Who does he think I am? "I absolutely HATE *The Giving Tree,*" I tell him.

"Thank goodness. That would've been the end of us, had that been your favorite book."

I would say the same if he'd chosen it. The tree in that book needs to stand up for herself. And the boy needs to be slapped.

"Here—take my arms! Take my legs!" I imitate.

"Take my head! Take my shoulders!"

"Because that's what love's about!" Really, I can't believe parents read the book to children. What an awful message to send.

"That kid is, like, the jerk of the century," A says.

"The biggest jerk in the history of all literature." It's nice to be agreeing on this point.

I put *Harold* down and move closer to him. I'm not going to need a purple crayon for what's coming next.

228

"Love means never having to lose your limbs," A tells me, leaning in.

"Exactly," I say, kissing him.

No sacrifice. No pain. No requests.

Love. Just love.

I am lost in it. Enjoyably lost in it. At least until someone yells, "What do you *think* you're *doing?*"

For a split second, I assume we've been caught by the librarian and are going to be fined. But the woman who's yelling at me isn't the librarian, or anyone else I've seen before. She's an angry, middle-aged woman spitting out words. Getting all in my face, she says, "I don't know who your parents are, but I did not raise *my* son to hang out with *whores.*"

I'm stunned. I haven't done anything to deserve *that.*

"Mom!" A shouts. "Leave her alone."

Mom. For a second, I think, *This is A's mother.* Then I realize, no, it isn't A's mother. A doesn't have a mother, not in the same sense that I have a mother. No, this must be the mother of the boy whose body he's in. The one who homeschools him. The one who let him out to go to the library, and has found this.

"Get in the car, George," she orders. "Right this minute."

I am expecting A to give in. I will not blame him for giving in, even though I am feeling really attacked. But instead of giving in, A looks George's mother in the eye and says, "Just. Calm. Down."

Now it's George's mother who's stunned. This innocent redheaded boy has probably never spoken to his mom like this before, although I have to imagine there have been plenty of times when she's deserved it.

While George's mother is thrown for a moment, A tells me we'll find a way and he'll talk to me later.

"You most certainly will not!" George's mother proclaims.

I kiss him again. A kiss that's *hello* and *goodbye* and *good luck* and *I've had a great time* all at once. I know these things are in there because I am putting them in there. Usually there are also questions in a kiss. *Do you love me? Is this working?* But this kiss is questionless.

"Don't worry," I whisper when the kiss is done. "We'll figure out a way to be together. The weekend is coming up."

I can't say anything more than that, because George's mother has grabbed his ear and has begun to pull. She looks at me again, trying to cut me down with her judgment—*whore whore whore*—but I don't give up any ground. A laughs at how silly it is to be dragged away by his ear. This only makes her tug harder.

When they get outside, I wave. He can't see me waving, but he waves back anyway.

It's not even three o'clock. I check my phone and find a text from Justin asking me where I am, and then another saying he's looked everywhere. I text back and tell him I wasn't feeling well, and left school early. I know he won't offer to bring me soup or check up on me, unless he wants to see if I'm lying.

So I turn off my phone. I disconnect.

If anyone asks, I'll tell them I was sleeping.

And I'll wait for A to wake me again.

Chapter Twenty-One

I spend Friday morning thinking about the weekend. This is not unusual—most people spend Friday thinking about the weekend. But most aren't trying to find a place to meet someone like A.

I come up with a plan. My uncle has a hunting cabin he never uses—and right now he's in California for work. My parents have a spare key they will never in a million years know is missing. All I need is an alibi. Or a few alibis.

I get an email from A saying he's a girl named Surita today, and not that far away. I'm ready to drop school entirely—it's Friday, after all—but A insists on meeting after school. I get it—there's no real reason to screw over Surita. But maybe A is a little nicer about that than I would be.

Justin's still annoyed with me. "Feeling better, I see," he says when we meet at his locker before class.

"Yeah. It must've been a twenty-four-hour thing."

He scoffs and I get defensive.

"Sorry I didn't text you a photo of my puke," I tell him.

"I didn't say a thing," he replies, slamming his locker.

I'm not being fair. I'm getting mad at him, when I'm the liar.

Then I add another lie.

"I'm glad I'm better, since we're going to see my grand-mother this weekend. And I wouldn't want to make her sick."

As soon as I say this, I remember Justin's own grandmother, who's actually sick.

"When are you leaving?" he asks.

"Tomorrow," I say. Then I realize what I've done, and add, "But I promised Rebecca I'd go over to her place tonight."

"Whatever," Justin mumbles. Then he walks away without saying goodbye, which is about what I deserve.

The reason I've mentioned Rebecca is because that's what I'm going to tell my parents—that I'm spending the weekend with her. They like Rebecca, so they won't mind. But I realize now I will have to at least spend tonight with her, since I've told Justin that's what I'm doing.

When I see her in art class, I ask her if she has plans. I pray that she doesn't.

"Nope," she tells me. "Any ideas?"

"How about a sleepover?" I suggest.

Rebecca looks so excited. "You're on! It's been a while since we had a *Mean Girls / Heathers* double feature."

"Or *Breakfast Club* and *Pretty in Pink*."

These were our go-to movies, back when we were sleepover age. It makes me happy that Rebecca remembers, since it's been a long time. Or at least it feels like a long time. That's my pre-Justin life. Another lifetime ago.

"I have to do a few things after school," I tell her. "With my mom. But how 'bout I come over around six?"

"Will you bring the cookie dough?" she asks.

"As long as you have the ice cream."

It feels so good to be talking like this that I almost forget all the lies that surround it. I almost forget all the things I'm not telling her.

I meet A back at the bookstore. Today he's this somewhat pudgy Indian girl. And I feel awful for thinking that right away, for noticing that first. It's A. I am spending time with A. Focus on the driver, not the car.

As we decide to go for a walk in the park, I stare hard at Surita and imagine her as a boy. It's not that hard. If you stare at anyone's face long enough, it's easy enough to imagine them as the other gender. Then I stop myself and wonder why I'm doing this. It's not like I would stare at her and imagine her white. That would be messed up. But I still want to see her as a boy, to think of A as a boy inside.

Part of the problem is words. The fact that there are separate words for *he* and *she, him* and *her.* I've never thought about it before, how divisive this is. Like maybe if there was just one pronoun for all of us, we wouldn't get so caught on that difference.

Part of me wants to ask A about this, to ask, *Are you a he or a she?* But I know the answer is that A is both and neither, and it's not A's fault that our language can't deal with that.

I'm sure A must notice. The fact that I'm not holding Surita's hand. The fact that there's not the same charge in the air as there was when A was in a guy's body. I want to undo this. I understand it's the wrong way to feel. But it doesn't feel like a knot I can actually untie.

A explains that Surita lives with her grandmother, and that her grandmother doesn't really pay attention, so she can be out as late as she wants. Which means I'm the one with the time limit today. I tell A about this, but then I also tell A I have a plan for the weekend, and that I know a place we can go. I don't tell A what it is, or where it is. I want there to be some surprise.

We get to the jungle gym, and since there aren't any kids around, we allow ourselves to become kids ourselves, climbing and swinging and laughing. A asks me who I hung around with in third grade, so I tell stories about me and Rebecca, me and my crush on this boy Peter, me and Mrs. Shedlowe, the lunch supervisor who would listen patiently to any problem I wanted to share. I know I can't ask A the same question, so I ask instead for things A remembers from being younger. And A tells me about a Valentine's Day his (her) mother took him (her) to the zoo, a birthday party where he (she) saved the day by finding a dog that had gone missing, and a Little League game where he (she) hit a home run, because somehow the body knew when to move, even if A didn't.

"Small victories," A jokes.

"But you made it through," I say. "That's the big victory."

"And this," A says, pulling closer, "must be the reward."

I know I should touch this girl's arm. I know I should draw him (her) close and find a way to nest inside the jungle gym. But instead I say, "Look—the slide!" and jump over to it, beckoning A to follow.

If A notices, A doesn't say anything. And even if we don't end up physically nesting in the space that's entirely ours, it still feels comfortable. It still feels like time is comfortable.

I'm good. Except for one moment, when I imagine Justin at home, playing video games. Sensing something wrong. Mad about it. But having no real idea how far I've strayed.

Then I think about what A would be doing if A weren't here with me. Lost in someone else's life. Erasing himself in order to be her.

After we slide, I suggest we swing. Instead of splitting into a push and a rise, we sit down on swings that are next to each other, and pump our legs to get moving in the air. At one point we're exactly even. A reaches out her hand, and I take it. We swing like that, perfectly even, for about twenty seconds. Then we start to pull apart, the difference in our weight, or in our strength, or in the angle of our bodies—something about our bodies—preventing us from continuing like that forever.

Back in the bookstore, I make A lead me back to *Feed*, to *The Book Thief*, to *Destroy All Cars* and *First Day on Earth*. I buy them all.

"You're so lucky," A says.

"Because they're good books?" I ask.

"No. Because once you have them, they'll always be there. You don't have to keep looking for them."

I'm about to offer to lend them to her, but of course I can't.

"But enough of that!" A says. "Who needs worldly possessions when you can have the world instead?"

The voice A is using is cheery. Maybe A actually believes this. Maybe I'm wrong to want things, and to want to have things. Or maybe A just gave me a glimpse of something he (she) didn't want me to see.

There's not enough time to explore this. I have to get over to Rebecca's. But A and I will have tomorrow. I remind myself we'll have tomorrow.

It's a hopeful farewell. It's only when I'm back in my car that I realize I could have kissed her when we said goodbye.

It didn't even occur to me.

That night, Rebecca can tell I'm thinking about something other than Lindsay Lohan and Tina Fey. She pauses the movie.

"Is something going on with you and Justin?" she asks. "Is that where your mind is right now?"

I'm immediately defensive—too defensive. "Why do you think there's something going on with me and Justin? There's nothing going on with me and Justin."

With this last sentence, I realize I've accidentally told her the truth. But she doesn't pick up on it.

"It's just—I mean, it's nice to have you back here. This is the first time we've done this since, well, the two of you got together. I wasn't sure we'd ever do this again."

Clarity. I've hurt her. I haven't even noticed, and I've hurt her over these past months. She's not going to tell me that, but it's there. I see it now.

"I'm sorry," I say, even though she hasn't asked me for it—or maybe because she hasn't asked me for it. "Things with him are fine. Really. But I also want to have more than Justin, you know? Like my best friends."

Best friends. It's like a gift I've been given and don't deserve.

But here I am, pointing out that I still have it, that I haven't returned it for something else.

"Do you want more ice cream?" Rebecca asks, picking up her bowl. "Because I want more ice cream."

"Sure," I say. Not because I want any, but because I know she wants to have more and doesn't want to have more alone.

As I sit there in the rec room I've known for most of my life, as I see photos of Rebecca and her family at all different ages, I realize this is one thing about us: Rebecca has to see me as more than just a body, because the body she's known has changed so much over the years. That must help a person see inside.

She comes back and unpauses the movie. Our double feature takes us well past midnight, for all the breaks we take for food and random things like seeing whatever happened to the guy who played Aaron and if he's still cute. (He is.) The only awkward moment comes when Rebecca asks me what I'm doing for the weekend. I know this is when I should recruit her to be my alibi, when I should warn her that my parents might call. But I use the grandmother excuse again. She tells me to say hello, and I promise I will.

I go to sleep wondering what I'm doing and wake up wondering what I'm doing, knowing for sure that whatever it is, I'm going to do it anyway.

Chapter Twenty-Two

The drive to Uncle Artie's cabin is about two hours, so I have plenty of time to think. I have the spare key in my pocket, as well as the bag I packed for my weekend at Rebecca's. Or my weekend at my grandmother's, depending on who you ask.

I'm excited to have time alone with A. I know it will only last until midnight—I hope that A will be able to come back tomorrow as well, but I know it's not a sure thing. It's funny to me that in all the time I've dated Justin, it never occurred to me to take him here. Maybe because we had his house. Or maybe because it never felt like we needed this kind of getaway.

Getaway. With enough time to think, I know that what I'm doing is technically cheating. I guess I knew that all along, but this is the first time I actually use that word in my head. It doesn't seem right to explain what I'm doing, but it doesn't seem entirely wrong, either. I feel I am in a messy middle ground of trying to figure it out. I know what Justin would say about that, and how he would see it. I am sure that I am doing to him something he has never done to me.

I am also mad at him for not noticing. Which is, I realize, completely unfair.

I could text him when I got there. I could break up with him that way. But he deserves more than that. And, more, he deserves an explanation. Only, there's no way to explain this.

I'm falling for someone I met when he was in your body for a day.

I've made sure to get there a little early to straighten the place up. I love Uncle Artie, but there's a reason his girlfriends always leave him. The cabin's basically one room with lots of stuff piled into it—including a lot of "trophies" from his hunts. The couple of times I came here with my parents when I was a little kid, it freaked me out to have glass-eyed animal heads staring at me from the walls. And it still freaks me out—but I've learned not to really see them anymore. There are one or two that are starting to get a little ragged, and I throw some sheets over those. The rest look on.

The problem with being early is it means there's a time when the groceries I've brought are put away, the floor's been swept, and I have nothing to do. I've brought *First Day on Earth* with me, but I'm too distracted to really pay attention, which doesn't seem fair to the book. I light a few candles so the air will smell more like vanilla and less like Uncle Artie. But the scent also starts to give everything a dreaminess. Or maybe I'm just tired.

I wake up when I hear a car outside. I come alive when I hear the car door open. Nobody else knows about this place, so it has to be A. I peek out the window and see this beautiful guy. My age. Him.

I open the door, wait and watch. Beautiful skin. Beautiful hair. Like the universe somehow knew what this day was for.

"You're really cute today," I say as he closes the door and comes closer. I expect him to have a bag, but of course he doesn't have a bag. He's only here for today.

"French Canadian dad, Creole mom," he explains. "But I don't speak a word of French."

"Your mom isn't going to show up this time, is she?" I joke.

He smiles. "Nope."

"Good," I say, getting closer. "Then I can do this without being killed."

I put everything into the kiss. All of the waiting, all of the desire. All of the today we have and the tomorrows we might not. I kiss him to tell him I'm here. I kiss him to tell him he's here. I kiss him to connect us, to meld us, to propel us. And he kisses me back with all of these things, and something else I can't identify. His arms around me, my arms around him, and both of us pulling, both of us pressing. His hands feeling me all over, giving me shape. No space between us. No space. Then I pull back a little to take off his coat, kick off my shoes. He kicks his off, too, and I lead him back, my mouth barely leaving his. I push him onto the bed. I'm pinning him down, we're meeting in the middle—still fully clothed but not feeling clothed at all. I kiss his neck, his ear. He moves his hands up my sides, kisses my lips again. There is not a single part of me that doesn't want this. I feel like I've been holding back my entire life, and now I'm letting go. Feeling under his shirt, following the trail to his chest. Keeping my hand there, feeling how hot the skin is. He is moaning and doesn't even realize it. I don't know his name and I don't need to know his name because he is A, he is A, he is A, and he is with me now. We are sharing this. Finger across my breast, finger along my back. Kissing lightly, kissing deeply. Shirts off, skin on skin. The only sense I have left is feel. Lips on shoulder. Hand under the back of his waistband. Arm on arm. Leg against leg. Fast then slow. Fast. Then slow.

"Hey," he says.

"Hey," I say back.

I lie on my back and he hovers over me. Finger along the side of my face. Side of his hand along my collarbone. I respond, tracing his shoulders, reaching down the valley of his back. I kiss his neck again. His ear. The space behind his ear.

There is nothing like this. In all the world, there is nothing like this.

"Where are we?" he asks.

"It's a hunting cabin my uncle uses," I explain. Even when I gave him directions, I didn't tell him where he was going. "He's in California now, so I figured it was safe to break in."

He looks around. "You broke in?"

"Well, with the spare key."

He lies back. I feel the center of his chest. The exact center. Then I move my hand to the right, heartbeat territory.

"That was quite a welcome," he says, his own hands unable to leave my body.

"It's not over yet," I assure him, turning his way as he immediately turns mine.

Closeness. That's what this is. Sex should have closeness.

Now there is closeness. Not just of our bodies. Of our beings. A is careful, but I am not careful. I don't want anything

241

between us. So I take off his clothes, and I take off my own. I want all of him, and I want him to have all of me. I want our eyes open. I want this to be what it's supposed to be.

Naked and kissing. Naked and needing. Naked and here. Moving in the inevitable direction. Sometimes moving quickly, but then slowing down and taking our time. Enjoying it.

It is dangerous, because I will do anything. But I will only do anything because I know it's not dangerous.

"Do you want to?" I whisper.

I feel him against me. The heat, the breath. I feel the momentum. I feel how right this is.

"No," he says. "Not yet. Not now."

Suddenly I feel the colder air around me. Suddenly I feel the world around me. I feel all the parts of it that aren't us.

I tell myself he's being considerate. I look at him and say, "Are you sure? I want to. If you're worried about me, don't be. I want to. I . . . prepared."

But he's pulling back, too, now. One hand still holds my side, but the other settles in the small space between us. "I don't think we should," he says.

I say, "Okay," even though it's not, because I don't understand.

"It's not you," he tells me. "And it's not that I don't want to."

Exit dream, enter nightmare. "So what is it?" I ask.

"It feels wrong."

He says it's not me, but who else could it be? I've pushed it too far. He must think less of me.

"Let me worry about Justin," I say. "This is you and me. It's different."

"But it's not just you and me. It's also Xavier."

"Xavier?"

He points to his own body. "Xavier."

"Oh."

"He's never done it before. And it just feels wrong . . . for him to do it for the first time, and not know it. I feel like I'm taking something from him if I do that. It doesn't seem right."

This seems more in line with the way the universe has treated me all my life. Send the perfect guy in the perfect body. But then make him a virgin whose first time I'll be taking away without him knowing it. There's no vocabulary in my head for dealing with this.

Closeness. I got so caught up in sex that I forgot what I was really after, what I really wanted. Even if we're not going to have sex, I don't have to give up on everything else.

That's what I wind up telling myself.

After a spell of being only in my mind, I return back to my body and press it closer to his. Turning so we're knees against knees, arms around backs, face to face.

"Do you think he would mind this?" I ask.

His body answers for him. I can feel the tension fall away. I can feel my welcome.

"I set an alarm," I say. "So we can sleep."

I roll over, and he presses his chest against my back, echoes his legs behind my legs. Gathering into a pocket of time, and refusing to leave it. Together, our bodies cool. Together, our breathing slows. Together, we feel unalone.

Our bodies can fit in so many different ways.

. . .

The current of sleep carries us at different wavelengths. Sometimes I wake and he's asleep. Sometimes he must be the woken
one. And other times, our wakefulness coincides, and we have
brief conversations as we remain holding on.

"Are you he or she?" I ask.
  "Yes," he replies.

"I know we don't talk about it," he says, many minutes, maybe
hours, later. "But why are you with him?"
  "I don't know," I tell him. "I used to think I did. But I don't
know anymore."

"Is this love?" I ask. But he's asleep.

He mumbles something. It sounds like, "Is your uncle Artie
tall?"

When we are both more awake, but still without any desire
to move from the bed, I face him and ask, "Who was your
favorite?"
  He puts his hand on mine. "My favorite?"
  "Your favorite body. Your favorite life."

"I was once in the body of a blind girl. When I was eleven. Maybe twelve. I don't know if she was my favorite, but I learned more from being her for a day than I'd learn from most people over a year. It showed me how arbitrary and individual it is, the way we experience the world. Not just that the other senses were sharper. But that we find ways to navigate the world as it is presented to us. For me, it was this huge challenge. But for her, it was just life."

"Close your eyes," I whisper.

I trust that he does. We feel each other's bodies as if we're in the dark.

Hours later, or maybe it's minutes, the alarm goes off.

The day is passing, and we let it. The light is fading, and we say nothing as it goes. This is all we want. Two bodies in a bed. Closeness.

"I know you have to leave," I say. My eyes are closed. I feel him nod.

"Midnight," he tells me. "I have to be back by midnight."

"But why? Why midnight?"

Now I feel him shake his head. "I can't be sure. But it's up to the body, and the body just knows."

"I'm going to stay here," I tell him.

"I'm going to come back tomorrow," he promises.

More time. More time together.

"I would end it," he says. "I would end all the changing if I could. Just to stay here with you."

"But you can't end it. I know that."

I don't sound mad or disappointed. I'm not mad or disappointed.

It is what it is.

We start to look at the clock. Knowing. It's time.

"I'll wait for you," I tell him as he gets dressed, as he gets ready to go.

"We'll both be waiting," he says. "To get back to this."

I have no idea what I am doing, and I am okay with that.

He kisses me goodbye. Like he is heading off to school. Or work. Like this is the future. Like we are used to this.

I don't know what to do after he's gone. There's no computer up here for email, no phone reception.

I pick up *First Day on Earth*. These are not his words, but they are words he's guided me to. For now, that's enough.

I have spent too much of the day sleeping. I read for a little while, and then spend the rest of the night dreaming.

Chapter Twenty-Three

I wake up really cold, then start the furnace and suffer as it gets way too hot. I guess these are my options.

I know A won't be back right away, but I also know that even if he wakes up five hours away, he'll find a way to be here. I just have to keep myself occupied until then.

I finish reading *First Day on Earth* and wish I'd brought a longer book, or even my homework. Artie doesn't have any books around that I can find. Only back issues of magazines like *Field & Stream*.

There's an old newspaper where the crossword hasn't been done. I try that, but I'm not very good at it. I play some games on my phone, and even walk around outside for a little in the hope of getting reception.

I am bored. So bored. And, even worse, I can hear Justin laughing at me, telling me, "What did you think would happen?"

"He's coming," I say.

"Yeah, right."

No. I cannot be having this conversation in my head. I look at the clock. It's after one. He should be here by now.

He's not coming.

But he promised.

I feel stupider and stupider as the day goes on. I'm wandering around in a T-shirt and boxers, it's so hot.

Finally, I hear a car coming. Driving up. Stopping.

All of the doubts I've been denying now turn themselves into relief.

I run for the door and throw it open. I'm about to jump into A's arms—when I realize the guy in front of me is very old and has a dead deer across his shoulders.

I scream.

He also screams, stumbling back.

I scream again and retreat into the cabin.

"Who the hell are you?" the man yells.

I want to slam the door, but I can't. He's still yelling.

"You're trespassing! Jesus, you nearly gave me a heart attack. Are you alone?"

He's looking at me now. Seeing a girl. Seeing my legs.

"I'm Artie's niece," I say. "Artie's my uncle. This is his cabin. I'm not trespassing."

He looks skeptical, and I really wish he'd put the deer down. It's making me nauseous.

"You're not supposed to be here," the man says. "If you even *are* Artie's niece."

"One second," I say. I scramble for my wallet, find my license. When I come back, he's put the deer back in his truck, thank God.

"You see," I say, holding out the license. "We have the same name."

"Fine. Doesn't mean you're supposed to be here."

"You can call him," I challenge, knowing there's no way, and hoping Artie will cover for me if there is. "He must've mixed things up."

"Well, you're about to get a whole lot more company. We've been hunting all morning, and Artie told us we could clean the skins here and do our business."

The vegetarian in me is horrified. But I'm stuck.

"One second," I tell the man again. I close the door and change into as many pieces of clothing as I can. I pack up all my things.

But I can't leave, because what if A comes? I am so mad at him for abandoning me but I can't risk abandoning him.

So I stay. As more men arrive. As they look at me funny. As they stare at me. They bring in more kills, and set up an area outside to skin the animals. I reread the only book I have. I go out to the car. I try to avoid everyone, but eventually I have to use the toilet, and there's no room to move.

I hold out for another two hours. Then I give up.

It's too late. A can't be coming. I need to get home.

The whole ride back, I seethe.

I check my phone as soon as I get reception. I expect an email. I expect some explanation.

Nothing. A's told me nothing.

He could have woken up paralyzed. He might be somewhere without a computer. He might not have a car.

I grasp for excuses. But I feel desperate doing it.

The worse answer is that A got what he wanted, and now it's over. Just like every other guy. And I am just like every other girl who's been stupid enough to think her guy would be different.

A isn't a guy, I remind myself.

But really, it doesn't matter.

I still feel stood up.

I still feel alone.

Chapter Twenty-Four

I wake up early, assuming A will wake up early, too, dying to explain to me what happened. I'll learn what was wrong with yesterday's body, why he couldn't make it.

But there's nothing in my inbox. No word.

The littler fears are giving up. The worse fears are coming closer.

I try to avoid Justin. Not because I've done something wrong (which I have), but because I'm afraid he'll smell it on me.

Rebecca asks me how my grandmother is doing. I tell her my grandmother is fine.

I keep checking my email. I keep finding it empty.

I think about ditching lunch, but then I figure there have been so many questions about my behavior lately that it's probably better to go along with the day as it usually is.

Luckily, Lindsay Craig threw a party on Saturday night,

which is all anyone at our table can talk about. Stephanie thought she saw Steve kissing a girl from another high school, but Steve swears that was all in Stephanie's drunk eye.

"I don't know, Steve," Justin says. "That girl was pretty smokin'."

I can't tell if he's trying to wind up Steve, wind up Stephanie, or get a reaction from me.

"You went to the party?" I ask stupidly.

"That okay with you?" Justin scoffs.

"Of course," I say quietly.

Rebecca notices this. I can sense her noticing. I also know that if she asks me if anything is wrong, I will start to scream. So I make sure to leave the table early.

I am lost in my own anger. I am angry at A. And I am angry at myself for getting into a position where A could mean enough to me to make me this angry.

I go to all my classes. We're doing softball in gym. I change into my gym clothes, and don't protest when I'm assigned to third base. I try to focus on the game, try to avoid embarrassing myself. I don't notice at first that there's someone waving. But then I realize he's waving at me. I don't recognize him, and that's how I know. He sees me staring at him and nods once. I wait until the play is over, then tell the teacher I have to use the ladies' room, because I'm not feeling well. She doesn't argue, and puts someone else on third base.

This guy doesn't look at all like Xavier from the cabin. He's got on this Metallica T-shirt and his arms are so hairy that they're almost as black as the shirt. When he sees me coming, he walks back inside, into the gym. Out of sight of the playing field.

I follow.

I know I should give him a chance to explain. I know that if he's here, it means he hasn't given up on me. But still, when he says "Hey" to me like nothing's happened, I launch right into him.

"Where the hell were you?" I yell. I don't even sound like myself. I sound much angrier than myself.

"I was locked in my room," he says. "It was awful. There wasn't even a computer."

I know this makes sense. I know this is actually possible. I know he's not lying. But the anger is still there.

"I waited for you," I tell him. "I got up. Made the bed. Had some breakfast. And then I waited. The reception on my phone went on and off, so I figured that had to be it. I started reading old issues of *Field & Stream*, because that's the only reading material up there. Then I heard footsteps. I was so excited. When I heard someone at the door, I ran to it."

I tell him who it was. I tell him what happened. I let him imagine me there alone with all of these men. Waiting for him.

"I wanted to be there," he says. "I swear, I wanted to be there. But I was trapped. This girl—there was just so much grief. She did this horrible thing and they wouldn't leave her alone. Not for one minute. They were afraid of what she'd do. She was denying it. But I wasn't. I figured it out. And it was painful, Rhiannon. You have to believe me—it was so painful. And even then, I would have left. I would have at least tried. But there was no way. She was in no state to leave."

"And this morning?" I ask, gesturing to Mr. Metallica. "Why couldn't he send me some word?"

"Because his family was leaving for Hawaii—and if I'd gone with them, I would have never made it back. So I ran. I took three different buses to get here, then had to walk from the station. I am sweaty and exhausted, and when I get back to this guy's house, it's either going to be empty or there's going to be hell to pay. But I had to get to you. All I cared about was getting to you."

The anger is going away, but it's not happiness that's taking its place—it's despair. Like I'm finally recognizing, for real, how absurd this is.

"How are we supposed to do this?" I ask him. "How?"

I want there to be an answer. I really want there to be an answer. But I suspect there isn't one.

"Come here," he tells me, opening his arms. No answer, and an answer. I give in. I walk right into those arms. He's sweaty and hairy and at that moment I don't care. This isn't about attraction. This is about underneath.

He holds me close, holds me for dear life. I close my eyes, tell myself we can do this. I can forgive him. We can adapt.

The door to the gym opens, and we both hear it. We pull away at the same time, not wanting to be seen. But we've been seen. I look over to the door, and there's Justin. I startle. Justin. It's like my mind can't accept it. Justin. Here.

"What the hell?" he yells. "What. The. Hell?"

I'll say he's my cousin, I think. *I'll say some great aunt died, and he's come to tell me.*

"Justin—" I start. But he's not going to let me finish.

"Lindsay texted me to say you weren't feeling well. So I was going to see if you were okay. Well, I guess you're real okay. Don't let me interrupt."

"Stop it," I say.

"Stop what, you bitch?" he shoots back, coming close.

Like he smells it on me.

I watch as A tries to block him. "Justin," he says.

Justin looks at him like he's scum. "You're not even allowed to speak, bro."

I'm about to explain. But before I can do anything, Justin is punching A full force—a fist right in the face, knocking him down.

I scream and rush to help A. Justin tries to stop me, pulling my arm back.

"I always knew you were a slut," he says.

I try to shake out of his grip, yelling, "Stop it!"

He lets go, but starts kicking A while he's down. I scream some more. I don't care who hears, if it will make Justin stop.

"This your new boyfriend?" Justin's shouting. "You love him?"

"I don't love him!" I shout back. "But I don't love you, either."

There.

Justin goes to kick A again, but this time A catches his leg and pulls him down. I try to reach A and get him back up, but I'm not quick enough, and Justin lands a kick right against his chin.

The door from outside opens, and the girls from softball start coming into the gym. They see me at A's side. They see the blood on the floor. Both A and Justin are bleeding.

Immediately, there's shock and gossip. Stephanie runs over

and asks me if I'm okay. Justin stands up and tries to knock A down again. But he misses, and A gets up.

"What's going on?" Stephanie's asking. "Who is that?"

A stumbles over to me, and Stephanie tries to block him. I realize this makes sense. Justin is my boyfriend. A is an outsider. I could lie now. I could pretend I'm on Justin's side. Only Justin would know the truth, and his pride might go along with the lie.

But I can't. I can't.

"I have to go," A is telling me. "Meet me at the Starbucks where we first met. When you can."

"A!" I call out. Because Justin is right behind him, is reaching for his shoulder. The hand lands, but instead of being pulled around, A frees himself and bolts.

There are tears in my eyes. I don't know how I'm finding the strength to stand. Our gym teacher is coming over. Stephanie is steadying me.

"You fucking bitch!" Justin yells. Everyone hears him. "I am through with you. Do you understand? Totally through. So you can go fuck any guy you want. You won't even have to do it behind my back. You think you're so great, but you're not. You're *not*."

I'm crying harder now.

"Justin, back off," Stephanie says.

"Don't try to defend her!" he yells at her. "She's the one who did this!"

The teacher's on us now, seeing my tears, seeing the blood. She has questions. Stephanie has questions. Lindsay, off to the side, gloats. A male teacher comes in and tries to take Justin to the nurse. Justin tells the teacher to fuck off, and pushes out of the gym. All eyes turn to me.

"It was nothing" is all I can manage to say.

Nobody believes me. And that makes sense, because nobody should.

Chapter Twenty-Five

I have to make some decisions, and fast. I have to figure out what my side of the story is so there can be a chance of people taking my side.

Even though I'm not hurt—at least, not physically—they take me to the nurse. She sees the state I'm in and makes me lie down. Stephanie asks permission to stay with me, but the nurse tells her to go to class. When the next class break comes, she returns with Rebecca and Preston, and I sit up in bed to see them.

"Rhiannon," Rebecca says. "Tell us what's going on."

"I messed up," I tell her, tell all of them. "It's over with Justin. I met someone else."

Rebecca tries to contain her surprise so I won't see it. Preston, however, lets out a "Hooooooo-eeeee!" Stephanie slaps his shoulder, but it can't be taken back.

"Who is it?" Preston asks. "Tell us tell us tell us."

Rebecca and Stephanie may act like he's out of bounds for asking so directly, but they're both hanging on my answer, too.

"I can't tell you," I say. "It's complicated."

"Is he married?" Preston asks.

"No! It's just . . . new."

"New enough for him to break into school to see you?" Rebecca asks.

"Is that what people are saying?" I want to know and I don't want to know.

"People are saying all kinds of things," Stephanie reports. "Justin's telling everyone he caught you going down on the guy. I've been telling everyone you were inside for maybe two minutes before we came in, and there was no evidence of him being, um, unzipped."

"We hugged. That's it."

"Well, that's enough," Stephanie says. "I mean, for the gossip. As far as Justin is concerned, you are the biggest slut to ever hit this school. But he's not exactly an unbiased witness."

Now that the punching and the kicking are over, it's really sinking in how much I've hurt him. What I did to him. What I did to us.

All that time. All those memories. I've burned it all down.

Rebecca leans in and hugs me tight.

"It's going to be okay," she tells me. "We'll get through it."

Preston and Stephanie echo this.

They might be all I have left.

The nurse lets me stay until the end of the day. When the final bell rings, I make a move to get out of the bed, but she gestures for me to hold off.

"Just let the halls clear," she says. "Allow yourself that."

She is so kind, I want to tell her everything. But I can only imagine what she'd think of me then.

I wait an extra hour. When I get to my locker, I find the photos of us that he kept in his locker and I kept in mine. He's torn them all up, to the point that if I didn't know what they'd once been, I'd never be able to guess.

That's the only damage he's done to my locker.

But it's enough.

Rebecca wants me to go over to her house. Preston and Stephanie keep calling. Even Ben texts to say he hopes I'm okay.

There's a part of me that wants to acknowledge the disaster I've caused, and take shelter with my friends.

But A is waiting. I know he's waiting.

I return to that Starbucks. He's cleaned up a little, but he still looks like a guy who's lost a fight.

I see him. I see him seeing me. I go to get some coffee, to give myself one more minute to think.

"I really need this," I tell him as I sit.

"Thank you for coming," he says. Like he wasn't sure I would. Like I'm doing him a favor.

"I thought about not coming," I admit. "But I didn't *seriously* consider it." Up close, he looks even worse. "You okay?"

"I'm fine," he says. He does not sound okay.

"Remind me—what's your name today?"

"Michael."

I look at him again. I remember that this boy is supposed to be in Hawaii right now.

"Poor Michael," I say.

"This is not how I imagine he thought the day would go."

"That makes two of us."

This morning seems like a million years ago. I was so mad at him. Now I'm just sad.

"Is it over now?" he asks. "With the two of you?"

How could it not be? I want to ask him. In what universe could Justin understand what I've done?

"Yes," I say. Then I add, unfairly, "So I guess you got what you wanted."

He does not appreciate this. "That's an awful way to put it. Don't you want it, too?"

"Yes. But not like that. Not in front of everybody like that."

He reaches up to touch my face, but it doesn't feel right. I flinch. He lowers his hand.

This makes me even sadder. What I'm doing to him.

"You're free of him," he says.

I would love for it to be that easy. It is not that easy.

"I forget how little you know about these things," I tell him. "I forget how inexperienced you are. I'm not free of him, A. Just because you break up with someone, it doesn't mean you're free of him. I'm still attached to Justin in a hundred different ways. We're just not dating anymore. It's going to take me years to be free of him."

I don't know why I'm saying this to him. Why I want us to hurt. Maybe I just feel less guilt if I feel more pain.

"Should I have gone to Hawaii?" he asks me.

261

I almost lost him. I have to realize I almost lost him. The thing I feared the most yesterday almost happened today. He did everything he could to stay, and now I'm punishing him for it.

I have to stop.

"No," I say, "you shouldn't have. I want you here."

His eyes light up with the chance I'm giving, with the possibility that even though everything's gone wrong, it might ultimately be right.

"With you?" he asks.

I nod. "With me. When you can be."

It's the best we can do. He knows it. I know it. And we also know we could settle for much less. We could give up.

He asks me more about what happened after he left, and I tell him. He wants me to understand why he had to run—he couldn't get Michael into even more trouble—and I tell him I understand.

We need to know there's no way Michael can be taken to Hawaii, so we use my phone to make sure all the last flights have left. Rather than have Michael take all the buses back, I offer to drive him—it's not like I'm in any rush to get home. I'm going to have to tell my parents I've broken up with Justin, before they hear it from someone else.

As we drive, I ask A to tell me more about who he's been. The damaged girl yesterday, and other people before that.

He lets the stories range all over the place—some sad, but most happy. As he's telling them, I realize that for each event, he has to remember two things, while the rest of us only have to remember one. Not only who he was with, but who he was.

Like with his first kiss. I remember my first kiss with Bobby Madigan—it was a dare in fourth grade that both of us had secretly wanted to take. When Mrs. Shedlowe wasn't looking, we sneaked at recess into the woods. I remember how soft his lips were. I remember how his eyes were closed. It hadn't occurred to me to close my eyes; if this was going to happen, I wanted to see it.

A tells me his first kiss was in fifth grade. He was in a basement and they were playing spin the bottle. He'd never played spin the bottle before, but the other kids seemed to know what to do. He spun and the bottle landed on a blond girl. He remembers her name was Sarah and that, before they kissed, she said, "Keep your mouth closed!" I ask him who he was at the time. He shakes his head.

"I'm not sure," he tells me. "All I remember is her. I can tell you she was wearing a dress—like a Sunday school dress—so maybe we were at a party for something. But I can't remember who I was."

"Not even if you were a boy or a girl?"

"A boy, I imagine—but, honestly, I wasn't paying attention either way."

It's strange to think about: All this time we're spending together, all of these days. I am trying to remember who he was each day. But A?

A will only remember me.

Eventually, the map on my phone tells us we're getting close to Michael's house.

"I want to see you tomorrow," A says.

"I want to see you, too. But I think we both know it's not just a matter of want."

"I'll hope it, then."

I like that.

"And I'll hope it, too," I say.

I float on that for a while, driving home. Then I remember everything else that's happened, and I start to sink. When I get home, I can't bear the thought of telling my parents about Justin, so I avoid them. My mom yells something about missing dinner, but I can't even begin to care.

I call Rebecca for a status report. She tells me, again, that everything's going to be fine. It will all blow over.

After I hang up, I stare at my phone. I click on the photo folder and it's like my whole history with Justin is there. He couldn't rip that up.

I know what I told A is true: It's not over.

Justin and I are in the bad part now.

Chapter Twenty-Six

School is brutal the next day. All the whispering. All the stares. All the talk. Some of it ridiculous. Some of it true.

Everyone in this building has gone years without caring about me. Now I do something wrong, and suddenly they care. It's disgusting.

There's no email from A when I wake up, and I don't check again. I feel I need to navigate this alone. A can't help me here. I need friends like Rebecca and Preston to help me.

It is amazing to me how many people are fine with calling me a slut to my face. Girls say it low and guys shout it out.

Justin has made it clear to my friends that they have to choose, and that he's the one who's been wronged. He doesn't care about Rebecca and Preston, which makes it easier for them. Stephanie, though, says she's going to have to keep her distance when Justin's around. Steve, too. She says she hopes I understand. I tell her I do.

"You're too nice," Rebecca says, overhearing this.

"No," I say. "I don't think niceness is my problem."

It's like it's not entirely real to me. There's a piece of me that's still calling out for Justin, that thinks we're still together, and meant to be together.

I can fix this, that piece believes. When, really, it's the broken part.

It also asks, *You gave up Justin for what, exactly?*

I don't know how to answer that.

I check my email quickly before third period. There's a message from A, saying he's on his way. I write back:

I don't think today is really a good day.

But I'm not sure the message will get to A in time. A's probably already kidnapped whoever's body he's in. I can't stop it.

I tell Rebecca that I'm going to skip lunch. I know she's going to offer to join me, but I tell her I'd rather be alone, to try to process everything. Mostly I want to hide, and it's easier to hide when you're just one person.

"Are you sure?" Rebecca asks.

I tell her I'm sure.

"Remember, this is the worst of it," she tells me. "The first day is always the worst."

This is a little less than credible from a girl who will no doubt now go find her boyfriend and sit with him at lunch. But I resist telling her that she's not allowed to talk to me until she cheats on Ben and he dumps her.

I don't know where I'm going to go after Rebecca leaves me. Some dark corner of the library should be safe. I've never seen a librarian turn a girl away because the whole school is calling her a slut.

I'm about to head there when a voice behind me says, "Hey."

I am not in the mood for someone else to give me an opinion on my behavior. I turn around and look at the person stopping me. It's a boy, I think. Maybe a freshman. Also maybe a girl.

I'm confused. Then I look in his/her eyes and am not confused.

"Hey," I say. "You're here. Why am I not surprised?"

I know I should be more excited that A's made it. But honestly? This is one more thing than an already hard day needs.

"Lunch?" A asks.

I guess I might as well. It's not really the hiding I'd planned, but I don't know how to explain that.

"Sure," I say. "But I really have to get back after."

"That's okay."

We walk down the hall. And you would think that maybe some people would be staring at the stranger next to me, a person they've never seen before. Maybe not the same guy I am rumored to have had sex with in the gym (there's no mistaking him for that), but still—someone different.

But no. I'm still the main attraction.

A's picking up on this, too. He sees them looking at me. He sees them turning away.

"Apparently, I'm now a metalhead slut," I explain. I genuinely don't care who overhears. "According to some sources,

I've even slept with members of Metallica. It's kind of funny, but also kind of not." I stop talking for a second and look at A. "You, however, are something completely different. I don't even know what I'm dealing with today."

"My name's Vic. I'm a biological female, but my gender is male."

A says it like this is obvious. I sigh and tell her, "I don't even know what that means."

"Well, it means that her body was born one way, but her mind—"

This is not what I want people overhearing. I interrupt, "Let's just wait until we're off school grounds, okay? Why don't you walk behind me for a while? I think it'll just make things easier."

I feel like a jerk asking this. But I also feel I need space. Just a little space.

I take her to the Philip Diner, which is like an old-age home that serves food. Nobody from school except the most die-hard hipsters ever eats there. And I figure I can take my chances with the hipsters. They have enough problems of their own to care about mine.

The waitress treats us like we're spies about to take away her Social Security. It's not until she's gone that we can talk.

"So how is everything?" A asks.

"I can't say Justin seems that upset," I reply. "And there's no shortage of girls who want to comfort him." *Thank you, Lindsay.* "It's pathetic. Rebecca's been awesome. I swear, there should be an occupation called Friendship PR—Rebecca would be ace at that. She's getting my half of the story out there."

"Which is?"

"Which is that Justin's a jerk. And that the metalhead and I weren't doing anything besides talking."

"I'm sorry it had to all go down like that."

"It could've been worse. And we have to stop apologizing to each other. Every sentence can't start with 'I'm sorry.'"

I should be sorry for snapping this out. I just don't have the energy. Especially with someone so complicated sitting across from me.

"So you're a girl who's a boy?" I ask.

"Something like that."

Oh, great. Now A's snappish, too.

"And how far did you drive?"

"Three hours."

"And what are you missing?"

"A couple of tests. A date with my girlfriend."

I can't help it. I ask, "Do you think that's fair?"

"What do you mean?" A asks.

"Look," I tell A, "I'm happy you've come all this way. Really, I am. But I didn't get much sleep last night, and I'm cranky as hell, and this morning when I got your email, I just thought: Is all of this really fair? Not to me or to you. But to these . . . people whose lives you're kidnapping."

"Rhiannon, I'm always careful—"

"I know you are. And I know it's just a day. But what if something completely unexpected was supposed to happen today? What if her girlfriend is planning this huge surprise party

269

for her? What if her lab partner is going to fail out of class if she's not there to help? What if—I don't know. What if there's this huge accident, and she's supposed to be nearby to pull a baby to safety?"

"I know. But what if *I'm* the one that something is supposed to happen to? What if I'm supposed to be here, and if I'm not, the world will go the wrong direction? In some infinitesimal but important way."

"But shouldn't her life come above yours?"

"Why?"

"Because you're just the guest."

It comes out sounding harsher than I mean it to be.

I go on, "I'm not saying you're any less important. You know I'm not. Right now, you are the person I love the most in the entire world."

"Really?" A sounds skeptical.

"What do you mean, *really?*"

"Yesterday you said you didn't love me."

"I was talking about the metalhead. Not you."

The waitress brings our grilled cheeses and our French fries.

"I love you, too, you know," A says once she leaves us alone.

"I know."

"We're going to get through this. Every relationship has a hard part at the beginning. This is our hard part. It's not like a puzzle piece where there's an instant fit. With relationships, you have to shape the pieces on each end before they go perfectly together."

· · ·

Relationship. I want to know if that's what this really is. But A is not the right person to ask.

Instead, I point out that A's piece changes shape every day. "Only physically," he argues.

"I know." I eat one of the fries. I'm tired of talking, but don't know how to get out of it without making A feel bad. "Really, I do. I guess I need to work on my piece more. There's too much going on. And you being here—that adds to the too much."

"I'll go," he says. "After lunch."

"It's not that I want you to," I try to assure him. "I just think I need you to."

"I understand."

"Good." I make myself smile. I need to change the tone. "Now tell me about this date you're going on tonight. If I don't get to be with you, I want to know who does."

Then I sit back and listen as he tells me about this girl named Dawn who this boy-born-a-girl, Vic, loves like oxygen and needs like nothing else in the world. It's a love story, pure and simple, and I find myself glad that someone in the universe gets to have one.

Even though I'm only meeting Vic this once and I've never set eyes on Dawn, I think about them after A leaves. I imagine the shit they must have to steer through to be together. It's the first thing today that feels perfectly timed. I have it bad, sure. But people can put up with a lot to get to the place they need to be.

I need to remember that.

• • •

After school, Rebecca, Ben, and Preston take me for ice cream. They want to know more about my Mystery Man—that's what they call him, and I don't know that they're far off.

I don't tell them much. They respect that. But it's also clear that their curiosity is going to continue, and I'm going to have to either invent some further lies or break up with Mystery Man pretty quick.

I am sure to make it home on time for dinner. Over chicken and potatoes, I tell my parents that Justin and I are over. To my extreme mortification, I start to cry. Even though I know it's the right thing, and even though I know it's my fault, saying it at the dinner table makes it more real than it's ever been before. I don't tell my parents about any Mystery Man. So the full story is that Justin and I are no longer together.

I know they've never liked him. I know they're not going to tell me to try harder, to make it work. I am grateful for that. My father says, "There, there." My mother says she's sure it's for the best. Then they just sit there and watch me cry. They wait for me to put myself back together. They change the subject, and ask me how Rebecca is doing.

I calm myself down as I tell them about an invented weekend—basically, I take the night with Rebecca and spread it out over two days. Lots of movies. Lots of talk. Lots of memories.

Justin isn't mentioned again.

I know that I owe A some kind of communication. Later that night, I send an email.

A,

Today was awkward, but I think that's because it feels like a very awkward time. It isn't about you, and it isn't about love. It's about everything crashing together at once. I think you know what I mean.

Let's try again. But I don't think it can be at school. I think that's too much for me. Let's meet after. Somewhere with no traces of the rest of my life. Only us.

I'm having a hard time imagining how, but I want these pieces to fit.

Love,
R

After telling so many lies to so many other people, it feels good to be honest with someone, and to know that honesty will be appreciated. If A is going to be the one true thing in my life, I have to keep it true . . . even as I wonder if I can make it real.

Chapter Twenty-Seven

I am ready to meet him wherever and whenever I have to. But when I finally get an email from A the next morning, it's to tell me he's woken up in the body of a boy whose grandfather has died. He has to go to the funeral today. There won't be any way to meet.

I want to type back that I'm sorry for his loss. But it's not *his* loss, of course. I actually feel bad for the boy whose body he's in, because he won't get to attend his own grandfather's funeral. It's not A's fault. But it's still not fair.

I don't know why the fact that I won't be seeing A sends me on a spiral, but it does. I should be used to it. I should know this is always going to be part of the plan—or the part that derails the plans. But with everything else such a mess, I was relying on it anyway. And now I'm feeling stupid for relying on it.

Going to school doesn't make it any better. I feel a distance from everything. Maybe this is self-defense—I can still hear people talking about me, can still see them looking at me like I'm awful. But I also know that nobody here can understand what I'm going through. Nobody here is in love with someone who may or may not show up on any given day. Nobody here doesn't know what form his or her love will take. And instead of feeling superior to them—instead of feeling smug because I have what they don't have—I find myself envying them. I want the same stability that Stephanie and Steve have. Or Rebecca and Ben. Which isn't stability—there are still fights and disagreements and bad days and good days—but it's at least more stable than the great unknown I'm not-quite-dating.

I am sixteen years old, I find myself thinking. *This is way too much.*

The one thing I'm not doing is wishing it were a few weeks ago, and that I was still entirely Justin's. But even that is shakable. Because when I see him for the first time since the gym, it sends me spiraling further. He's coming out of math class, and I am just another body in the hall. What I see isn't pretty. It's much more sad than angry. He has always hated being here, and now he hates it even more. I'm sure, if he saw me, the hate would be shot in my direction. But since he doesn't see me, there's nowhere for it to go. Instead, it loops in on itself, chews on its own tail.

A week ago, I would be rushing over to comfort him. I would be trying to unknot that anger, that hate, to get him to breathe. That was what I did. That was what he needed, and what he always resented.

I turn away and move in the direction I know he won't be going, even though it's not the direction I need to go. It's bad enough already. I don't want to make it even worse.

• • •

The next day, A says he can see me. But it comes with a warning.

> I'm not sure this guy is your type. He's pretty huge. I
> just want to prepare you, because the last time you
> saw me, it wasn't like this.

Type. Suddenly A is worried about my type. I don't want him to be thinking that way. It will only make it harder for both of us. And since I really keep thinking of A as a "he" now, I almost want to tell him that at least he's got half of my type right, if he's a guy. But what does that even mean? How wrong am I to think that way?

Love the person inside, I remind myself. *This will only work if you love the person inside.*

The problem is—and I think about this all through school—I have a mental image of the person inside. When I picture A, I picture him as this attractive guy, shimmering like a spirit or a ghost, jumping from body to body. That is the person I am in love with. And in my mind he's a guy, and in my mind he's white, and in my mind he has dark hair, and in my mind he's lean. Not buff. Not superstar beautiful. Just an ordinary attractive. I can even see him smile.

This mental picture should make it easier for me, should make A more real to me. But it only makes it harder, because I know the mental picture is about what I want, not what A is.

• • •

He is waiting for me outside the Clover Bookstore after school. He's dressed up in a button-down shirt and a tie, which I appreciate. But there's no way around it—he's big. Really big. And that's hard for me to deal with. Not because he's ugly. There's actually something sweet about him, in that tie. But he's just so much bigger than me. I'm intimidated. And, yes, it's really hard for me to adjust from seeing A in Vic-the-girl-who's-a-boy's body one day and this body the next time I see him.

"Hey," he says when I get closer. I guess that's our code word now. Our greeting. But it still sounds weird coming in this voice, so low.

"Yeah, hey," I reply.

It's even worse when I'm next to him. I feel miniscule.

"What's up?" he asks, like this body is no different from any other.

"Just taking you all in, I guess," I say. It's like a test. *Let's make A as different as possible from last time, and see how you deal.*

I'm not in the mood to be tested. I've been tested enough.

"Don't look at the package," A says. "Look at what's inside."

I get it. I do. But still, I don't like the assumption that this is natural.

"That's easy for you to say," I tell him. "I never change, do I?"

God, I don't want to be fighting. I think this even though I'm the one who's being fighty.

And then I take the thought one step further, and think, *It's like it was with Justin.*

No. It's not. With Justin, I fought because he backed me into corners.

A is not doing that.

Like now. A could easily say, *Yeah, sure you change—the girl I met was really nice, and the girl talking to me right now is acting like a bitch.*

But the thing is: A wouldn't say that. Which is why I'm here.

Instead of confronting me, A says, "Let's go." Taking it forward instead of getting stuck here.

"Where to?" I ask.

This gets a smile. "Well, we've been to the ocean and to the mountain and to the woods. So I thought this time we'd try . . . dinner and a movie."

Ha. Not what I was expecting. But much better than trying to find a desert.

"That sounds suspiciously like a date," I say, smiling myself.

"I'll even buy you flowers if you'd like."

I like the sound of that. "Go ahead," I tell him. "Buy me flowers."

I'm both joking and not joking. And he's serious, because instead of going into the bookstore, he finds a florist and buys me a dozen roses. It's a little crazy, but this whole thing is a little crazy, so I accept it.

He gives me options from the movie theater down the road, and I say if this is a date, then we have to go see one of those superhero movies that seem designed for dates—enough action for the guys and enough banter for the girls. Of course, as soon as I say this, I realize that this equation doesn't take into account people who are neither boys nor girls—and also makes some pretty big assumptions about what guys want and what girls want.

A doesn't call me on it, though. Instead, he tells me it's something he wanted to see, without telling me why.

When we get to the theater, it's mostly empty. The only other people there on a Thursday night are a posse of teenagers who clearly don't care about homework or school tomorrow. I can see them staring at us and making sniggering comments—maybe because of A's size, maybe because I'm this girl going to the movies with a bouquet of roses, like it's Valentine's Day or something.

It's funny because A is clearly having a little trouble navigating in this guy's body. It makes sense—he's not used to being this big, and he has to adjust. He barely makes it into the chair next to mine—and even though he does, it's clear I'm not going to have any part of the armrest. He tries to move his arm around me, and it's awkward—I'm basically stuck in his very active armpit. But honestly? I think it bothers A more than it bothers me. By the end of the previews, he's given up, and moves one seat away so we can have some breathing room. But that's not exactly what you should do on a date.

To make things better, he moves his hand to the seat between us. I know what this means. I move my own hand there, too, and as the movie starts and the world is threatened with destruction, we hold hands. It's nice—but not as nice as before. Partly because his hand is so much bigger than mine. Partly because of the angle. Partly because it's sweaty, and because he keeps shifting in his seat. Eventually, I give up, and he doesn't try to get me back. I would be okay leaning against him—his body would be really good for leaning. But he's moved too far away. So we just sit there in our separate spaces for most of the movie. I don't mind, but it doesn't feel like a date.

After the movie, we head to an Italian place. I still don't know what to do with the flowers, and wish I'd never asked for them. In the end, I put them under my chair.

He asks me again about how school is going, and I give him the update. I also tell him about letting my parents know, and about Rebecca calling him Mystery Man.

"I hope that's not how you think of me," he says.

"Well, you have to admit you have more mystery to you than the usual guy. I mean, person."

"Like what?"

"Like why you are the way you are? Like where you come from? Like why you do the things you do?"

"Yeah," he says, "but don't we all have those same mysteries? Maybe not where you came from—but do you really know why you are the way you are? Or why you do the things you do? I don't know why I was born this way—but you don't know why you were born your way, either. We're all in the dark. It's just that my dark is a little more unusual than yours. For all we know."

"But there's more about me that's explainable. You have to admit that."

"You can drive yourself crazy looking for explanations for

every single thing. I can't do that. I'm happy to let things just be what they are. I don't need to know why."

"But you have to be curious! *I'm* curious."

"Well, I'm not. And if this is going to work, I need you to take it at face value."

"Face value? Really?"

"Okay. Bad choice of words. Inside value. Soul value. Self value. Whatever you want to call it."

"What do *you* call it? What do you think you are?"

"I'm a person, Rhiannon. I'm a person who happens to go into other people for a day. But I'm still a person."

Chastised. I feel like I've disappointed him. I've fallen into the same trap as everyone else. I haven't understood.

We stop talking to eat. But I can't help watching him. Searching.

"What is it?" A asks, catching me looking.

"It's just that . . . I can't see you inside. Usually I can. Some glimmer of you in the eyes. But not tonight."

I'm not sure if this is his fault or mine. The connection needs to be plugged in on both ends, and maybe it's loose in me tonight.

"I promise I'm in here," he says.

"I know. But I can't help it. I just don't feel anything. When I see you like this, I don't. I can't."

"That's okay. The reason you're not seeing it is because he's so unlike me. You're not feeling it because I'm not like this. So in a way, it's consistent."

"I guess," I say. But it's not what I want to hear. I've never heard him disown one of the bodies before. I've never heard

281

him say, *This isn't me.* Is it because he feels that way, or is it because I'm making him self-conscious? He knows I'm uncomfortable, and it's making him uncomfortable. He, who can adapt to everything, and has been doing it for as long as he's been alive, is seeing himself through my eyes, and because of that, he's finding himself lacking.

I need to stop. But what am I supposed to do? Try to not see him as this huge guy? How can I ignore that? How can I not feel different relative to that?

All of these thoughts, and I can't say any of them aloud. Because that will only make it worse.

So instead we talk about the movie. The food. The weather.

This is disturbing. Disturbing because we're not talking about us. And also disturbing because I realize that when you're sixteen and in love, there isn't much to talk about besides yourselves.

This isn't about the body you're in, I want to tell A. *It's about where we are.*

He doesn't call me on it until we're walking to get our cars.

"What's going on?" he asks me.

"Just an off night, I guess." I try to smell the roses, but the scent is worn out. "We're allowed to have off nights, right? Especially considering . . ."

"Yeah. Especially considering."

It's not the one thing, it's everything. If he were in the body from the cabin, I would be kissing him good night. If he were the girl-boy from the other day, I wouldn't be. Or if he were Ashley with her Beyoncé looks. Or if he were Nathan from the basement. I wouldn't be. And if he were the picture in my mind, this night would have been different. Right now would be different.

It's not how it should be. But it's how it is with me. At least until I can get more used to it. If I can get more used to it.

I couldn't even kiss him goodbye if I wanted to. Not lightly. Not without him coming down to my level.

So instead of trying for that, I raise the roses up. I let him breathe them in instead of a kiss. I try to make it a nice goodbye that way.

"Thanks for the flowers," I tell him.

"You're welcome," he says.

"Tomorrow," I say.

He nods. "Tomorrow."

We leave it at that.

But is it enough?

We keep saying tomorrow. We keep promising it, even though there's no way to promise it for sure.

My parents are already asleep when I get home, but the quiet house gives me too much space to think. Dinner and a movie. The most basic elements of a relationship, of dating. But we failed it, didn't we?

I think maybe I'll feel different in the morning.

I don't.

I lie there in bed, wondering where A is and what he looks like.

I imagine having to think that every morning. Maybe not for the rest of my life. But even for the rest of high school.

It feels like too much.

I email A.

I really want to see you today.

We need to talk.

Chapter Twenty-Eight

A emails back to say that today he's a girl named Lisa, and that he'll meet me anytime I want. I say after school, and tell him to meet me at this park by my high school.

I spend the whole day wondering what to do. I want A in my life. I know he's a good thing, and that he cares about me in a way few people have. What we have is love. I'm sure it's love. But does that mean it can be a relationship? Does that mean we're bound to be together? Can't you love someone without being together?

After school, I find A on a bench in the park—he's exactly where I asked him to be. The girl he is today looks like someone I could be friends with—similar style in clothes, similar hair. I still have to adjust, but it's not as hard, because it's more familiar.

She's reading a book, and doesn't even notice me until I sit down next to her. Then she looks up and smiles.

"Hey," she says.

"Hey," I say back.

"How was your day?"

"Okay." I don't want to come right out and say all the things I've been thinking. So instead I tell A about class, and about the homecoming game that everyone's excited about tomorrow, and how Rebecca is insisting that I go, even though I don't really want to go. A asks me why, and I admit it's partly because I don't want to see Justin and partly because . . . well, it's a football game.

"It's supposed to be good weather, at least," A says before launching into the forecast for the weekend.

I have to interrupt. If we start talking about whether or not it's going to rain on Sunday, I am going to scream.

"A," I say, even though A's not finished. "There are things that I need to say to you."

A stops. And it's not like yesterday, when he felt so distant inside the body. Now he's floating to the surface of this girl. So nervous. So scared.

I wish I could tell him it will all be okay. I wish I could ask him to the homecoming game. I wish I could have him meet all my friends. I wish I could say that I want to kiss this girl as much as I want to kiss everyone else. I wish I could say what he wants me to say.

But I refuse to lie. That's the one thing we can have—honesty between us. Everything else—whatever it is—can be built from that.

"I don't think I can do this," I say.

He knows what I mean. He doesn't say *What?* He doesn't look confused. Instead, he asks, "You don't think you can do it, or you don't *want* to do it?"

"I want to. Really, I do. But how, A? I just don't see how it's possible."

Now he asks, "What do you mean?"

I spell it out. It hurts to do it, because I know it's not something he can control. But he has to see that I can't control my own self, either.

"I mean, you're a different person every day. And I just can't love every single person you are equally. I know it's you underneath. I know it's just the package. But I can't, A. I've tried. And I can't. I want to—I want to be the person who can do that—but I can't. And it's not just that. I've just broken up with Justin—I need time to process that, to put that away. And there are just so many things you and I can't do. We'll never hang out with my friends. I can't even talk about you to my friends, and that's driving me crazy. You'll never meet my parents. I will never be able to go to sleep with you at night and then wake up with you the next morning. Never. And I've been trying to argue myself into thinking these things don't matter, A. Really, I have. But I've lost the argument. And I can't keep having it, when I know what the real answer is."

This is it. As honest as it gets. But he doesn't give in when I force him to face it.

"It's not impossible," he tells me. "Do you think I haven't been having the same arguments with myself, the same thoughts? I've been trying to imagine how we can have a future together. So what about this? I think one way for me to not travel so far would be if we lived in a city. I mean, there would be more bodies the right age nearby, and while I don't know how I get passed from one body to the next, I do feel certain that the distance I travel is related to how many possibilities there are. So if we were in New York City, I'd probably never leave. There are so many people to choose from. So we could see each other all the time. Be with each other. I know it's crazy. I know you can't just leave home on a moment's notice. But eventually we could do that. Eventually, that could be our life. I will never be able to wake up next to you, but I can be with you all the time. It won't be a normal life—I know that. But it will be a life. A life together."

I want to be the girl who can believe this. I want to be the girl who can run away from her life and do this. For one person. For the right person.

But right now, I don't think I'm that girl.

I try to picture it. I can see living in New York City. Having an apartment. Living a life there.

The problem is, when the door opens and A comes home, it's my mental image of A. He's that guy. The guy he'll never be.

I can't picture it with a different person every day. That doesn't feel like a life. That feels like a hotel.

I know he wants it so badly. And it kills me that I can't give it to him.

"That will never happen," I say, trying to make my voice as comforting as possible. "I wish I could believe it, but I can't."

"But, Rhiannon—"

I'm crying now. It's too much. "I want you to know, if you were a guy I met—if you were the same guy every day, if the inside was the outside—there's a good chance I could love you forever. This isn't about the heart of you—I hope you know that. But the rest is too difficult. There might be girls out there who could deal with it. I hope there are. But I'm not one of them. I just can't do it."

A is crying, too. I mean, the girl sitting with me on this bench is crying, too.

"So . . . what?" she asks. "This is it? We stop?"

I shake my head. "I want us to be in each other's lives. But your life can't keep derailing mine. I need to be with my friends, A. I need to go to school and go to prom and do all the things I'm supposed to do. I am grateful—truly grateful—not to be with Justin anymore. But I can't let go of the other things."

"You can't do that for me the way I can do that for you?"

"I can't. I'm sorry, but I can't."

And I don't want him to do it for me, either. I don't. We are not worth that.

"Rhiannon . . . ," A says. But then it stops there. As if he's finally realizing what the truth is. And what it means for us.

We could argue about it for hours. For days. We could keep coming to this bench, A in a different body each time. It wouldn't matter. I know this. And I think that A is starting to know it, too.

I lean over and kiss him (her) on the cheek.

"I should go," I say. "Not forever. But for now. Let's talk again in a few days. If you really think about it, you'll come to the same conclusion. And then it won't be as bad. Then we'll be able to work through it together, and figure out what comes next. I want there to be something next. It just can't be . . ."

"Love?"

No. "A relationship. Dating. What you want."

I stand up. I have to go now. Not because I'm going to

change my mind if I stay. I know I'm not going to change my mind. But I also know it will hurt A more to keep trying and failing.

"We'll talk," I promise.

"We'll talk," he says. It's a statement, not a promise.

I hover there. I don't want to leave it like this.

"Rhiannon, I love you," he says, her voice breaking.

"And I love you," I say.

I know it's something. It's not enough, but it's something.

I give a little wave, then head to my car. I don't look back. I keep myself together. It isn't until I'm in the car, until I've put on my seat belt, that it all comes out. My body needs to release this. So I let it go. I let myself be the mess my life has become. And when I'm done, I blow my nose, wipe my eyes, turn the key in the ignition, and find my way home.

Chapter Twenty-Nine

As soon as I get to my room, I want to email A, to take it back.

But I have to be stronger than that. Because I know that would be a lie, and I need to live with the truth.

I have no intention of going to the homecoming game, and Rebecca and Preston have no intention of letting me get out of it. I might be able to resist one of them, but their combined force is too much for me.

They call me on speakerphone from Rebecca's house.

"You have to come," Preston insists.

"I don't care if Mystery Man is planning on taking you on a tour of Europe this weekend," Rebecca says. "This comes first."

"Because we want you there."

"We *need* you there."

"But Justin will be there!" I point out.

"So what?" Preston says. "We can take down that skinnyass whiner if we have to."

Rebecca sighs. "What Preston means is, you can't avoid

Justin forever. Our school just isn't that big. So the sooner you get the first time over with, the better. And we'll be with you the whole time."

"Plus," Preston adds, "you'll go crazy if you stay home all weekend."

True. All of this is true.

Also, I miss them.

"Fine," I say. "But you're talking to me the whole time. You are not going to expect me to watch high school football for two hours."

"You've got yourself a deal," Rebecca says, and Preston cheers.

I become hyper-preoccupied with what to wear. Which was never an issue when I was going to see A—I guess I figured if he was going to show up in whatever body, I could show up wearing whatever. Or maybe I didn't feel like I was auditioning for him all the time, like I did with Justin.

Rebecca, Preston, and Ben pick me up and we head to the high school. It feels like the whole town is here—even though our football team sucks, homecoming is a sort-of big deal. Stephanie and Steve are with Justin and a few more friends, and Stephanie has promised to text updates about their location. I tell Rebecca that's not necessary—I don't need to be treated like there are restraining orders involved. I'm not worried Justin will attack me. I'm just worried about how sad it will feel to see him.

Luckily, the stands are packed, and Justin's group is nowhere near us. As promised, we talk through the game—mostly

Preston giving running commentary on the fashion choices of various people in the bleachers, with even Ben throwing in a remark every now and then. At one point, Preston says he's going on a pretzel run and Rebecca volunteers to join him, leaving me and Ben alone together for the first time in a while.

At first, I think we're just going to watch the game until Preston and Rebecca get back. But then Ben says, "I'm glad you did it." He's not even looking at me—he's watching the field as he says it. But I know he's talking to me.

"Thanks," I say.

Now he looks at me. "No thanks necessary. It's just nice to see you out from his shadow. Because things don't grow in shadows, you know? So it was frustrating to see you standing there . . . and really cool to see you step out of it. I don't know who this new guy is, but make sure when you're with him, you're not standing in his shadow. Stand where everyone can see you."

The crowd starts to cheer, and Ben turns back to the game in time to see one of our players heading to the end zone. "Come on!" he yells, along with the rest of the crowd. The guy is tackled a few yards short. "Oh man!" Ben sighs. "Can you believe it?"

"So close," I say.

"Yeah," Ben says with a nod. "So close."

I should have known there'd be an after-party.

"It'll be fun," Rebecca promises, taking my arm and leading me to her car. "We won't leave your side."

The truth is, I don't need much convincing. I'm having a

good time. An uncomplicated, good time with my friends. For a long time, I couldn't have had this—there would have always been the counterweight of Justin, the obligation of being in a couple instead of hanging with a couple of friends. This is part of freedom—not looking for anything, not missing anything, just happy with the friends who are here.

"Sure," I tell Rebecca. "Let's go."

It's not that late, and barely dark out. There's an official after-party at some restaurant owned by a former high school quarterback, but the less-than-football crowd is gathering at Will Tyler's house, which is very conveniently located across the street from a water supply area that's never patrolled for trespassing.

Will Tyler's this guy from the grade above us who sold a fantasy novel to a big publisher when he was fourteen. He has a banner over his door that says FOOTBALL IS FOR WUSSES; QUIDDITCH IS FOR GODS. Preston whoops when he sees that.

If the geekiness of the sign isn't enough to ward off Justin, I'm sure the complete lack of alcohol will be. Instead of beer and vodka, Will and his parents have stocked up on every single soda that's ever been created—or at least it seems that way. The bottles are lined up in identical pairs in the kitchen, like this is some kind of carbonated Noah's ark. Some people are grumbling or pulling out flasks to spike their Fanta. But I'm into it. It's been too long since I've had a Cherry Coke.

A would love this. I have no doubt A would love this. I wish he were here—not for us to be together, but so he could sample any of the sodas he never got as he bounced around his childhood.

"Will Tyler's no fool," Preston says, cheersing me with a red cup of purple pop. "This is a party we'll all remember."

"Why, thank you," a boy behind him says. His voice has a slightly Southern twang. "Glad you could be here, Preston."

Preston turns to the boy and blurts, "You know my name?"

Will laughs. "Of course I know your name! It's a very nice name."

Preston smiles.

Will smiles.

And I'm like, *Wow. Yes. Go.*

"I need to find Rebecca," I say, even though Rebecca is all of ten feet away from me, pouring herself a Barqs.

"Don't look now," I whisper when I get to her, "but I think Preston's found someone on his team."

Of course Rebecca looks over. When she turns back to me, her eyes are wide.

"Why didn't we think of this sooner?" she asks me.

"All in due time," I tell her.

"And I'd say that time is due!"

Ben shuffles over. "Do any of you have any idea what Vernors is? I'm trying it, and it's not bad. But I'm not sure what it's supposed to be."

"Out," Rebecca says. "Out out out."

We shuffle away from Preston and Will, into the den, where Ellie Goulding's "Lights" is playing on high, and the lights themselves are playing on low. Looking around, I see we're mostly surrounded by smart kids—Rebecca and Ben's crowd. But I don't feel unwelcome.

I think this would be A's crowd, too. I mean, he could have turned into anyone—a jerk, a druggie, a social climber, a sociopath. But after all he went through, he's basically a smart kid.

I scan the crowd, looking for that recognition even though I haven't asked him to be here. If he's here, it will have to be coincidence. Fate.

Someone suggests charades. The music is turned off, the lights are turned up, and Preston and Will come out of the kitchen. They're on the same charades team, of course. And when either of them is giving clues, it's the other he's looking at.

More people show up—more smart kids who stopped off for dinner before coming over. It isn't until nine that the official after-party breaks up, and a whole different wave comes. Some are drunk, and some want to be drunk. Rebecca checks her phone and there's a text from Stephanie, saying they'll be here soon.

"Do you want to leave?" Rebecca asks me.

And I say no. I'm happy here. I don't want to leave.

But still, it's awkward when Stephanie comes into the den, and I know that means Justin's somewhere in the house. It's awkward when I hear him yelling in the kitchen, asking someone where the booze is being hidden.

"Steve will keep him in there," Stephanie promises me.

But Steve can't keep him in there, not when there isn't any booze. Justin comes jumping out into the den, and there it is: me and him, in the same room.

The look on his face when he sees me is awful. Like he's been tricked. Like I'm the trap.

"What the fuck is she doing here?" he says. He must be

296

three or four beers closer to drunk already. I can tell. He turns to Stephanie. "You knew she'd be here, didn't you? Why the fuck didn't you warn me?"

Now Steve's on the scene, telling Justin to calm down.

"Shit!" Justin says, knocking the nearest cup to the floor. It doesn't really have the effect he wants. It's plastic. And full of Sprite.

I'm standing there, and it's as if I've stepped away from myself for a second. I am watching this from a distance. Calmly, I am wondering what he's going to do next. Yell at me? Spit at me? Throw another cup? Burst into tears?

Instead, he looks at Steve and says, with more feeling than he'd want me to hear, "This *sucks*." Then he bolts from the room, out the front door.

Steve moves to follow, but I surprise everyone in the room—including myself—by saying, "No. I've got this."

Steve looks at me curiously. "Are you sure? I have his keys."

"I'll be right back," I tell him. Then, seeing the look on Rebecca's face, I say it to her, too. "Really. I'll be right back."

It's not hard to find him. I can actually see the glow of his cigarette across the street in the water supply area. It figures he'd head straight to the NO TRESPASSING signs.

I let him take a few drags before I get there.

"I'm coming in," I warn. Then I skirt around a tree, and end up right in front of him.

I can't help it. The first thing out of my mouth is, "You look like shit."

Which means the first thing out of his mouth is, "Well, you made me feel like shit, so that kinda makes sense."

"I'm sorry."

"Fuck you."

"I'm really sorry."

"Fuck you."

"Go ahead. Get it out of your system."

"Why, Rhiannon? *Why?*"

This is worse than the *Fuck you*. Much worse.

Because now his body is transparent. I see right inside, right to who he is. And he is so upset. So wronged. So surprised.

All along, I've wanted to see how much he cared. And now I get to see it. Now, when it's over.

"How long, Rhiannon? How long were you screwing some other guy? How long were you lying to me?"

"I never screwed him."

"Oh, that makes me feel *so much better*. The best kind of slut is one who won't put out!"

I've humiliated him. I've been so busy being humiliated that I haven't realized how badly I've humiliated him.

"I am so, so sorry," I say.

I should be crying. But what I feel is different from sorrow. It's horror.

"It's okay if you hate me," I say.

He laughs. "I don't need your *permission* to hate you. Jesus! Listen to yourself!"

I wish I could blame A. I wish I could say it's A's fault. But all A did was show me who Justin wasn't. And instead of dealing with that, I ran away. I pretended. And then I was caught.

"I don't just hate you, Rhiannon," Justin says. "I hate you

more than I ever thought it was possible to hate anyone. Do you know what's worse than being destroyed? It's being destroyed by someone who was never worth it. If you want me to let you off the hook—if you want me to tell you that I'm okay with everything—well, all I have to say to that is that I hope you stay on this hook for as long as you fucking live. I hope you feel it every time you kiss that guy. I hope you feel it every time you think about kissing anyone. I hope it keeps you awake at night. I hope you never sleep again. I hate you that much. So go back to that lame-ass party and drink soda and get out of my face."

"No," I say, faltering. "No—we need to talk. I need to tell you—"

"Fine. New plan. I am going to go back there, get Steve and my keys, and drive the hell away. You can stay here. I hereby give you custody of this shitty reservation. Do not follow me, and please do not talk to me ever again."

He flicks his cigarette to the ground and walks away. I jump forward—not to follow him, but to make sure the cigarette doesn't set everything on fire.

What have I done what have I done what have I done?

Even as I'm thinking this on repeat, I'm also thinking it's a little too late to be asking this question.

I want to wake up tomorrow in another body, another life. But I don't really want that. What I'm realizing is that for all the time I've spent with A, for all the time I've thought about A and A's life, I missed the most important part: *Do no damage.* Somehow A can manage it in the course of a day, but I couldn't manage that in the course of a real, continuous life.

I can't go back to the house, but I also can't just stand here, waiting to see Justin and Steve leave. So I walk deeper into the woods, trespass more definitively. Once I'm out of the streetlamp range and the neighborhood glow, it's completely dark. As I walk among the trees, I realize this is as close to bodiless as I'm going to get. Just a mind walking through the night. Unseen. Unfelt. Unreal.

Justin was careless with me. That's undeniable. But it doesn't excuse me from being so careless with him. It explains it, but it doesn't excuse it.

I lose all sense of time until I hear my name being called. More frantic with each repetition. Rebecca's voice. Preston's. Ben's. Stephanie's. Will's.

"I'm here!" I shout, then keep shouting it until they find me.

Chapter Thirty

I call my parents.

I tell them I'm sleeping over at Rebecca's.

Then I sleep over at Rebecca's.

The next morning, Will invites us back to his house for a picnic.

"Are you sure he's not just inviting Preston?" I ask. It's eleven in the morning and I'm not out of bed yet.

"Nope," Rebecca says. She's been up for at least an hour, I'm sure. "All of us. Me and Ben. Steve and Stephanie. Will and Preston. And . . . you. Do you want to ask your Mystery Man?"

"I can't," I say.

"Come on. Isn't it time we met him?"

"I just can't."

"What? Are you ashamed of us?" She's teasing, but I can tell there's a worry that it's true.

"No," I say. Because the truth is that I'm sure A would love nothing better than a picnic with me and my friends. A would fit in perfectly. It hurts me to know this.

"Then why not?"

"Because I don't think it's going to work out," I say. "With him and me. I just don't think—"

I can't finish the sentence, because it feels so strange to say it out loud.

Rebecca sits down on the bed next to me and gives me a hug. "Oh, Rhiannon," she says. "It's alright."

I don't know why she's treating me this way, but I guess I'm crying or something. I want to tell her they're tears of confusion, not sadness. *Was all of this for nothing?* I think of Justin last night. I think of A out there somewhere. And I think, *No, this wasn't for nothing.* Even if I'm not going to be with A, I needed to stop letting Justin determine my life. I needed to find my own life. A, in a way, got me there. And it wasn't for nothing. A and I still have something, even if it's not the kind of something where he can come to a picnic with my friends.

I get myself together. "Sorry," I tell Rebecca.

"No need to be sorry," she assures me.

"I know."

"Do you want to talk about it?"

Yes, I want to talk about it.

No, I cannot talk about it.

"It's just a long-distance thing. It's hard," I say.

Rebecca nods, sympathetic. I know she wants to ask me more.

"Let's get ready for the picnic," I say.

• • •

We hang out in Will's backyard and pretend it's Central Park. Nobody mentions Justin. Nobody mentions the Mystery Man. Except my thoughts. They mention Justin and A all the time.

I am glad Justin isn't here. If he were here, it wouldn't be like this. Rebecca and Ben arguing over whether it's pretentious to pronounce *croissant* in a French accent when you're speaking English. Will and Preston finding every possible opportunity to touch each other on the arm, the leg, the cheek. Steve and Stephanie chilling out—Stephanie asking Steve to peel her a grape, and Steve actually doing it, both of them laughing at how messy a process it is. If Justin were here, he'd be bored. And he'd be letting me know how bored he was. I wouldn't be able to enjoy any of my friends, because I would be so stuck on how Justin was feeling.

But if A were here. It's Mental-picture A at first. But then it's any of the A's. Because even if he was a pretty girl, or even if he was a huge guy, or even if he was poor Kelsea, back from wherever her dad sent her—there'd be a place for A. Because A would appreciate this. A would understand how much this matters, to spend a day lazing around with your friends, telling inside jokes and feeling inside of them. A has never had that. But I could give A some of mine.

I could email. I could say, *Come on over.* But I'm worried he won't understand why I'm asking. He'll think I mean we can be together. A couple.

Plus, it wouldn't be fair to the person he's in.

I have to remember that, too.

• • •

I think about contacting him a thousand times. For the rest of the day—in the fun moments with my friends, or in the quiet moments when I'm at home. Back at school, when I see things it would be fun to tell him about, or when the minutes seem hours long and class never ends. I want to tell him about Justin, and how now when we see each other in the halls, we ignore each other, as if we're strangers, even though the way we ignore each other isn't like strangers at all. I want to tell A that he was right about Justin but also wrong about Justin. Yes, he wasn't good for me. But, no, it's not that he didn't care. That much is obvious now.

Finally, on Monday night, I give in. Instead of telling A everything, I keep it simple, to make sure that it's okay to keep in touch.

How are you?

R

Within an hour, I get his response.

It's been a rough two days. Apparently, I may not be the only person out there like this. Which is hard to think about.

A

And just like that, I feel myself being drawn in again. I start to write a response—a long response—but after a few paragraphs I think, *No. Stop.* I thought there would be distance, but there isn't any distance. I know that if I involve myself again right now, it will be the same as before. And it can't be.

I hold off. I call Rebecca and talk about other things.

I need to build a life without A before I let him back in.

Chapter Thirty-One

My friends gather around me. In school. After school. On the phone at night.

Will effortlessly joins our circle. He and Preston look so happy together. And I'm happy for them. I am. But I'm also angry, because Will can join us so effortlessly, in a way A never could.

Nobody mentions my Mystery Man anymore. Rebecca must have told them not to.

Part of me still expects him to show up. Expects the universe to send him into the classroom next to mine. Or into Rebecca's body. Or Steve's. Just to say hello. Just to be near.

But I can't think that way. I know I can't.

I find myself looking into people's eyes more than I ever did before. And I realize, that's where we stop being a certain gender or color. Just look right into the center of the eye.

I know I haven't answered him. It weighs on me. I know I'm not being fair. There's no point in spending all this time thinking about A without answering. I have to be honest and clear about where it can go. That's all. That's it.

First thing Thursday morning, I write.

I want to see you, but I'm not sure if we should do that.
I want to hear about what's going on, but I'm afraid that
will only start everything again. I love you—I do—but I
am afraid of making that love too important. Because
you're always going to leave me, A. We can't deny it.
You're always going to leave.

R

All through the day, there's no response. And I think, fine, I
deserve that.

But it's still disappointing.

Then, Friday at lunch, a response.

I understand. Can we please meet at the bookstore
this afternoon, after school?

A

To which I say:

Of course.

R

I'm nervous as I drive over. Everything's changed, and
nothing's changed. This is going to be hard, but it feels so

easy. Mostly, I want to see him. Talk to him. Have him be in my life.

All the other obstacles have fallen away. I am even starting to believe, deep in my heart, that if I told my friends the truth, if they met A the way I met A, on multiple days, they would believe it, too.

The only obstacle, really, is his life.

Which I know is too big an obstacle. But in the rush to see him, it doesn't seem as big as maybe it should.

I get there first. I scan the café and know that none of these people could be him. If he were here, he'd be looking for me. He'd know when I arrived.

So I sit down. I wait. And the minute he walks through the door, I know. Like there's a shiver of lightning between us. Today he's this thin Asian guy wearing a blue T-shirt with Cookie Monster on it. When A sees me, his smile is wider than Cookie Monster's.

"Hey," he says.

And this time I say it back gladly. "Hey."

So here we are. I'm trying to remind myself to not fall back into it, to not start thinking it's possible. But with him right here, that's hard.

"I have an idea," he says.

"What?"

He smiles again. "Let's pretend this is the first time we've ever met. Let's pretend you were here to get a book, and I happened to bump into you. We struck up a conversation. I like you. You like me. Now we're sitting down to coffee. It feels right. You don't know that I switch bodies every day. I don't know about your ex or anything else. We're just two people meeting for the first time."

The lie we want to believe. That feels dangerous.

"But why?" I ask.

"So we don't have to talk about everything else. So we can just be with each other. Enjoy it."

I have to tell him, "I don't see the point—"

"No past. No future. Just present. Give it a chance."

I want to. I know I want to. So I will. I know it's not as easy as that, but it can at least start by being as easy as that.

"It's very nice to meet you," I tell him. I feel like I'm a bad actress in a bad movie.

But he likes it. "It's very nice to meet you, as well," he says. "Where should we go?"

"You decide," I tell him. "What's your favorite place?"

He thinks about it for a second. Whether he's inside his own thoughts or this boy's thoughts, I don't know. His smile gets wider.

"I know just the place," he says. "But first we'll need groceries."

"Well, luckily, there's a food store down the street."

"My, how lucky we are!"

I laugh.

"What?" he asks.

" 'My, how lucky we are!' You're such a goofball."

"I am happy to be your ball of goof."

"You sound like Preston."

"Who's Preston?"

He really doesn't know. How could he? I've never told him.

So as we walk over to the grocery store, I introduce him to all of my friends. He knows Rebecca, and vaguely remembers Steve and Stephanie, but I tell him more about them, and about Preston and Ben and even Will, too. It's weird, because I know I can't ask him the same questions back. But he seems okay with that.

Once we get to the grocery store, A says we're going to go down all the aisles. "You never know what you might miss," he tells me.

"And what are we shopping for?" I ask.

"Dinner," he says. "Definitely dinner. And as we do, keep telling me stories."

He asks me about pets, and I tell him more about Swizzle, this evil bunny rabbit we had who would escape his cage and sleep on our faces. It was terrifying. I ask him if he had a favorite pet, and he tells me that one day he had a pet ferret that seemed to understand it had a guest in the house, so it made his life as difficult as possible—but also gave him something to do because no one else was home during the day. When we get to the produce aisle, he tells me a story about this time at camp where he got hit in the eye by a flying greased watermelon. I tell him I can't remember being injured by any fruit, although there was a good few years when I made my mom cut up apples before I'd eat them, because someone at school had told me about psychos who put razor blades inside.

We get to the cereal aisle, which isn't really going to help us for dinner. But A stops there anyway and asks me for my life story told in cereals.

"Okay," I say, getting what he means. I begin by holding up a cylinder of Quaker oatmeal. "It all starts with this. My

310

mother barely eats breakfast, but my dad always has oatmeal. So I decided I liked oatmeal, too. Especially with bananas. It wasn't until I was seven or eight that I realized how gross it was." I pick up a box of Frosted Flakes. "This is where the battle began. Rebecca's mom let her have Frosted Flakes, and like everyone else, I'd seen the commercials for them a zillion times. I begged my mother to let me eat them. She said no. So I did what any law-abiding girl would do—I stole a box from Rebecca's house and kept it in my room. The only problem was, I was afraid my mom would catch me putting the bowls in the dishwasher. So I kept them in my room. And they began to stink. She threw a holy fit, but my dad was there and he said he didn't see the harm in Frosted Flakes if that's what I wanted. The punch line being, of course, that once I had them, they disappointed me. They got so soggy so fast. So my mom and I reached a compromise." I walk him over to the Frosted Cheerios. "Now, I'm not sure why Frosted Cheerios are any better than Frosted Flakes, but my mom seemed to think so. Which brings us to our grand finale." I make a production of choosing from the ninety kinds of granola before landing on my favorite cinnamon-raisin kind. "In truth, this probably has just as much sugar in it as anything frosted, but I have at least the illusion of health. And the raisins are satisfying. And it doesn't get soggy right away."

"I used to love how the Frosted Flakes turned the milk blue," A says.

"Yeah! When did that stop being cool and start being gross?"

"Probably the same time that I realized there was not, in fact, any fruit in Froot Loops."

"Or any honey in Honeycomb."

"Or any chocolate in Count Chocula."

"At least the Frosted Flakes had flakes in them."

"And frostedness."

"Yes. And frostedness."

Talking like this, I am forgetting that this isn't A. I am forgetting that we're not on a regular date.

"Moving on . . . ," I say, taking us to the next aisle, and the one after.

We pick up a ridiculous amount of food. As we're nearing the checkout, I realize there's no way I am going to be getting home when my parents are expecting me.

"I should call my mom and tell her I'm eating at Rebecca's," I tell A.

"Tell her you're staying over," he says.

My phone is in my hand, but I don't know what to do with it. "Really?"

"Really."

Staying over. I think about the cabin. About what happened. I mean, what didn't happen. And how that felt.

"I'm not sure that's a good idea," I say.

"Trust me. I know what I'm doing."

I want to trust him. But he also doesn't know what it was like. And he might have the wrong idea of what a night might lead to.

"You know how I feel," I say.

"I do. But still, I want you to trust me. I'm not going to hurt you. I will never hurt you."

Okay. I look into his eyes and I feel like he knows. There's a plan—there's definitely a plan. But it's not going to be a repeat of the cabin. He knows what he's doing, and I do trust that.

I call my mother and tell her I'm at Rebecca's and will be staying there. She's annoyed, but I can deal with that.

The harder part is calling Rebecca.

"I need you to cover for me," I say. "If my mom calls for any reason, tell her I'm over."

"Where are you?" she asks. "Are you okay?"

"I am. I promise I'll tell you about it later—I can't right now. But I'm okay. I might not even be out the whole night. I just want to make sure I'm covered."

"Are you sure?"

"Yes. Really. It's good."

"Okay. But I expect a full explanation this time. Not your usual evasion."

"I promise. I'll tell you everything."

She says to have a good time. I think it's remarkable that she's trusting me. But she is.

"You'll tell her you met a boy," A says once I've hung up.

"A boy I just met?"

"Yeah. A boy you've just met."

It's strange to think of that conversation. No longer a Mystery Man. Just a boy.

If only it were that easy.

I follow him in my car. This is the moment I could decide not to go. All I need to do is turn the steering wheel. All I need to do is return to the highway.

But I keep going.

• • •

His name is Alexander Lin and his parents are away for the weekend. A tells me both things at once.

"Alexander," I say. "That's easy enough to remember."

"Why?" he asks.

I thought it was obvious. "Because it begins with A."

He laughs, surprised. I guess it wasn't as obvious, from the inside.

The house is a very nice house. The kitchen is about twice the size of our kitchen, and the refrigerator, when we open it, is already pretty full. Alexander's parents did not leave him to starve.

"Why did we bother?" I ask. I can barely find space to put away what we bought.

"Because I didn't notice what was in here this morning. And I wanted to make sure we had exactly what we desired."

"Do you know how to cook?"

"Not really. You?"

This is going to be interesting. "Not really."

"I guess we'll figure it out. But first, there's something I want to show you."

"Okay."

He reaches for my hand, and I let him take it. We walk like this through the house—up the stairs, to what is clearly Alexander's bedroom.

It's amazing. First of all, there are sticky notes everywhere—yellow squares, pink squares, blue squares, green squares. And on each of them, there's a quote. *I don't believe in fairy tales, but*

I believe in you. And *Let all the dreamers wake the nation.* And *Love me less, but love me for a long time.* I could spend hours reading his room. *In a field, I am the absence of field.* —Mark Strand. Most of the quotes are in one handwriting, but there's other handwriting, too. His friends. This is something he shares with his friends.

There are pictures of these friends, too, and the way they arrange themselves looks like the way my friends would arrange themselves. Not Justin. Never Justin, who didn't like having his picture taken. But Rebecca and Preston and the others. They would like it here. There's a lime-green couch to hang out on, and guitars to strum, and what looks like the full collection of *Calvin and Hobbes.* I look at the records he has leaning against the record player. Bands I don't know but like the sound of. God Help the Girl. We Were Promised Jetpacks. Kings of Convenience.

I read more of the sticky notes. *We are all in the gutter, but some of us are looking at the stars.* I check out the books on his shelves. Most of them have sticky notes sticking out—pages to be collected, words to be remembered after they've been forgotten.

I like it. I like it all.

I turn to A, and know he likes it, too. If he could have a room, this would be it. How cool that he's found it. And how depressing that he'll have to leave it in a few hours.

But I'm not going to think about that. I'm going to think about now.

I see an almost-finished pad of sticky notes on Alexander's desk, and put it in my pocket, along with a pen.

"Time for dinner," A says.

He takes my hand again. We head back into the world—but not too far into it, not too far away from this.

I find some cookbooks. We choose, by and large, to ignore them.

"Improvise," A says. And I think, yes, that's what we're doing. Improvising. Living by instincts. It's a big kitchen, but we make it feel like a small space. We fill it with music from Alexander's iPod and steam from the boiling pots and smells as different as basil picked from the stem and garlic sautéed against a flame. There's no plan here, just ingredients. I am sweating along and singing along and I am not stressed, because even if none of it ends up edible, it's still worth it just to be putting it together. I think about my parents, and how they've missed this sensation of working together, or putting your hands on the back of the person as he stands at the stove, or having one person start the sauce but the other person take it over without a word. We are a team of two. And since it's not a competition, we've already won.

In the end we have a kale salad, garlic bread, a huge pasta primavera, a quinoa and apricot salad, and a pan of lemon squares.

"Not bad," A says. And what I want to tell him is that now I understand why people want to share a life with someone else. I see what all the fuss is about. It's not about sex or being in a couple when you hang out with other couples. It's not for ego gratification or fear of loneliness. It's about this, whatever this is. And the only thing wrong with it right now is that I'm sharing it with someone who's bound to leave.

I don't say any of this. Because the last part makes all the rest of it harder to say.

"Should I set the table?" I ask instead. The Lins have a very nice dining room table, and a feast like this seems fit for a very nice dining room table.

A shakes his head. "No. I'm taking you to my favorite place, remember?"

He looks through the cupboards until he finds two trays. The food we've made barely manages to fit on them. Then A finds a bunch of candles and takes them along, too.

"Here," he says, handing me one of the trays. Then he leads me out the back door.

"Where are we going?" I ask. I don't even have my jacket. I hope we're not going far.

"Look up," he says.

At first, all I see is the tree. Then I look closer and see the tree house.

"Nice," I say, finding the ladder.

"There's a pulley system for the trays. I'll go up and drop it down."

These parents have thought of everything.

As I balance the trays, A heads up the ladder and sends a platform down. I'm not sure how balanced it's going to be, but I put one of the trays on, and A manages to pull it up without anything falling off. We repeat this for the second tray, and then it's my turn to go up the ladder.

It's like something I've read about in a book. It never occurred to me that kids could actually have tree houses in their backyards.

There's an open door at the top, and I climb right through.

A has lit some of the candles, so the air flickers as I pull myself inside. I look around and see what's basically a log cabin stuck in the air. There isn't much furniture, but there's a guitar and some notebooks, a small bookshelf with an old encyclopedia on it. A has put the trays in the middle of the floor, since there isn't any table and there aren't any chairs.

"Pretty cool, isn't it?" A says.

"Yeah."

"It's all his. His parents don't come up here."

"I love it."

I take the plates, napkins, and silverware from one of the trays and set the table that isn't a table. When I'm done, A serves—some of everything for each of us. As we sit across from each other, we comment on the food—it's all turned out better than it has any reason to be. The sauce on the pasta primavera tastes like a spice I can't quite identify—I ask A what it is, and he doesn't remember. He thinks I might have put it in. I don't remember, either. It was all just part of the improvisation.

There's a carafe of water on one of the trays, and that's all we need. We could have wine. We could have vodka. We could have Cherry Cokes. It would all be the same. We're drunk on candlelight, intoxicated by air. The food is our music. The walls are our warmth.

As the first candles diminish, A lights more. There isn't brightness, but there's a glow. I've just taken my first bite of a lemon square, its tartness still on my tongue. I catch A watching me and assume I have some powdered sugar on my face. I move to wipe it off. He smiles, still looking.

"What?" I ask.

He leans over and kisses me.

"That," he says.

"Oh," I say. "That."

"Yes, that."

We hang there, waiting for the kiss to leave the room, to float off into the night.

I have no idea what I want.

No. Not true. I know exactly what I want. I'm just not sure if I should want it.

"Dessert," I say. "You need to try a lemon square."

He smiles. It's okay to let the kiss leave the room.

Already, I feel others knocking on the door.

I look at his lips. The powdered sugar on his lips.

I remind myself they're not really his lips.

I'm not sure I care.

When we're done, I gather up the dishes. I put everything on the trays, and then I push the trays aside. We've been sitting too far from each other. I want us so much closer.

I move right next to him. He puts his arm around me, and I take the pad of sticky notes out of my pocket, along with the pen. Without saying a word, I draw a heart on the top sticky note, then put it on Alexander's heart.

"There," I say to A.

He looks down at it. Then back up at me.

"I have to tell you something," he says.

For a moment, I think this will be the *I love you* that's even greater than the others. If he says it, I will respond.

But instead he says, "I have to tell you what's been going on."

Instead of leaning in to him, I move so I can see his eyes.

"What?" I ask. Irrationally, I wonder if he's met someone else.

"Do you remember Nathan Daldry? The boy I was at Steve's party?"

"Of course."

"I left him on the side of the road that night. And when he woke up—he knew something was wrong. He suspected something wasn't right. So he told a lot of people. And one of the people who found out—he calls himself Reverend Poole. But he's not Reverend Poole. He's someone in Reverend Poole's body."

"This is what you were talking about when you emailed and said you thought you weren't the only one."

A nods. "Yes. But that's not all of it. Whoever's inside Poole is like me, but not entirely like me. He says he can control it. He says there's a way to stay in a person's body."

I try to wrap my mind around what he's saying. "Who told you this? Did you email him? How do you know he's real?"

"I saw him. I met him. He used Nathan to set a trap, and he almost got me. He says we're the same, but we're not the same. I don't know how to explain it—I don't think he uses the same rules as I do. I don't think he cares about the people he inhabits. I don't think he respects what we are."

"But you believe him? When he says you can stay?"

"I think so. And I think there might be others, too. On the Internet—I think I've found others. Or at least, other people who were inhabited, like Nathan or you. You at least know what happened. And Nathan knows now. But most of them never know. And if Poole's right, there may be others who've been taken over permanently. Someone like me could go into them, and then not leave."

"So you can stay?" I ask, not believing this is what he's telling me. Suddenly anything is possible. *We're* possible. "Are you saying you can stay?"

"Yes," he answers. "And no."

It can't be both. I don't want to hear it's both.

"Which one? What do you mean?"

"There might be a way to stay," he tells me. "But I can't. I'll never be able to stay."

"Why not?"

"Because I'd be killing them, Rhiannon. When you take over someone's life, they're gone forever."

No. He can't be saying this. He can't be saying it's possible and impossible at the same time.

I can't deal with it. I can't. I have to stand up. I can't be sitting on the floor in the middle of a tree house having this conversation with him.

Once I'm up, I start to boil over. "You can't do this!" I'm telling him. "You can't swoop in, bring me here, give me all this—and then say it can't work. That's cruel, A. Cruel."

"I know," he says. "That's why this is a first date. That's why this is the first time we've ever met."

Not fair. This is not pretend. This is life.

"How can you say that?" I ask. "How can you erase everything else?"

He stands up and comes over to me. Even though I'm mad, even though I don't understand what he's doing, he wraps his arms around me. It's not what I want, and I try to tell him I don't want it. But then I feel the shelter of his closeness and I want it, and I stop trying to pull away.

"He's a good guy," A whispers in my ear. "He might even be a great guy. And today's the day you first met. Today's your first date. He's going to remember being in the bookstore. He's going to remember the first time he saw you, and how he was drawn to you, not just because you're beautiful, but because he could see your strength. He could see how much you want to be a part of the world. He'll remember talking with you, how easy it was, how engaging. He'll remember not wanting it to end, and asking you if you wanted to do something else. He'll remember your asking him his favorite place, and he'll remember thinking about here, and wanting to show it to you. The grocery store, the stories in the aisles, the first time you saw his room—that will all be there, and I won't have to change a single thing. His pulse is my heartbeat. The pulse is the same. I know he will understand you. You have the same kind of heart."

No. This is not what I want. Can't he see what I want?

"But what about you?" I ask, my voice stained by my sadness. I can't keep it away from him.

"You'll find the things in him that you find in me," he answers. "Without the complications."

He says it like it's easy.

It's not easy.

"I can't just switch like that," I tell him.

322

His arms draw me closer. "I know. He'll have to prove it to you. Every day, he'll have to prove he's worthy of you. And if he doesn't, that's it. But I think he will."

A's giving up. Whether or not I want him to, he's giving up.

"Why are you doing this?" I ask.

"Because I have to go, Rhiannon. For real this time. I have to go far away. There are things I need to find out. And I can't keep stepping into your life. You need something more than that."

I know this makes sense. But I don't want to make sense. I don't want anything to make sense.

"So this is goodbye?" I ask him.

"It's goodbye to some things," he says. "And hello to others."

This is where I turn.

This is where I stop being held and decide to hold.

This is where I loosen myself from his arms, but only to unfold my own arms and welcome him there.

I am not saying yes, but I am agreeing that there's no point in me saying no.

I hold him with everything I have. I hold him with so much that he will have to remember it. He will have to remember me, wherever he is.

"I love you," he says. "Like I've never loved anyone before."

"You always say that. But don't you realize it's the same for me? I've never loved anyone like this, either."

"But you will. You will again."

• • •

This is where it stops. This is where it begins.

Every moment. Every day.

This is where it stops. This is where it begins.

I haven't been looking at the clock, but now I look at the clock.

It's almost midnight.

Where it stops. Where it begins.

"I want to fall asleep next to you," he whispers to me.

This is my last wish.

I nod. I'm afraid to open my mouth. I am afraid I will not be able to say what he wants me to say.

We leave the trays in the tree house. It doesn't matter, if this is what he's going to remember anyway. Climbing down the ladder. Running back to the house. Heading to his room.

We will remember this together. All three of us.

I want to stop time. I know I cannot stop time.

Holding hands. Then, inside the room, stopping to take off our shoes. Nothing else, just shoes. I crawl into the bed. He turns off the lights.

Only the glow of the clock. He gets into the bed next to me, lying on his back. I curl into him. Touch his cheek. Turn his head.

Kiss him and kiss him and kiss him.

"I want you to remember that tomorrow," I say when we come up for air.

"I'll remember everything," he tells me.

"So will I," I promise.

One more kiss. One last kiss. Then I close my eyes. I steady my breathing. I wait.

If I could hold on to him, I would.

Lord, if I could hold on to him, I would.

I do not sleep. I wish I could sleep. But I cannot sleep.

Instead, I lie there, eyes closed, safe in the dark.

I feel him reach over and touch my heart.

I hear him say goodbye.

I feel him close his eyes. I feel him fall.

I open my eyes. I turn.

I look for the moment. I want to see the change.

But instead I find a beautiful someone, beautifully asleep. Left behind by another beautiful someone, now also asleep in some other house, in some other bed.

I want to wake him. I want to ask him if he's still there.

But I don't wake him, because I don't want Alexander to ask me why I'm crying.

It isn't until I'm turned back to the wall, until I've decided to will myself to sleep, that I feel the sticky note on my shirt.

The heart I gave him.

He's taken it, and given it back to me.

Chapter Thirty-Two

I open my eyes. There is sunlight.

"Good morning," Alexander says.

At some point in the night, I must have turned toward him. Because he's right there in front of me, also waking up.

"Good morning," I say.

He doesn't look confused. He doesn't look surprised. He understands why we're in his bed, fully clothed. He remembers the tree house. He remembers meeting me in the bookstore. It's unusual, for sure—it's not the kind of thing that happens every day. But it's possible. On a very lucky day, it's possible.

He looks so happy. And completely unafraid to show it.

"Why don't I make breakfast?" he says. "I seem to recall my parents left us with plenty of breakfast options."

"Breakfast would be good," I say, sitting up and stretching out.

"Okay," he replies. But he doesn't make any move to go. He just looks at me.

"What?" I ask.

"Nothing," he says, bashful. Then he corrects himself. "No.

Not nothing. The opposite of nothing. I'm just really glad you're here. And I'm looking forward to another day with you, if you'll do me the pleasure."

"Breakfast first," I say. "Then we can figure this out."

"Sounds good," he says, bouncing out of bed. "Help yourself to clothes, towels, shampoo, books, Post-its—whatever you need."

"Will do."

He teeters in the room for a moment. He looks so sweet.

"I love this, whatever it is," he says.

I can't help but smile back at him. "Yes," I say. "Whatever it is."

"No oatmeal, right?"

"Yup. No oatmeal."

He whistles as he heads downstairs. I listen until he's too far to hear.

His laptop sits on his desk, beckoning me.

I know what I should do. I know what A wants me to do.

Only, I'm stubborn now.

I like Alexander. But I want A.

I want to find A.

ACKNOWLEDGMENTS

Since I usually create a book as I'm writing it, without really knowing what will happen until it's happening, this book was particularly challenging to write, and I feel the need to acknowledge accordingly.

First, thank you to all the readers of *Every Day* who have shared their reactions with me. I think it's very safe to say that without your meaningful enthusiasm, the story would have ended there.

As always, I want to thank my friends, family, and fellow YA authors for their support. I am always tempted to attempt a full list to back up this acknowledgment, but live too much in fear that I'll inadvertently forget someone. So instead I will limit myself to the people who have actually shared a house, room, car ride, and/or coffee shop with me as I've drafted this book: my parents, Libba Bray, Zachary Clark, Nathan Durfee, Nick Eliopulos, Andrew Harwell, Billy Merrell, Stephanie Perkins, Jennifer E. Smith, Nova Ren Suma, Chris Van Etten, and Justin Weinberger. Joel Pavelski has the distinction of having been with me in Montreal when I began the book and then, a year later, with me in Montreal when I neared finishing it. Thanks, too, to Rainbow Rowell, for the conversation that led to the title, and for conversations in general. And to Gayle

Forman, for being my reference point in this particular literary endeavor of shifting perspectives while sticking to the same story. Also, for conversations in general.

This book also wouldn't exist without the accidental suggestion and very deliberate support of everyone at Random House Children's Books. Thank you especially to Nancy Hinkel (more about her in a sec), Stephen Brown, Julia Maguire, Mary McCue, Adrienne Waintraub, Lisa Nadel, Laura Antonacci, Barbara Marcus, and everyone (I mean, everyone) in the sales, marketing, publicity, production, manufacturing, and legal departments.

Thank you also to Bill Clegg and Chris Clemens, for guardian angelhood. And to Stella Paskins, Maggie Eckel, and everyone at Egmont UK; to Penny Hueston, Michael Heyward, Rebecca Starford, and everyone at Text Publishing; and to all the foreign-language publishers and translators who've supported *Every Day* in such an astonishingly global way.

As for Nancy . . . I'll linger here, your words in my margins, dear, and sing till dawn a song of you and me and what and why. The what being the book in your hands, and the why being the way that you care.